The supply columns blew up – un-recognisable lumps in the gorge of death. You can eat bark, leaves, even earth to help your hunger – but thirst?

We discovered a shell hole full of water out in no-man's-land. A horde of rats was drinking avidly from it and we flung a grenade at them, then flung ourselves down and drank . . .

By the afternoon bursting shells had emptied the hole. On the bottom were some distended corpses. They had been there a long time. We spewed our guts up – but the next day we found another shell hole and drank again.

This was Monte Cassino . . .

Also by Sven Hessel

Wheels of Terror
Legion of the Damned
Comrades of War
Liquidate Paris
March Battalion
Assignment Gestapo
SS General
Reign of Hell

and published by Corgi Books

Sven Hassel

MONTE CASSINO

CORGI BOOKS

A DIVISION OF TRANSWORLD PUBLISHERS LTD

MONTE CASSINO
A CORGI BOOK 552 08168 X

First publication in Great Britain

PRINTING HISTORY
Corgi edition published 1969
Corgi edition reprinted 1970
Corgi edition reprinted 1970
Corgi edition reprinted 1971
Corgi edition reprinted 1971
Corgi edition reprinted 1972
Corgi edition reprinted 1973
Corgi edition reprinted 1973
Corgi edition reprinted 1974

Copyright © 1969 by Sven Hassel

This book is set in 10-11 pt. Plantin

Corgi Books are published by Transworld Publishers Ltd.,
Cavendish House, 57-59 Uxbridge Road,
Ealing, London, W.5.
Made and printed in Great Britain by
Hunt Barnard Printing Ltd., Aylesbury, Bucks.

NOTE: The Australian price appearing on
the back cover is the recommended
retail price.

This age of compulsory military service has shown that whether a man is dressed in this uniform or that, whether he is on the side of the executioner or the victim is not necessarily a question of deserts or even of character.

ROLF HOCHHUTH

This book is dedicated to those who
fell at Monte Cassino, monastery
and fortress.

I

God! how it rained! It poured and poured. Everything was sopping. Our mucky rain-capes were long since wet through.

We were sitting under some trees in a sort of tent made by buttoning capes together. They were SS capes and better than ours and we were relatively dry. Tiny had also put up his umbrella.

We had finally got the stove from the big house burning and we were getting ready to dine. We had forty starlings which we were roasting on long sticks, and Porta was making marrow-balls. It had taken us two hours to scrape that marrow out of the bones of two dead oxen. We had found some fresh parsley. Gregor Martin knew how to make tomato ketchup, which he was mixing in an American steel helmet. Steel helmets were practical things, capable of being used for lots of purposes. The only thing they were useless for, was the purpose for which they were made.

Suddenly, we burst out laughing. It was Tiny's fault. He had made a classic remark without realising that it was classic.

Then Porta held up his yellow top hat and announced that we were to inherit it, when he died. And we bellowed at that.

Then by mistake Heide pissed into the wind, and we rolled about with laughter, and we were still laughing as we ran back with our food between the bursting shells.

Once I heard a padre say to one of the staff officers:

"How can they laugh like that?"

That was the day we were laughing over Luisa Fatarse's knickers which Tiny was wearing tied round his neck, and I swallowed a piece of potato the wrong way and had to have my back pummelled with a hand grenade. Laughter can be pretty dangerous.

"If they didn't laugh as they do," the staff officer replied, "they would not be able to carry on."

Porta had a masterly hand with marrow-balls. He made only

7

ten at a time, otherwise they went soggy, eating his own share in between. We ate over 600 between the nine of us, which is quite a lot, but then we were all night at it.

God, how it rained!

THE LEATHERNECKS LAND

The thunder of the guns could be heard in Rome, 170 miles away. We could not see the great men-of-war out at sea, but every time they fired a broadside, it was like volcanoes erupting on the horizon. First there was a dazzling flash of fire, then a thunderous roar.

They knocked our grenadiers cold. In the course of a few hours our weak panzer regiments were rolled up. From Palinuro to Torre del Greco the coast was a flaming furnace, whole villages were wiped out in a matter of seconds; one bunker a bit to the north of Sorrento, one of our biggest that weighed several hundred tons, was sent flying high into the air along with the entire crew of its coastal battery. Then out of the south and west came swarms of low-flying Jabos* that shaved the roads and paths clean of all that lived. One hundred miles of Highway 19 disappeared altogether, and the town of Agropoli was razed to the ground in twenty seconds.

Our tanks, devilishly well camouflaged, were standing in readiness among the cliffs. The grenadiers of the 16's were with us, lying under cover of the heavy brutes. We were to be the great surprise when they did come, those men from across the sea.

Thousands of bursting shells churned up the ground and transformed a hot sunny day into dark night.

An infantryman came running up the slope without his rifle, arms flailing, crazed with fear, but the sight made no impression on us. He was one of many. That morning I myself had been in the grip of the paralysing fear that strikes one rigid. It could come over you as you were marching along, turning you into a corpse, except that you were still on your feet. The blood drained from your face, making it deathly white, and your eyes

* Fighter-bombers.

stared: As soon as the others noticed what had happened, they began pummelling you with their fists. If that was not enough, they used their feet and rifle-butts, and when you collapsed sobbing, they just kept hitting away. It was brutal treatment, but it nearly always worked. My face was badly swollen after the treatment Porta had meted out to me, but I was grateful. If he had not been so thorough, I would probably have been on my way to the rear in a strait-jacket.

I looked across at the Old Man lying between the tracks of his tank. He smiled and nodded encouragingly.

Porta, Tiny and Heide were throwing dice, using a piece of green baize that Porta had "organised" in Palid Ida's whore-house.

A company of infantry on its way down the mountainside ran right into a salvo from the ship's guns. It was as if a giant hand had just brushed them away. There was not a thing left of 175 men and their hill-ponies. The Jabos came when the sun was low in the West and right in our eyes. Swarms of landing craft spewed infantry over the beach: old tanned veterans, professional soldiers and young anxious recruits called-up only a few months before. It was a good thing their mothers couldn't see them. Dante's hell was an amusement park compared to what they had to go through.

Our coastal batteries had been knocked out, but behind every stone and in every shell hole lay grenadiers, mountain troops, paratroops, with their automatic weapons, waiting. Light and heavy machine guns, trench-mortars, panzerfausts, flame-throwers, automatic cannon, assault carbines, rocket-projectors, machine pistols, rockets, hand grenades, rifle grenades, mines, Molotov cocktails, petrol bombs, phosphorus shells. So many words, but what terrors they harboured for an advancing infantryman!

Under cover of their ship's guns they shot ropes up the cliffs and clambered like monkeys up the swinging ladders or went tumbling down from the jutting top. Flocks of them ran in circles about the white sand, while our phosphorus consumed them. The beach was a sea of flame, that turned the sand into lava.

We were silent spectators. Our orders were "no firing".

The first wave was destroyed. They did not get even 200 yards up the beach. A grim sight for the men of the second wave when it followed. They too were shrivelled up. But fresh hordes kept pouring ashore. A third wave. With guns raised well above their heads, they ran through the roaring surf, flung themselves down on the beach and hammered away with their automatic weapons. And they did not make even a yard's progress.

Then the Jabos came, bringing phosphorus and naphtha; yellowy-white flames shot up towering into the sky. The sun went down, the stars came out and the Mediterranean played lazily with the charred bodies, cradling them gently at the water's edge. The fourth wave of infantry landed. Star shells rose into the sky. These men also died.

Just after sunrise, an armada of assault craft roared towards land. These were the professionals, the Marines who were to have established themselves, once the others had opened the way. Now they were going to have to do both, open the way and establish themselves. Their main task was to deprive the enemy of Highway 18. Their armoured cars remained at the water's edge like so many burning torches, but, tough and ruthless, the veterans made their way forward. These men from the Pacific killed everything that crossed their path, shot at every corpse. They had short glinting bayonets on their assault carbines, and many of them had Japanese Samurai swords flapping against their legs.

"US Marines," Heide growled. "Our grenadiers will get it now. Those lads haven't lost a battle in 150 years. Each one of them is worth a whole company. Major Mike'll be glad to see his old chums from Texas."

It was our first encounter with the Marines. They seemed to have tricked themselves out in whatever they liked: one went storming up the beach with a bright red open parasol fastened to his pack, followed by a huge sergeant wearing a Chinese bast hat on top of his helmet. At the head of one company ran a little officer with a Maurice Chevalier straw hat on the side of his head, a rose beckoning gaily from its light blue ribbon. They stormed forward quite regardless of the death-bringing fire from our grenadiers' automatic weapons.

One German infantryman tried to run, but a Samurai sword severed his head from his body. The American who had wielded it called something to his companions, waved the grim weapon above his head and kissed its bloody blade.

A swarm of Heinkel bombers dived down over them. The entire beach seemed to rise up towards the clear sunny skies and the soldier with the Samurai sword lay writhing in a pool of blood on the smoke-blackened sand.

Leutnant Frick came crawling up.

"Withdraw singly. We're pulling back to Point Y."

The Marines had got through our positions. Fresh landing craft were being run up the beach. Amphibian craft roared ashore while bombers and fighters fought savagely in the clear sky.

A group of grenadiers surrendered, but they did so in vain for they were mown down ruthlessly. Some of the Marines stopped to plunder the bodies of their medals and badges.

Porta grinned and said: "Collecting fanny-attractors."

"*Bon!* Now we know the rules. Good thing we saw that," said the Legionnaire.

We fell back to a couple of kilometres south of Avelino, knowing that the German Command counted on being able to defeat the invading force, once it had got ashore. They were hoping for another battle of Cannae, but they had failed to take into account the Allies' enormous material superiority. Where Field Marshal Alexander and General Clark had only hoped for a bridge-head, they were presented with a proper front. Position after position was taken, but still we weren't sent in. We had very few casualties. but we were pulled back to north of Capua, stopping long enough in Benevento to drink ourselves silly in a wine cellar. After we had helped to bury several thousand dead at Caserta, the regiment dug itself in at the fork where Via Appia parts company with Via Casilina. We dug our Panthers half in. We had a barrel of wine from Caserta stowed behind the engine hatch on ours; a spit-roasted pig hung from a pole over the turret. We lay on the forward hatch, throwing dice on Palid Ida's bit of green baize.

"How would you feel about plugging the old Pope and smashing the Vatican organisation?" Barcelona asked, in the middle of a good throw.

"We do what we're ordered to do," Porta replied laconically. "But why should we have to plug His Holiness? We haven't even fallen out with him."

"Yes, we have," Barcelona said, pluming himself with being in the know. "That time when I was One-Eye's orderly, I saw a RSHA* order on the NSFO's† desk at Corps HQ and read it. The boys in Prinz Albrecht Strasse are very keen to get the Pope to come out openly on the side of the hook noses. They have *agents provocateurs* in the Vatican. As soon as the holy wallah has been induced to take sides, the whole lot are to be smoked out. Every crow is to be put to the sword. I can give you the end of this nice little document word for word: 'On receipt of the code word "Dog-collar" a special duties Panzer regiment, demolition engineers and panzer-grenadiers from the SS Tagdkommando will go into action.'"

"But, damn it, you can't shoot the Pope," Heide exclaimed, forgetting in his surprise that he had thrown a winner.

"They can, and a lot more," said Rudolph Kleber, our minstrel, who used to be with the SS. "Six months ago a friend of mine in the Bible Research Section told me that they were very anxious to get to work on the crows. They are laying trap after trap for the Holy Father. In Prinz Albrecht Strasse they regard him as Adolf's worst enemy."

"Bugger that," said Barcelona, "but would you plug the holy man, if you were ordered to?" We looked questioningly at each other. Barcelona had always been a stupid swine capable of asking the most idiotic things.

Tiny, our six foot illiterate from Hamburg and the most cynical killer of all time, held up his hand, like a child at school: "Listen here, you scholars, which of us is a Catholic? Nobody. Who here believes in God? Nobody."

"*Attention, mon ami!*" The Legionnaire raised an admonitory hand.

But there was no stopping Tiny once he had got into top.

"My Desert-Roamer, I know you're a Mohammedan, and I say like Jesus, Saul's son," Tiny was getting his bible history

* Reichssicherheitshauptamt (Security HQ).
† Nazi Welfare Officer (political).

a bit mixed up, "Give me what's mine, and slip a coin or two into the emperor's palm. What I would like to know is this: is this fellow Pius in Rome, whom you've been talking such a hell of a lot about, is he just a high priest in white, a sort of Church general, or is he deputy of the commander-in-chief in Heaven, as that nurse who gave me some ointment for my eye told me he was the other day?"

Porta shrugged. Heide looked away. He was playing with a couple of dice. Thoughtfully Barcelona lit a cigarette. I was changing the fuse in a rocket. The Old Man ran his hand across the breech of the long gun.

"I suppose he is," he muttered thoughtfully.

Tiny drummed on his teeth with the nails of his left hand. "Obviously none of you is quite sure. You're on uncertain ground. Obergefreiter Wolfgang Ewald Creutzfeldt is a tough lad and one dead man more or less does not matter a shit to him. I'll shoot anybody: private or general; whore or queen, but not the holy man."

"God does exist," said the Legionnaire. "Lay hands on a Mohammedan and you insult God. The Pope is great, greater than anyone. But let's wait until we see the order, before we discuss what we're going to do. There's always a way out. We could even turn the guns the other way and paint a couple of keys on the turret."

"You're crazy," Porta jeered. "They'd send a couple of SS divisions against us and they'd soon burn us out."

"The Legionnaire's idea is not all that mad," put in the Old Man thoughtfully, "They have their own broadcasting station in the Vatican. Suppose the world heard that a German Panzer regiment was defending the Vatican against a German attack. That would make headline news Berlin wouldn't like."

"You're pretty naïve," Heide said sarcastically. "We know that they've smuggled *provocateurs* into the Vatican, and they won't hide in the cellars when the fun starts. They'll make straight for the transmitter and tell the world that the Holy Father has asked for German protection, and once the Pope's paid a little visit to Prinz Albrecht Strasse, he'll dance to SS Heini's pipe."

"Your talk's on the level of your intellect," Porta said, "but at the moment we're sitting here waiting for a pack of baying Yankees. You shake the double and you are entitled to six throws."

We forgot the Pope for the dice. There were six of them, golden dice with diamond eyes that Porta had "borrowed" from a gambling joint in France. He had had a machine pistol with him the evening he borrowed them and a woman's stocking pulled over his face. The Military Police spent a year running round in circles searching for the culprit, who was considerably nearer than they ever realised.

A horde of infantry came storming past our hide-out.

"They're in the hell of a hurry," Porta remarked. "Think they've met an ogre?"

Another lot came running along, as if the devil himself was after them. The Old Man climbed up onto the tank and had a look towards the south through his glasses.

"It looks as though the whole front's disintegrating. I haven't seen running like this since Kiev."

One-Eye came bustling up with Leutnant Frick at his heels. "Beier," he called excitedly to the Old Man.

"Yes, One-Eye," the Old Man replied, for General Mercedes insisted on being addressed thus, when we were in action.

"You are to hold this position. Porta, give me a schnaps." Porta held out his leather field water-bottle.

The obese general drank, wiped his mouth with the back of his hand. "Slivovits," he growled appreciatively. "Don't be surprised, if you suddenly see Japs in front there. The 100th Battalion is made up of naturalised US-Japanese. Don't let them near. Kill them. They have Samurai swords and are as fanatical fighters as their fellow-countrymen in the Pacific. There'll be Moroccans too. You may come across Gurkhas. They'll cut your ears off to flaunt when they get home. At the moment, you're the Southern Army's one fixed point. Everyone else is running."

"Herr One-Eye," croaked Tiny nervously, as usual putting up a finger. "Will these devils really cut our ears off?" Major-General Mercedes nodded. "That's all right, then," Tiny announced happily. "From now on I'd recommend the chaps on the other side to wrap their ears up carefully, because now

I'm collecting listening-flaps too."

"I prefer gold teeth," Porta said. "Cranium fins have no commercial value."

"You can expect the whole lot pretty soon," the general went on. "And God have mercy on you, if you do a bunk."

"We know the programme, One-Eye," Porta cackled. "To the last man and the last cartridge."

One-Eye nodded assent.

"It'll be an unpleasant little surprise, when they run into our Panthers. So far they've only met our P III's and P IV's. They laugh at those. There'll be an SS-division on the way. They'll take over from you, if there're any of you left. Look out for Jabos. They're shaving the roads. They've already landed half a million men. Another schnaps, Porta, please."

"That's a whole litre you owe me, One-Eye," Porta remarked drily, as he handed the general the water-bottle for the second time.

Then the fat general disappeared over a mound of earth with Count Frick at his heels.

Porta rolled up Palid Ida's green baize, brushed his yellow top hat on his sleeve and edged himself in through the driver's hatch. I jumped into my place at the periscope, Tiny got his shells ready and we tested the electrical equipment. Porta started up the many horse-powered motor and rocked the tank backwards and forwards a bit, then put her into neutral. Another flock of infantry sped past, most of them without their helmets and rifles.

Porta laughed maliciously. "They're in a hurry, aren't they? They seem to have tired of being heroes, and I always believed what Adolf said." Imitating Hitler's voice, he went on: "German women, German men, our barbarian enemies, Russian swamp-dwellers and American gangsters, French syphilitic alfonses and homosexual English aristocrats, say that the German armies give way, but where a German soldier has once set foot, there he stays . . ." Porta laughed. "Unless I've got shit in my eye, at this moment the German soldier is very busy doing a bunk."

An infantry feldwebel stopped beside me, gasping.

"Get out of here," he called. Then he leaned exhaustedly

16

against the front of the tank. "Got a mouthful of water? They've wiped out the whole of my lot." He drank greedily from Heide's water-bottle.

"Come now," said the Old Man reassuringly. "You've been seeing things. Tell us what's happened."

"Tell?" the feldwebel gave a tired laugh. "All at once they were behind us, in front of us, over us, swarms of tanks and Jabos. In ten minutes my unit had gone, crushed in their fox-holes by the tracks. They aren't taking prisoners, just shooting the wounded. I saw one group surrender, engineers from my own division they were. They snuffed them out with their flame-throwers."

"Which is your Division?" the Old Man asked steadily.

"16th Panzer. 46th Panzer grenadiers."

"And where are your 46th grenadiers?"

"In hell."

"The tram for Berlin stops just round the corner," Porta said with a malicious grin. "You'll probably get a seat on the back if you hurry. I've been told that Adolf's driving it."

"You'll soon be laughing on the other side of your face," said the feldwebel angrily. In three days there won't be a live German soldier in Italy."

"Oh, rot," said the Old Man.

"Best start up your old crate and bugger off," the feldwebel suggested.

"Can't do that," Porta said with a sorrowful smile.

"Haven't you any petrol?"

"Masses, but Adolf said we weren't to. And we're good little boys, who always do what they're told."

"Arse-holes," was the reply. "You should have seen our freshwater-salts, who were supposed to hold the coastal forts. They were roasted by the first Jabo swith napalm. Our grenadiers chucked their shooting irons away and tickled the soles of the angels' feet, but the Yankees haven't time to take prisoners. They just lay you flat."

"How many times have you shat your pants since you saw your first Coca-cola drinkers," Porta asked sarcastically.

Leutnant Frick walked up to us, a wry smile on his face. He had heard Porta's remark to the agitated feldwebel.

"How many tanks have you seen, Feldwebel, and what type were they?" he asked quietly. He produced a map and spread it out on the Panther's fore-hatch. "Show me where you last saw them."

The feldwebel bent over the map, casting a nervous glance towards the South. It was obvious that he was wanting to bolt and cursing himself for having stopped and spoken to us. Now he was caught.

"We were in positions north of Bellona. They were across the Volturno before we even realised what was happening."

"But they couldn't have got across without a bridge," Leutnant Frick protested.

"Herr Leutnant, I don't suppose you'll believe me, but they drove across."

Thoughtfully Frick lit a cigarette. "You saw tanks crossing the river?"

"Yes, and trucks, Herr Leutnant."

"Ordinary military trucks?"

"Yes, Herr Leutnant, big trucks and the river's deep, I know."

"Partisans," said Frick, thinking aloud. "Under water bridges. A fine mess." He looked at the feldwebel searchingly. "And once they were across, you did a bolt."

"It was all so quick, Herr Leutnant. They crushed every single man in the fox-holes. And they're not taking prisoners."

"How many tanks were there?"

"Several hundred, Herr Leutnant."

Porta guffawed. "You're confusing tanks and foot-sloggers, you idiot!"

"Just wait till they come along and blow that yellow tile off your dome. I was at Stalingrad, but I've never seen war like this."

Frick held out a cigarette, smiling. "Take a deep breath and think. Where were all these hundreds of tanks?"

"In Alvignano."

Frick consulted the map.

"Were they all in the village?" Porta asked spitefully. "It must be a bloody great village. How many tanks can you see here? A thousand? Are you quite sure you haven't come from

Rome and are bolting in the wrong direction?"

"Shut your mouth," the feldwebel snarled furiously. "There were so many we couldn't count them."

This was a familiar phenomenon. The infantry always saw double, when they were ridden down by tanks. In all probability the feldwebel had seen twenty-five tanks and not one more. With wide, staring eyes, he explained to Leutnant Frick how these numbers of tanks had wound in and out among the houses in the village, shooting down all living creatures. It was obvious that the man had been through hell.

"Come now, Beier. We must go forward and see what's happening. And you, feldwebel, show me the way," ordered Leutnant Frick.

"Yes, but, Herr Leutnant, the American gangsters are in the village now," he said.

"We'll go and see," Leutnant Frick said.

"Herr Leutnant. There are Japanese too, with Samurai swords."

Leutnant Frick laughed quietly and fanned some dust off the cross that hung round his neck. He was the most dapper officer in the division. His black panzer uniform was always immaculately clean, his tall boots shone so that you could see yourself in them. His left sleeve was empty. He had lost that arm at Kiev, crushed by the turret-hatch, when his tank was hit by a 4-inch shell. He turned to the rest of us.

"Two volunteers to come with us."

The Legionnaire and I stepped forward. We had to, for we took it in turn to volunteer. I swung the light machine gun over my shoulder and we got down into the ditch. Leutnant Frick went first.

II

We were in Milan being re-equipped. We drifted round while the others did the work. We threw our weight about in Biffi and Gran Italia, having rows with officers of different nationalities. They couldn't stand us, because we smelled of death and talked in vulgarly loud voices, but we made friends with Radi, the waiter. He composed our menus. That was at Biffi opposite La Scala. In the galleries and terrace cafés we drank fresa, which has a wonderful taste of strawberries.

Heide and Barcelona had a fit of megalomania. They went to La Scala every night. They thought that was the right thing to do, for anybody who was anybody in Milan went there.

I fell in love. You do, when you drink fresa at one of the small tables in the galleries. She was twenty. I wasn't much older. Her father kicked her out, when he found us in bed; but when he saw my uniform he turned pleasant. It was the same with most people in Europe in those days, at all events as long as we were within sight and hearing, they were as pleasant as could be.

I decided I was going to desert, but unfortunately I got drunk on fresa again with its lovely taste of strawberries and confided in Porta. After that they would not let me go out alone any more. Deserting was a stupidity that could have unpleasant repercussions on one's friends.

We played a football match with an Italian infantry team. The game was a draw because both spectators and the two teams began fighting.

When they chucked us out of Biffi's, we fornicated behind the pillars in the galleries and then drank ourselves silly with the ack-ack gunners on the roof.

People said there was a lot of unrest in Milan, but we never noticed any. Perhaps that was because we were drinking chianti and fresa with the partisans.

When Biffi closed, we often went back to Radi's. He lived in a basement that had patches of damp on the walls and springs protruding from the mouldy seats of the chairs.

Radi would take off his shoes and pour mineral water over his feet. He said it helped them.

PANZER ATTACK

We could hear violent gunfire to the south-west – the wicked, sharp reports of tank-guns mingled with the uninterrupted barking of machine guns; flashes and flames spurted up beyond the trees.

An amphibian came lurching along the road, braking so fiercely that it skidded sideways for quite a distance. Even before it stopped, a colonel with the red stripes of the General Staff had leaped from it, spattered all over with mud. The edelweiss in his beret showed that he belonged to the Mountain Brigade.

"What the hell are you doing here?" he called excitedly. "Are you from the 16th?"

"Forward reconnaissance, Herr Oberst," Leutnant Frick answered. "No. 2 Troop, 5th Squadron, Special Duties Panzer Regiment."

"Panthers," the Colonel exclaimed delightedly. "Just at the right moment. Where have you got your crates?"

"In the woods, Herr Oberst."

"Splendid, Leutnant. Bring them up and bowl the gangsters over. Get the old goloshes moving, gentlemen. The Division was to be pulled out, but forget that."

Leutnant Frick clicked his heels together.

"Very sorry, Herr Oberst, but it's not as easy as that. I have first to investigate what's going on. Then I must report my observations to my Company Commander. A tank, Herr Oberst, cannot attack blindly. Excuse me, Herr Oberst, I'm not trying to teach you your business."

"I should hope not, my dear fellow or I'll have something to teach you." The colonel's voice boomed. It was a voice accustomed to command.

Leutnant Frick studied his map.

"There should be a bridge here, Herr Oberst, but can it take the weight of our 50-ton Panthers?"

"Of course," the Colonel stated with the utmost self-assurance. "Our assault guns were driven across it several times."

"Allow me to say, Herr Oberst, that there is an essential difference between assault artillery and a Panther tank. Fully laden, our tanks weigh nearly twice as much as an assault gun and our tracks are three times the width."

The colonel's voice took on a dangerous, quiet note. "Let me just tell you this, Leutnant, that's nothing to do with it, but if you don't bring up your tanks pretty sharp and clear the village of the Americans, you'll have a hurricane on your hands."

"I'm sorry, Herr Oberst, but I have orders from my regimental commander to find out what's in the village, and so I cannot carry out your order."

"Are you out of your mind?" the colonel roared. "Your army book!"

"I cannot show you my army book, Herr Oberst. I have no guarantee that you are what you say you are. I am Leutnant Frick, troop commander in No. 5 Squadron of Special Duties Panzer Regiment, and our regiment, Herr Oberst, comes directly under C-in-C South."

"Now you come under me. I'm Chief of Staff of the Division in this area. I order you immediately to fetch your squadron. Refusal smacks of cowardice."

"Herr Oberst, I cannot carry out your order."

"Arrest that man!" the colonel roared furiously. None of us moved. He pointed to the Legionnaire.

"Didn't you hear? Take hold of that man!"

The Legionnaire smacked his heels together with a tired movement.

" *Je n'ai pas compris, mon commandant.* "

The colonel's red, brutal face gaped.

"What the hell's this?" He turned to me. "Arrest that officer." His amazement only increased when I answered him in Danish, gaping at him with an uncomprehending expression on my face. He was almost beside himself with fury and kicked

23

at a stone; and when he turned back to Leutnant Frick his roar had become a shrill squeak and the words came tumbling over each other. "You, Leutnant, order your scarecrows to arrest you! Hell's bells, do something." He cursed, swore and threatened.

All at once, Leutnant Frick had had enough. He swung his machine pistol up under his arm and ordered:

"Reconnaissance group, single file, after me!"

The colonel tore his pistol from its holster and his voice thundered.

"Halt or I shoot!" It was a roar that could have stopped a division in flight. And it stopped us for a moment. Then we walked on without looking back.

A burst of pistol shots followed.

"Il est fou," snarled the Legionnaire, as the bullets whistled round our ears.

The colonel was roaring savagely behind us. A fresh burst of fire pursued us.

I glanced across my shoulder. He had gone amok. He was kicking at the amphibian; then he leaped into it, tried to start it, but it had gone on strike. He leaped out again, pistol in hand.

"Look out!" I yelled and flung myself in the ditch. The next moment Leutnant Frick and the Legionnaire lay beside me.

Only the strange feldwebel did not have time to fling himself flat and the entire burst hit him in the back. He collapsed with blood spurting from his mouth and his helmet rolled homeless across the road.

"Jamais vu si con," swore the Legionnaire. "Pot him, Sven!"

I pulled the LMG's legs down.

"No," muttered Leutnant Frick. "It's murder."

"Shut your eyes, Herr Leutnant," suggested the Legionnaire, "or comfort our dying pal there."

I tucked the butt into my shoulder, set the visor, loaded, turned the LMG. The colonel had put a fresh magazine in his machine pistol. A rain of bullets spattered round us. His great figure was balanced neatly in my sight.

"Nice fine bead," I grinned to the Legionnaire, but I had

aimed short and the bullets spattered the road a couple of yards in front of the colonel, who gave a bellow and leaped for cover behind his car, roaring: "Mutiny!"

A whining swish almost burst our eardrums as a shadow swept across us and we rolled into the bottom of the ditch as a Jabo straffed us. Its cannon banged and a couple of rockets registered bulls on the colonel's amphibian, flinging it away into the trees, where it was consumed in fire, leaving no more than a charred mummy of the man who had so short a while before been a colonel.

Leutnant Frick got to his feet, shouting: "Follow me."

I broke off half the dead feldwebel's dog-licence and took it with me. We crept right up to the village, on the outskirts of which our infantry and gunners were still running about wildly, hotly pursued by Americans drunk with victory.

A captain landed literally in our arms, sobbing: "Finished. The regiment's wiped out. They overran all our anti-tank guns. I managed at the last moment to get out of the window of the room I was sitting in with my NCO. Hand grenades came flying round our ears. I was the only one who got out alive. The entire company office was wiped out."

"But hadn't you put any pickets out?" Leutnant Frick asked, amazement in his voice.

The captain tore the cap from his head.

"We felt so safe. Yesterday evening they were 100 miles away. A couple of their regiments had been pushed back. We had some prisoners brought in from the American 142nd Infantry Regiment and they weren't worth much. We were getting ready to celebrate a victory and I had only set ordinary sentries. Our anti-tank guns were in position behind the houses with muzzle covers on, their shells packed away in the trailers."

"But what about sentries?" Leutnant Frick asked.

"The Amis throttled them with steel nooses." The captain sat down wearily between us. He was quite old and had white hair and was the kind that had believed in the invincibility of the German soldier right up to the moment when the Americans' Shermans overran his regiment; a learned chap, a doctor of something or other at the university in Freiburg, the kind of person who regards anyone under thirty as a child. But the twenty-year old American tank men had taught him differently. He had seen 4,000 troops go up in flames in twenty minutes and now he was sitting in a ditch being questioned by another twenty-year old, a young puppy in a black tank uniform with a decoration round his neck, who was telling him what he should have done.

"One should never feel safe," Leutnant Frick smiled. "When I go to bed, I have my machine pistol in my arms. Your experience was a common one in Russia. War is all cunning and foul play."

The captain regarded his iron cross from the first world war. "In '14–18 things were different. I was in the Uhlans, attached to Count Holzendorf*. I was only called-up again three months ago. This is an evil war." Leutnant Frick nodded. "And I believe we're going to lose it," the captain whispered.

Leutnant Frick did not answer. Instead, he watched for a moment the macabre spectacle being enacted in front of us before he let his glasses drop onto his chest.

"What happened out there, Captain? Could you tell us quickly, we're in rather a hurry."

The Legionnaire lit a cigarette and stuck it in Frick's mouth. The captain gaped.

"They were just suddenly there," he resumed.

Leutnant Frick laughed. "That I realise," he said.

The captain looked reproachfully at the laughing lieutenant. He picked up a stick and drew in the sand.

"I imagine they must have come in here."

Leutnant Frick nodded. "Obviously. I would have broken in there too. Then they knocked out your guns according to the book."

"I suppose so." He hid his face in his gloved hands. "I cannot understand how I escaped. My No. 2 lay across the table with his back torn open. He was full of promise. We had just been saying that he must come to Freiburg. He knew everything about Kant."

Leutnant Frick laughed ironically.

"It would have been better, if he had been a specialist in

* C-C of the Austro-Hungarian army in 1914–18.

automatic cannon and lateral security. It's soldiers we need just now, not philosophers."

The captain looked up. "There's another time coming, young man."

"Most certainly. But in all probability you won't see it, any more than your philosopher-second-in-command."

"Are you intending to report me for dereliction of duty," the captain asked anxiously.

"Wouldn't dream of it," Leutnant Frick answered casually. "How many tanks do you estimate there are in the place?"

"At least a battalion."

"Hm," Leutnant Frick snorted. "Sounds incredible, but you must know what you've seen. But do you realise how much space a tank battalion occupies? 80 to 100 tanks plus all the accessories. It's traffic enough to make the hair of even a French policeman stand on end."

"It was absolute slaughter," said the captain defending himself. "I saw my batman being crushed under a Sherman. He was a law student, from a good Viennese family. We had a lot of promising young men in our battalion, academically, I mean. Now they've all been killed. We had a sort of lecture-circle. The regimental commander was a university professor. We honoured the academic spirit."

"I can't say anything about that," Leutnant Frick remarked drily. "But it seems to me, it would have been better if you had been military-minded. You might have saved half of your battalion, if you had." He brushed an imaginary grain of dust from his sparkling grand cross. "The philosophic approach is no use for commanding a battalion."

"You are a soldier, Leutnant, decorated for bravery – and very young."

"Yes, I'm a soldier and have been one since they fished me out of the class-room. In your eyes, perhaps, I'm only a child, but now the child had got to pull the chestnuts out of the fire for you and your intellectual aristocrats. Lying behind me, there, is a man who has been a soldier for thirty years. He has learned his craft thoroughly with the French, and the ensign there by the LMG is one of those you despise. In your eyes he is just a product of the gutter. He and the little NCO there know nothing of Kant and Schopenhauer, but they do know the cruel laws of Mars."

The captain gazed steadily at the young lieutenant. A tired smile appeared on his face.

"You would kill your own mother, if your superior ordered you to do so?"

"Certainly; just as I would run over her if she stood in the way of my tank."

"Poor world," whispered the academic in uniform. He got to his feet, chucked his pistol and cap into the ditch and walked off down the road, alone.

The Legionnaire lit a new cigarette from the old, as he watched him go.

"A generation will disappear with that naive idiot. *C'est fini.*"

Leutnant Frick righted the order on its ribbon that he had been given for smashing a battalion of Russian tanks. "He believes his ideas. Let him keep his illusions till he pegs out. We'll write a nice report about him, when we get back; we'll have him manning an anti-tank gun, the last survivor of his battalion."

We sneaked back along a sunken road and the dry bed of a stream and rejoined the squadron.

Major Michael Braun, known as Mike, our new squadron commander, who before the war had served in the US Marines, listened in silence to our report. He turned, grinning, to the radio-operator "Barcelona" Blom and, in a gruff beery voice, ordered: "Call up the regiment, ask for the code word for starting general slaughter." He shot a jet of tobacco juice at an industrious lizard and hit it on the tail.

Barcelona called into his microphone.

"Rhinoceros calling Sow, Rhinoceros calling Sow. Over."

"Sow here. Come in Rhinoceros. Over."

We hung our heads in through the hatch and listened to their conversation, complete gibberish to the uninitiated.

"Rhinoceros here calling Sow, Rhinoceros calling Sow. Point 12 AZ water 4/1. One litter of pups drowned. Four mothers. Not clear if more. Wild pigs scattered. No pikes. Code word desired. Mike. End. Over."

"Sow here calling Rhinoceros. Do it yourself. Responsibility Mike's. No extra wild pigs. Good luck. End."

"What a change," grinned the Major. "The responsibility is to be mine. I've been a pistol-cooly for a hundred years now but I've never yet heard of the responsibility not being the squadron boss's." He perched on the nose of 523, which was our tank. "Tank commanders to me!" He placed one of his giant cigars bang in the middle of his mouth.

The tank commanders came trotting up, their silk neckscarves glowing with all the colours of the rainbow. Each tank crew chose its own colour. Mike surveyed us.

"Park your arses on the sward and listen. I haven't time to repeat anything, and the pisser who doesn't get what I say will have to deal with me. We have had our code word and that means: clear the bog! My old friends the Yankees have just roasted a couple of regiments of our coolies and are busy marking them on the arse with their bayonets. They think they're all ready to pull on the zabarotsch* and have begun writing postcards home reporting their victory. Quick victories induce megalomania, and now we're going to take them down a peg or two." He jumped down from the tank. "Out with your maps. We must be over them like thunder and lightning. There's a gap here." He pointed to the map. "We'll go through there. We've two miles on the other side of the wood, the hell of a big open stretch, but we've got to cross it. At all costs. And it's all up to us. We've no help. We're on our own. No infantry support, no artillery support. The lads from Texas have shot 'em all up." He enveloped himself in blue tobacco smoke. "I thought we'd do the trick this way." His cigar swung from one side of his mouth to the other. "Four Panthers smash slap through into the village. We'll catch the Texas bums at their coffee and cakes." He swept his cigar from his mouth and held it up admonishingly. "The Yankees must have no idea of our existence until we're right in among them administering emetics, so," Mike raised one big bushy black eyebrow, "no pooping off. All safety catches on. And the Yankees must not be allowed to start shooting either."

"Well, we'd better send them a postcard about that," said

* Russian = shirt of victory.

Porta disrespectfully from one of the back rows.

"Shut up and listen. The first two tanks drive straight through the gap and close the door, so to speak, at the far end. You can see from the map that there's no emergency exit; then it's about turn, muzzles pointing the other way. The troop commander fires off a red Verey light, when he's slammed the door. Then four other tanks pound up as well. With eight Panthers we should be able to clear up that pisspot all right. Leutnant Herbert," he turned to the new leutnant, who had joined us only three days before, and let a fat, dirty finger travel across the map, "you'll remain here on the fringe of the woods with the remaining eight Panthers and you'll follow us only, note this, only if and when you see a yellow three stars." He seized the young leutnant by his tunic – "And God have mercy on you, if you move from here before you see that triple star decorating God's heaven. Do that, and I'll pull your arse-hole over the top of your head and you'll look like a tired monk at midnight."

Major Mike spat out the stump of his cigar, pulled a rusty tin out of his pocket, drew a deep breath through his nose, hawked, spat, opened the tin and pulled out a two-foot roll of juicy chewing tobacco. Curling his lips back, he bit off a piece, then handed the roll to the Old Man.

They were the only two of us who chewed tobacco. The major always placed his quid between his lower lip and his teeth; while the Old Man preferred his against his right cheek, where it looked as if he had an enormous gumboil.

"This is good stuff," was the Old Man's laudatory comment.

Leutnant Herbert shook his head. Here was a major, a Prussian officer, sharing chewing tobacco with a feldwebel, a common joiner from the slums of Berlin. What next, in Heaven's name! If he told his father, he would refuse to believe him.

"As I said, we're going into that gap as fast as we can and as soon as the two leading tanks send up their red light, we'll liquidate the bastards in a couple of shakes. Anything that moves, wipe it out." He stuck a finger into his ear and stirred it round. "Oberfeldwebel Brandt, you'll take up position with your wireless tank in that dried out stream. Glue yourself to the fourth Panther. Camouflage yourself at once and up with your prick. You'll listen until your ear-drums get inflamed. Put your pornographic magazine away so you don't forget to alternate. If I have to wait even a second to come in, you'll have me to deal with – and the longest part of your life behind you. A red Verey light starts the ball. Yellow triple star, general attack. Eight tanks in reserve. We have no need of a withdrawal signal. Either we liquidate the cowboys or they wipe us out. Any questions?" Porta stepped forward and the major frowned. "Joseph Porta, I'll tell you here and now, if you try to make a fool of me . . ."

Porta pretended to be embarrassed, wiping the palm of his hands on the seat of his trousers. "Herr Major, does a weak heart exempt a chap from this picnic?"

"I should bloody well think not. Neither weak heart nor bad prick. Any more?"

Tiny put up a finger from the back row.

"What is it now?" Mike growled. "Anyway, you don't understand any of this."

"Herr Major, according to the Military Service Act of 1925, that General Blomberg made, a soldier who has served for more than seven years, does not have to take part in action. Herr Major, I have nine years service. May I have permission to step out by the back way?" Tiny then made as if to produce his army book to prove his point, but Major Mike waved him away.

"Even if you had served for 109 years, you'll park your broad arse on the gunner's seat in 523, and you can wipe that same arse with General Blomberg's Military Service Act. If anyone else has a question, keep it till Christmas, and hang it on the tree."

"Amen," Porta murmured, turning up his eyes.

"Get aboard. Start engines."

As Tiny swung his leg over the reserve tank and let himself slide down in through the right turret hatch, he called:

"Porta, we're off to the wars again! To think we volunteered for this shit. I must have had inflammation of the speculanium that day." He bent over the shell locker inside the turret, stuffed his black panzer tunic behind the battery, pulled his shirt over his head and stowed it in the same place; then he knotted round his neck the pink chemise he had got from broad-bummed Luisa the last time we patronised Palid Ida's whorehouse. He caught a couple of lice in the thick hair on his chest and smeared them across the range finder. "And this sort of war, Porta, is dangerous. You can get your prick and balls shot off. You can be most horribly maimed, Porta, but war can also lead to undreamed of wealth. Have you got your dental forceps, Porta?"

"You bet," Porta grinned and produced the ghastly instrument from the leg of his boot. Then he bent over his instrument panel, tested petrol and oil gauges, tried the clutch, checked the brakes, swung the heavy tank round in a circle.

Major Mike climbed into the command tank and swinging his right hand above his head as a signal to start engines, he called to the Old Man: "Beier, you stick to my tail. Legionnaire and Barcelona follow him. The rest in arrow-head formation P-a-n-z-ers March!" He pumped his fist up and down several times: the signal for full speed ahead.

The many thousands of horsepower roared. The ground quivered. The whole wood shook with the tremendous vibration, as tank after tank swung out. A tree that was in the way fell with a crash. The Major waved encouragingly from the turret of 005. He took another bite of his rope of tobacco. The Legionnaire waved back from his turret, lit a cigarette and tied his blue-red-white scarf round his neck. Barcelona moved his dried-up talisman orange from Valencia from his right to his left pocket. Porta bent over and spat on the accelerator, and with his finger drew a cross in the dust on the instrument panel. I tied a garter round the range-finder. Tiny placed Luisa Broad-bum's lipstick firmly above the fuse lamp. Heide, our super-soldier, checked to see that the feed pipe to the flame-thrower was in order, undid the safety catch of his forward machine gun, arranged its long cartridge belt. Then he tied a small blue cloth elephant round his neck.

All our radios were checked. They were important and had to be working perfectly, for much depended on them. The loaders climbed out to remove the muzzle-covers of the cannon as we drove along and tank after tank reported itself ready for action.

"Rhinoceros ready for action," Mike's voice said on the wireless.

Then we were out of the wood that until then had hidden us safely and we could see the Americans who were guarding the northern exit from the village with three tanks.

As we tore across the open tell-tale stretch as fast as we could make the tracks turn, Porta sang in a care-free voice:

"Eine kleine Reise im Frühling mit Dir,
    Sag'mir, bitte, leise,
    Was gibst du dafür . . ."

He was standing on the accelerator and we expected any moment that the pistons would jump from their bearings. None of the others could keep up with us. On the radio we could hear Barcelona's stream of curses:

"Caramba, crucifix, sacramento! How the hell does he get it to go like that?"

"That only Allah knows," answered the little Legionnaire, cursing his own driver to the uttermost pit of hell.

Everything now depended on speed. At first, the three Shermans on the fringe of the village failed to react at all. God knows what they thought, but they were certainly inexperienced. Not one shot was fired.

We made the centre of the village first, closely followed by Major Mike. The Legionnaire who was a hundred yards behind us saw that the Sherman's turrets were beginning to swing, stopped, swung his cannon round like lightning and in ten seconds it was all over. The three Shermans in flames.

The rest all happened as quickly. We tore round in the narrow streets shooting at anything with a cockade or a white star on it, the range point blank so we couldn't miss.

An M.5. mounted flame-thrower came round the corner of a house, spitting out a flame many yards long, but a shell drilled into it and it splintered into a thousand pieces.

A 42-ton T.14. came waddling out from an orange grove, its turret swinging wildly.

"Fire," the Old Man shouted.

I pressed the trigger and in the next instant the enemy tank was on fire, oily black smoke welling out from its hatches brightened by the sharp tongues of red flames. An officer tried desperately to get out of the turret, but the turret hatch fell forward and he remained hanging there. The flames leaped across his uniform, caught in his hair and he half rose up, screaming, desperately trying to put the flames out with his bare hands. More flames shot up through the turret; he held his hands to his face, where they slowly charred. Then he disappeared into the glowing interior of his tank.

A suffocating smell of burned flesh reached us. Someone swung a mine to throw it at us – but he never did. He was crushed beneath the tracks.

A group of infantry squeezed back against a wall in the naive hope we might not see them. Heide laughed wickedly. His forward machine gun chattered and they collapsed one on top of the other with perforated stomachs.

A soldier cook was running across the open space of the square, hoping to hide behind one of the four burning Shermans, but a short spatter from the turret MG stopped him as though he had run into a wall. He clapped his hands to his head and gave a loud, piercing shriek, his helmet rolled on across the dusty square; he spun half round, then collapsed with a kick or two. A Sherman came bursting out from some bushes. Two 8.8 armour-piercing shells bored into it and it blew up with an ear-splitting explosion. Its turret was flung high into the air to descend with a whine to bury the long muzzle of its gun deep into the ground.

Another Sherman appeared. A direct hit knocked its turret off and flung it into a house. We could see right into the tank. There was only the lower part of the commander's body left, for he had been shorn through the middle. The remains of the loader hung there caught between the breech and the shell-racks.

Mike's tank, which had two heavy flame-throwers mounted on the turret, burned up a group of infantry. Though some put their hands up in surrender, they died beneath our tracks, for tanks can't take prisoners. The grinning death's-heads on our lapels were well suited to our arm.

And so it was all over and not one of them had escaped. We

had surprised them as completely as a few hours before they had surprised our infantry. We had had our revenge.

Jumping out, we pushed our goggles up onto our foreheads, went to the drinking fountain in the square and drank and drank, tried to wipe some of the oil and powder off our faces. The acrid fumes in the air inside the tanks had made our eyes bloodshot; our throats and lungs smarted and breathing was painful.

Some terrified survivors emerged and stared at us. One of them knew a word or two of German.

"Nicht schiessen, Kamerad. Wir nicht Juden, nicht Japsen. Wir von Texas. Wir O.K."

A few minutes later we were chatting away, showing each other pictures, exchanging souvenirs, beginning to laugh together. We had lost one man: the gunner in Leutnant Herbert's tank. The hatches had been shut tight and it had not been noticed that the ventilator had shorted. The gasses had suffocated him. We also had two wounded: one was Feldwebel Schmidt, the commander of 531 tank who had bent down to pick his map off the bottom of the turret just as the gun recoiled smashing his right arm to pulp. A couple of needle-sharp bits of bone stuck out from his shoulder.

One of the American prisoners, a medical orderly, gave him a blood transfusion beside the drinking fountain, while we stood round watching. It was most interesting. Feldwebel Schmidt was lucky; for him the war was over, but if the American had not been there with his transportable blood bank, Schmidt would have been dead.

The other wounded man was one of the loaders, who was relatively new. He had been hit in the lung by a pistol bullet. His tank commander, Oberfeldwebel Brett, had been loading his pistol, when it had gone off and hit the loader.

We hid the American who gave Schmidt the blood transfusion, a corporal from Lubbock, from the unit which came round collecting prisoners. Four days later we took him in a tank to within a few yards of the American position and let him jump out. Before that we gave him a black eye and knocked out one of his teeth, a gold one that, strangely enough, neither Porta nor Tiny would have. We also banged his shin with a belt buckle so that it swelled up enormously. He was half-Jewish.

Looking like that, he told us when he asked us to do it, he would be sent home to the States and never see the front again. Only an idiot stayed at the front voluntarily, but of course there were some of those on either side. I won't say we despised them. Most of us had volunteered originally, so in our heart of hearts we had a sort of admiration for the tough guys who shrank from nothing and accepted all the consequences of their volunteering.

We laid the wounded out in rows along the side of the road and sent a wireless call for amphibians and SPWes,* which we filled with bloody, whimpering bodies.

Porta and I lifted up a man and found that a bit of lung was bulging out from a gaping wound in his back; Tiny came up carrying a corporal, half of whose cranium had been shot away, baring the brain. Behind a midden, we found an officer, whose face had been shaved off by a shell splinter. We piled the dead in two great heaps. Many were little more than charred mummies. Thousands of flies buzzed round them. We dug a common grave. Not a deep one, just enough to make sure they were covered with earth. The sweet smell of corpse was nauseating.

One of the prisoners, a staff sergeant, who was sitting on the front of Major Mike's tank chatting, had been given schnaps and was half-drunk. He gave everything away, telling us that they had sent back the green signal that reported the area clear of the enemy. Some of his companions looked at him contemptuously. Then he saw the same contempt in our eyes and realised the ghastly thing he had done. He snatched Barcelona's pistol, shoved the muzzle into his mouth and pulled the trigger. We could have stopped him, but none of us moved.

Major Mike gave the body a contemptuous poke with the toe of his boot.

"War's a bloody thing," the Old Man muttered.

The Major scribbled down a message for the radio NCO to send back:

"Rhinoceros to Sow. Chief. 36 tanks liquidated, 10 trucks, 17 cars. Unknown number of killed. Own losses: killed – one private; wounded – one Feldwebel and one NCO. Awaiting

* Troop-carrying tanks.

36

contact with enemy. Continuing on own responsibility. Breaking off link. End."

We grinned understandingly, knowing that Major Mike wanted to deal with the enemy regiment on his own. Having risen from NCO to major, he was determined to shine and to do that the red tabs had to be shown that they were not the only ones who could do things. It was pretty ingenious, breaking off radio communication. For the next three or four hours nobody would be able to get hold of us. It was playing for high stakes, but if Major Mike could bring it off, he would be a big man. If things went wrong and he returned alive, he would land in Torgau. That was the hard law of the Army.

"Mount," ordered Mike. "Tanks – fo-r-ward."

We leaned out of our opened hatches as we drove through a belt of young trees and then down to a river bed with stinking water and mud, where some swollen bodies of dead cattle made the air putrid.

Leutnant Herbert's tank stuck. It just shoved the mud in front of it, till it got itself well and truly stuck.

Major Mike swore furiously, leaping from his tank and wading across up to his knees in mud. When he had kicked at a dead rat and glared evilly at Leutnant Herbert in his turret, he asked "What the hell do you think you're doing, man?"

Leutnant Herbert muttered something about it being an accident that might have happened to anybody.

"There's no such thing in my squadron," bellowed Major Mike. "You aren't pissing about the Kurfürstedamm now. You're in a war and in charge of a tank costing a million Reichmark. I don't care about the million, but I need your bloody tank. What bloody fool promoted you Leutnant. Pull him out, Beier!"

Tiny and the gunner of the unfortunate tank together fastened the towing wires to the tank's hooks.

The thick steel wires sang, taut as violin strings. They could break any moment, and if they hit you, you would be killed on the spot. We'd seen it happen.

The loader became so nervous that he let go his grip on the hooks and took cover behind the tank. Tiny threw a handful of mud, for want of better, at him.

"Wait till I get hold of you, you cunt-thief!" Then he leaped up onto the wires and hung on to the hooks for all he was worth.

"If they part," the Old Man muttered, "they'll mash him."

"*Un bon soldat*," said the Legionnaire with an approving nod.

"But as dumb as the hole in a cow's arse," Porta said with a grin.

"Don't go too far," Heide threatened. "I'm not so bloody dumb. No NCO has passed out with higher marks than I in the last twenty years. Who of you pissers can floor me on tactics?"

"March, march!" shouted Major Mike.

Slowly the stranded tank moved up out of the mud. Tiny lay on his belly across the wires, and the major helped him keep them firmly on the towing-hooks, cursing and swearing at Leutnant Herbert, who stood gazing forlornly from his turret. As soon as the tank was on firm ground again, Leutnant Herbert had to leave the turret, where Unteroffizier Lehnert took his place. No one exulted over the unfortunate. We had seen a hauptman fired as company commander and his place taken by a feldwebel in the middle of an attack.

We took up position behind a long dyke and at once set about camouflaging the tanks, removing the broad marks of the tracks with little rakes and by sticking grasses in them and laying twigs and branches over them. This was essential in case planes came over. It was the Russians taught us the art of camouflage. Three Jabos came screaming out of the clouds, just as Porta and I were out checking that all was as it should be. We pressed ourselves flat. The next moment they began firing. It was like an invisible grass-cutter sweeping across the ground. Hundreds of little fountains of earth spurted up. We were lucky, because they were using armour-piercing, not explosive shells. One of the pilots showed himself to be bloodthirsty by rising up almost vertically and diving back at us, his cannon spitting murderously.

The other two Jabos circled round. The first one passed over us so low that we thought he would rip up the belly of his machine. Then with a thunderous bang he disappeared over the hill after his companions.

Major Mike called the crews to him and we squatted among the bushes with him in the middle.

"In front of you," he said, "are two miles of visible road. When those buggers come, the first is to get as far as the curve where the road disappears into the wood. That will be your tank, Beier. You are on the left wing. Frick, you're on the right wing. You will plaster the last tank in the column the moment it emerges from the curve round the hill, but I warn you: no shot is to be fired before I give the word. I personally will shoot any gunner who presses his trigger too soon." He almost swallowed his big cigar in his vehemence, then he went on in a more kindly tone: "All sixteen guns are to fart off simultaneously. Every shell must hit. After the first salvo, the sector will be divided into fields of fire. Each tank is to weed out its own field." He spat a long jet at a feeding bird, hit it and grinned broadly. He bit a piece off his length of twist and, as usual, handed it to the Old Man. "And I would advise any gunner who sends a shell into space to follow it, before I reach him. Keep cool heads, lads. Let them come to the scaffold. They have no idea we are here. They can't possibly see us. The three Jabos are proof of that. We'll stay here quietly and wait for them."

We eased ourselves into our seats. We tested our radios, checked the electric firing mechanism. Heide conversed in low tones with the radio-operators in the other tanks. Feldwebel Slavek had just married by proxy and we congratulated him and made him describe in detail what he had done with his fiancée, whom he had only known for a week.

As we waited, we passed the time dicing. All at once Tiny said, a crafty expression on his great face:

"Who's your heir, Porta? I mean, if you get killed? You're mine, you know," he hurried to add. "All the gold in the green bag round my neck is yours, if one day they make a stiff of me."

Porta smiled wryly, shaking the dice over his head, and said: "Smart, aren't you? Am I to have your gold? I know what you're thinking. Did you really work that out all alone?"

"You can't possibly know what I'm thinking," Tiny protested indignantly. "Word of honour, you're to get my gold. I've made a will on a bit of paper, like that woman in the book

39

we were reading the other day."

"Shut up," growled Porta. "No need to worry about me. When I was in Roumania, I had my fortune told by a respectable chap herding a lot of old nags out on the puszta. By night he stole from the big houses. One still evening, when he and I were enjoying a cup of slivovits, he offered to read my fortune in coffee grounds. It was quite uncanny. After staring into the stuff for ten minutes, while I was thinking about a pretty little piece of cunt I'd discovered in Bucharest, he suddenly uttered a ghastly howl.

" 'Porta, I can see your glowing face surrounded by a shining halo. Sorry, that was a mistake, it's neon lights. Tremendous. Your name shining out over all Berlin. You're going to be a big business man. You understand the good things of life. You'd never cheat a poor whore. You give the pawn-broker his due and the brothel-keeper what is hers. You will steal without letting yourself get caught. A nasty war's coming. Both enemy and friends will be after your scalp, but you'll come through. You'll survive the lot of them, go to many of their funerals, but your own is so far in the future, that I haven't yet seen it in the grounds. You'll live to over a hundred. I can't see death here, though normally you can see it a hundred years ahead.' "

"Do you think I ought to have my fortune told some time?" Tiny asked, interested, lovingly rubbing the green bag of gold teeth that hung from his neck.

"Never does any harm," Porta said. "If the chap tries to hand you out a lot of shit, you give him one on the nut. If it's good, you give him a coin or two and swallow it all. But I do recommend, Tiny, that you keep away from wills. Those are dangerous things, especially if your heirs have any idea how rich you are."

Tiny became so deep in thought that he forgot to shake the dice and when he threw, it was a hopeless one. He looked up at the opening of the ventilator, wiped his thumb over the control lamp on the loading mechanism, then his eyes began to twitch nervously and he exploded: "You lousy devil! You damned great bullock! Would you murder a friend for the sake of a tiny bit of gold?"

Porta shrugged: "I'm only human and the devil is a difficult chap to stand up to. He can put the craziest ideas into people's brainboxes, but as I said: Wills and testaments – that's all a load of shit."

Tiny flung the dice from him in a rage, dealt a kick at a shell and shouted excitedly: "You can't make a fool of me. I've got grey matter too, you know. I'll get the better of you, bet your life."

Porta laughed and withdrew to safety behind the driver's seat. He said with a grin: "The really important thing when you make a will, is to make yourself safe against the men of darkness. You say that I'm your sole heir. I'm a business man and for all their white collars and polished nails, business men are a lot of ugly devils. If one of them gives you a cigar, you can be sure he's counting on getting a full box of them in return. All business people are in direct liaison with the devil. The world of business is a blacked-out jungle. Remember, Obergefreiter Wolfgang Creutsfeldt, only the toughest can float on the surface. Countless people have tried the game, but only a few are chosen. Those who don't know how to secure themselves on all sides, soon end in the gutter. There are competitors everywhere just waiting to strip you of your last rags, but if you know how to play the game, the money will flow into your pocket, and, even if no one can stand you, they will all vie for your company and kiss your arse if you ask them. The bigger and more hated you are, the more bowing and scraping you'll get. Spit on the parquet in your enemy's house, and he'll think it a great joke. You can ring up a judge in the middle of the night and he won't mind. Everything you do is right. Wave a sheaf of ducats and they all come running, from kings to pimps. You mustn't be particular about your methods. You must know a few thugs, who can arrange the occasional street accident. And a sawn-through front axle on your competitor's Jaguar can be a great help at times."

"But that's being a gangster," Tiny objected.

"Which is what every big business man is. Otherwise he would have gone under. You have to have lots of cunt out spying for you. Put 'em in your competitor's beds and they'll have lots of interesting things to tell you in the morning;

41

dolls're the army scouts of the business world."

Tiny's face lit up. "You've just to build it all on a military basis?".

"Correct, and that's why I always pay attention when we are lectured on tactics. Your sales managers are the armoured troops; your thugs the paratroops."

"What about the infantry?" Tiny asked, athirst for knowledge.

"That's all the poor fools who labour away for tiny wages. The pen-pushers and typewriter-hammerers in the offices. When a skirt's done you a really big service, you wrap her in Persian lamb."

"Never seen that," Tiny exclaimed. "What's it look like?"

"Black and curly."

"Like One-Eye has on his hat?"

"Not on your life," Porta snorted contemptuously. "What One-Eye has is the remains of a moth-eaten poodle some Jew palmed off on him as Persian lamb."

The radio whistled.

"Enemy tanks in sight. Action stations. Break off radio contact."

I edged in behind the periscope; Porta started up the dynamo; Tiny checked the fuses and shoved an armour-piercing shell into the chamber. The heavy breach block closed with a smack.

"Loaded, safety catch released," he reported automatically, already with a new armour-piercer in his arms. The long shells stood there in rows, glinting at each other, looking so innocent; but in a few minutes they would spread death and horror, start blazing bonfires, make men scream in torment and terror. Through our open hatches we stared intently at the enemy tanks rolling along in close column down the sunlit asphalt road.

I depressed the pedal slightly. The electric motor hummed. The turret revolved quietly. My target was to be exactly between two trees.

Major Mike was peering over the edge of the turret. His glasses were lying in front of him, camouflaged under a turf. We were to fire, when he tore his beret off.

42

There was a whole regiment of them. The sort of sight a tank commander dreams of.

"You could hardly believe it," whispered the Old Man. "If they don't discover us, it'll be all over in ten minutes."

A lark was pouring out its trills in the blue sky, a herd of heifers stood on the fringe of the trees staring inquisitively at the tanks, and two farmhands were sitting on a muck cart drinking chianti, taking a rest with no idea of what was lurking the other side of the dyke. In a few seconds, they would be right in the middle of it. They waved gaily to the Americans, who called back witticisms. We were so tense that we did not even dare speak aloud. My eyes were glued to the rubber surround of the periscope.

A dog came gambolling up to the farm cart. One of the men threw a stick for it. A couple of bees buzzed about the flowers that camouflaged the guns. A lizard darted across the turret. A magpie was belabouring a big snail. The Americans were singing.

Then the first tank came in to view in my range-finder. Apart from the driver, the entire crew was sitting perched on the outside.

Mike's beret went sailing through the air.

"Fire," ordered the Old Man.

Sixteen heavy tank guns thundered simultaneously, the blast bending the bushes horizontal. Every shell went home. Bodies went flying through the air. There were flames everywhere.

A second salvo thundered out, smashing more tanks.

I swung the turret slightly. Tiny used his forehead to undo the safety catch. The sweat was pouring down his bare back. Shell after shell left the muzzle.

The horses in the muck cart bolted. One of the men clung to the reins and was swept along with the clattering, jolting cart. The heifers burst in panic through their fence and ran straight into the field of fire.

Every tank in the road was in flames.

"Use the high explosives," Major Mike ordered.

Then, shells started bursting among the screaming, desperate men. Those already killed were tossed up into the air and

43

smashed all over again. Finally, we fixed S-shells and the road was transformed into an all-consuming sea of flames.

"Start motors," ordered the Major. "Tanks forward."

Then it was the turn of our machine-guns and flame-throwers. We drove along that blazing hell, turrets revolving, machine guns barking, while dead and wounded were lashed by our bullets. One man reared up out of a pile of bodies, crazily stretched out his hands as though to ward us off, his mouth wide open, eyes staring wildly. A flame-thrower licked him with its tongue of yellow flame and he was transformed into a shrivelled black something.

Mike signalled to cease fire, "Form column of march. Destination: Regiment!"

Wireless contact was reopened. We laughed to each other. They had not fired a shot. We had not even had our paint scratched and we had destroyed a whole regiment, thanks to an American sergeant.

Major Mike called up regimental HQ. We could hear the delight and pride in his voice:

"Rhinoceros calling Sow. Over."

"Sow here. Come in Rhinoceros. Over."

"Rhinoceros, commander, enemy tank regiment liquidated. No prisoners. No own losses. Consumption 1500 armour-piercing shells, 800 high explosives, 300 S-shells. For air observation: Map 3, road 6, Point A2. Over. End."

"Sow to Rhinoceros. Congratulations. Report back. Commander. End."

III

"I prefer withdrawal to advancing," Barcelona said. "Here we can drink fresa, but if we go forward, we should have to dip our snouts in puddles of filthy water. When we go forward, they give us anything. And I'm tired of Ida's tarts."

"Tomorrow," Porta said, eyes beaming as he held up two marrow balls for us to admire, "I should like to sleep in the imperial bed and rape the queen and all the princesses."

"Perhaps they would be glad to do it," Gregor Martin said dreamily. "Perhaps they would like being pawed by fists that smell of corpses."

"We are just a phenomenon of the times," said the Old Man. "One day all this will be over, and we shall have to wash."

"If there's time when I get to Rome," Heide said, "and if they aren't too close on our heels, I shall first fling myself into a great big four-poster bed with silk curtains. Keep all my rags on. Make a mess of it all. Then I'll sleep my fill, then go out and find myself some fine lady, with very superior underclothes, and I'll roger her again and again. Then I'll drink myself silly and carry on retreating."

"More fresa," called Porta, "we'll carry on like this all the way; drink all they have, whore with all their women, mess up their beds. Rome, Milan, Innsbruck and end up in Berlin with the party to end all parties."

A whistle recalled us to reality.

"Take your arms, fall in in front of your tanks!" ordered Major Michael Braun.

"I'm a bit too sleepy," growled Porta.

We staggered up to the front of the No. 5; we were all exhausted for we hadn't slept for four days.

"I'll fall asleep as we go along," Porta threatened.

45

Mike swore at him. His own eyes were swollen and red-rimmed from lack of sleep.

We moved off.

Two tanks went over the edge, because their crews had fallen asleep.

helmets dangled from hooks on their belts.

Hoffman came out from the office, followed closely by Eagle carrying the board with the day's allocation of duties and the six coloured pencils. He kept exactly three paces behind the hauptfeldwebel, halting and moving at exactly the same second. You could almost have thought they worked off the same differential. Hoffman took up position, legs straddled, in front of the squadron, opened his mouth till it was like a large red steaming hole, then, from the depths, came a savage roar of command: "Squadron: right dress. Eyes front!" He waited a couple of minutes to see if anyone would venture to move, then gave a grin of satisfaction and ordered: "Stand at ease. You pink zebra-stallions imagine you can pull off the maintenance trick with me, do you? Well, today's the last time, you stinking scrotums. Mechanics to the right."

Two-thirds of the squadron moved to the right, while the rest stood gazing vacantly into the air.

Hoffman strode up to them, followed by Eagle.

"You there," he called, pointing to an obergefreiter. "Where did you get that pistol you've got on your broad bum?"

The *obergefreiter* had to hand over his pistol.

Hoffman grinned delightedly. He loved that sort of thing. He knew how much a pistol meant to an ordinary soldier. To deprive him of one was like stealing his soul.

Three times Hoffman hounded them through the bog, on the pretext of bad carriage and undisciplined behaviour.

When the group had fallen in again in front of him, now covered with mud and duck pond, he gloated: "Well, you lice, you will perhaps have realised that you have joined a proper Prussian company, where there is discipline. You will see that you are less than the rump of a castrated hippo. Here I am the one who says what is what, and only I. If I feel I would like to knock your bloody heads off, I shall do it; if, contrary to all probability, I should discover among you swamp-fish a desert cow with a tiny bit of grey matter, I'll make him an NCO."

When we had fallen out and Hoffman had disappeared Eagle came and hovered about for a while before he told us: "The major wants a word with you all and to have a look at the newcomers. He's crazy today. He's hounded the clerks through the office window five times already."

"Do you know what I'm going to do," Porta said with a crafty grin. "I'm going to take you up to the front line one day and send you across to the Gurkhas or the Moroccans with a couple of severed ring fingers in your pocket. *Come trista la vita!*"

Eagle disappered hurriedly.

Rudolph Kleber, our minstrel, who had been with the SS, sounded a tattoo on his bugle.

"*Mille diables!* He won't become much older," said the Legionnaire with a laugh.

We fell in as we were, dipping our hands into the waste oil first. We were supposed to be on maintenance and Hoffman might take it into his head to look at our hands.

Major Michael Braun was there already, waiting for us. He was leaning up against a wall, playing with the large cigar in his mouth. We had heard the strangest rumours about Major Mike. Some people said that he wasn't a German at all, but an American. Julius Heide, who was always well-informed, said he had been a corporal in the American Marines. He had been born in Berlin, and been taken to America just after the first world war with his grandparents and seven brothers and sisters. There his mother had married an American business man, who thought of nothing but business and women. He dealt in textiles and didn't give a damn for race or politics. For him the U.S.A. was the entire world and its surrounding planets. Anybody who didn't subscribe to this was a damned nigger.

When Michael Braun returned from a tour of duty in Hawaii with some rather peculiar notions, he was discharged and told that he was a blot on the escutcheon of the United States. He lived off his discharge gratuity until he became gigolo to an actress in Los Angeles. One day in a drug store in Lincoln Road he let his tongue run away with him and said a good deal too much about her. When he returned to her bower, he found her very het up by nine whiskies, two gins, three genevers and an account of what he had said relayed to her over the telephone. Between them they managed to smash most of the furniture before Michael was dismissed.

Then he tried his luck as shoeblack at the end of the long Pier. Unfortunately he had not yet learned caution. He went to bed with a guardman's wife, a blackhaired Mexican nympho. The guardman, an Irishman, could not live up to her requirements and paid two Japs from Yokohama to keep her happy. One of these had a laundry in Little Street. The other worked in a bakery, where an immigrant from Vienna made Wiener-bröd such as no Viennese would have recognised.

Michael got involved in a sex orgy that ended in an almighty rumpus. There was a lot of talk of hidden cameras and it was quite a scandal. The guardman became a sergeant and the two Japs started their own laundry, which is still there in Little Street. They make a lot of money. They have a way with old shirts.

Things did not go well for Michael. He was put in clink accused of responsibility for the photographs. Yet he was lucky in a way. He could have got ten years, but as the judge had lunched well that day and was in a good humour, he got let off. Also the judge liked the photographs which were attached to the evidence. A great many prints were made of these which were handed out to judges, counsel and the police.

Having got out of prison, Michael Braun jumped a goods train to New York. When he reached rock bottom in Millwall Dock, he went to the army recruiting office in Washington Road. He swaggered in rather arrogantly; after all, he was an old marine and, what is more, one from Shuffield Barracks, but a lousy sergeant with three rainbows on his breast pocket – he had been on the Somme and still boasted of it – asked for his certificate of conduct. Braun tried to talk round his year in Los Angeles jail. Grinning, they invited him into a bedroom, where he was given the best thrashing he had ever had and made to understand that he was a criminal swine that the army wanted nothing to do with.

He then went back to Millwall Dock, sneaked aboard the HAPAG line's ship, *Bremen*, and was discovered 375 miles east of Halifax. He then learned to his immense surprise exactly how many plates a man can wash in the course of a day. Every time he dropped one, the head waiter hit him on the head with a larding board. When the ship reached Hamburg he was handed over to the security officer. The beating-up he had had from the three recruiting sergeants in New York was nothing compared to that meted out to him in 8 Stadthausbrücke.

He spent nine months in Fulsbüttel under Marabu, the most hated of all high-booted SS-Obersturmbannführers. Intuitively, Braun realised that if he was to get out alive, he must kneel before the twisted Nazi cross and swear loyalty. His old soldier's flair told him who was the stool pigeon in the cell. Very carefully he began telling them about the US Marines and Shuffield Barracks, describing prisoners' work in the quarries, the inhuman marches under a blazing sun, and also let fall a phrase or two about the new semi-automatic MI carbine. He also let it be thought that he was familiar with Pedersen's Garaud rifle.

The Marabu became interested. For two hours Mike stood at attention, as only a marine could. The Marabu nodded approval and subjected him to various tests. In the first, he disarmed three tough SS men with just his hands.

The Marabu was amazed. He had been standing behind a curtained window on the first floor, watching. Then Mike had to walk the two-mile long outdoor track after starving for six days. They put him in an ice cellar, and he was all but dead when they released him. Then they tied him to a radiator and chucked a bucket of water over him every quarter of an hour. He began longing for the garrison prison at Shuffield, where Scar-face, the worst of all evil staff sergeants, held sway.

The Marabu spat on Mike, but at the back of Mike's brain he could hear the familiar trumpet call from Shuffield. Marabu had made the mistake of giving an old sweat treatment devised for political fanatics. Mike stood at attention and saw the Marabu through a veil of mist. The Marabu struck him in the face four times with his hippo-whip.

Seventy-three days later Mike was transferred to a labour camp near Eisenach. By devious ways he managed to acquire connections in the Party. He became friends with a gauleiter and the two of them discovered a flair for deals, especially shady ones. So in record time, Mike became company commander in an Allgemeine SS Company. One day a good friend whispered in his ear that a police investigation was in the offing. Somewhere in the higher echelons someone had begun wondering why so many rationed goods were disappearing without trace in Eisenach. Mike realised that the time had come for a change of scene and he let fall a few pompous remarks to the effect that he felt it his duty to serve with the army, if the army would have him. His regional commander SS Gruppenführer Nichols, swallowed the bait and so, one cold rainy day in April, he reported to the 121st Frontier Infantry at Tibor Camp. However, the Commander of No. 2 Company there, Hauptmann Tilger, could not stand this peculiar semi-German, so he was sent to Tapiau on the Polish frontier, just about as far away as they could get him. He spent six months there in the 31st Machine-gun Battalion, where he attracted a certain amount of attention by his skill in shooting. He got the army championship for his battalion. When his commander asked him what his rank had been in the US Marines the former corporal impudently replied:

"First lieutenant, Herr Major."

A report was sent to Berlin about Michael Braun and eight days later he was a feldwebel with a reserve officer cadet's braid on his shoulder straps. Three months later he was Fahnenjunker and at the end of a year Oberfähnrich. By chance he discovered that they were thinking of sending him to the Military Academy at Potsdam. There it would not have taken more than an hour or two to show him up for the gigantic liar he was, so he contacted his connections in the Party and went on his travels again.

For a time he was with the 2nd Engineer Battalion at Stettin, where he learned with much swearing and sweating to make pontoon bridges. So, each time there was any talk of the Military Academy he managed to get himself transferred. There were few German garrisons that had not had the honour of his company by the time war broke out in 1939. He ended the Polish campaign at Lemberg as leutnant in command of a company. There he was a welcome guest on the other side of the demarcation line, where he drank many a good glass of vodka with the Russian officers.

He fell out with his C.O. who insisted that the time had

come for Michael Braun to attend the Military Academy and as a result he left the 79th with this eloquent description in his soldier's book: "Undisciplined, insubordinate, quarrelsome. Unfitted for independent command."

Obviously, such an entry did not make for an easy start in his new units. For six months he went about Germany commanding the transport company of a Service Unit, and one fine day he and his laden lorries drove into Eisenach, where half the loads disappeared into the roomy warehouses of his friend, the gauleiter.

That was the end of Leutnant Michael Braun's service with the transport company. He became a hauptmann in record time and was promoted major five months later, all thanks to the gauleiter. The astounding thing was that Major Michael Braun had never been within a hundred miles of an officer training school. He was always given the dirty jobs and the insoluble tasks, and somehow or other, he managed to accomplish them, while others got the credit. His last commander added yet another uncomplimentary opinion to those already recorded in his soldier's book, and he was sent to a Special Duties regiment, all because when drunk, he had flung a mug of beer at Hitler's portrait and said 'Prosit!'

But now, he no longer had a gauleiter friend to help him, for the latter was then breaking stones for a new autobahn and the mere fact of having known him was dangerous. Mike hastened to forget him.

That was how Major Michael Braun found himself standing in front of our company introducing himself to the newcomers. He could swear for an hour and a half at a stretch and never repeat himself.

"Well, you arse-holes," he bellowed, "I'm your commander. I will not stand for any form of funny stuff. If any of you should get the crazy idea that he would like to bump me off from behind, let him write his will and testament before he tries. I have eyes in the back of my head." He pointed to Tiny and said: "Creutzfeldt, who's the toughest company commander you have ever had?"

"You, Mike."

The major grinned broadly. Then he pointed to the Legionnaire. "On the right wing there you see NCO Kalb. Listen to him and you have a chance to save your lives. He has been with the Moroccans and knows every dirty trick there is. That long lout with the yellow necksquare on the left of No. 1 platoon has been one of the fieldmarshal's paratroopers, but he was too good with his knife and they kicked him out. You can learn close combat from him. From NCO Julius Heide there you can learn order and discipline; from Feldwebel Willie Beier, the Old Man, learn knowledge of people and humanity, though you won't have much use for the latter. Obergefreiter Porta can teach you to steal, and, if you are in need of spiritual comfort, go to our padre, Father Emanuel. Don't make a mistake with him. He can knock a bull unconscious with his left fist." He drew his heavy P. 38 from its yellow holster. "As you no doubt have noticed, I have a service pistol and not one of those arse-ticklers most pansy boys trick themselves out with, and the dirty swine who shows the least sign of cowardice when the skull-crackers appear will have a bullet from it sent through his dome by me. Don't think you have come here to get an Iron Cross. With the SS you have to be recommended twice before you get one, here it is six times. You are the scum of humanity, but you are going to be the world's best soldiers." He drew a deep breath and restored his pistol to its yellow holster. "Take lessons from the men I've just recommended." Then he turned to Hauptfeldwebel Hoffman. "Two hours special drill in the river. Anyone who kills a comrade gets three weeks leave. Every tenth cartridge and every twentieth grenade will be live. I want to see at least one broken arm. Otherwise, four hours extra drill."

Then began one of Mike's usual exercises. We hated him because of them, but they made us hard and inhuman. If you are to be a good soldier, you have to be able to hate. You have to be able to kill a man as you would a louse. We had had many CO's, but the German-American Major Michael Braun, who had never been to an officers' school, taught us all this in a way none of the others had been able to do. He would jeer and spit at you at eleven o'clock, hound you into death at twelve and drink whisky and dice with you at one.

He made super soldiers out of gutter snipes. He introduced

55

goose-stepping in a bog, where we were up to our eyes in squelch, headed by a band: ten trumpets, ten flutes and ten drums. He had even got permission for our minstrels to have bearskins round their helmets.

Quite a number of cartridges had been filed, in readiness for the back of his head, but even so Porta and the Legionnaire had twice humped him back from No-man's land, and he never even said thank you. When there was anything particularly tough to be done: rolling-up the enemy line, blowing up a special objective, covering a withdrawal, mine-clearing, swimming a river under water with the engineers, capturing an enemy general, Mike nearly always took part, dressed as a private. Once he brought three wounded back, and the next morning he went back for a fourth who was lying out on the wire.

Another time our own artillery was firing short and Mike crawled out to the forward observation post, arrested the observer for dereliction of duty, and for the next two hours directed the guns' fire so that we were able to take the enemy positions almost without a casualty. On another occasion he waited ten minutes beyond the time laid down by the Staff for an attack, with the result that it was successful beyond all expectations, but only thanks to Major Mike.

He could make us stand up to our necks in icy water at night doing rifle drill, but he always saw that we had dry straw to come back to, when we came out of the line. And, woe betide the cook who did not bring his grub right up to the line, even if a barrage was being laid down two miles behind the front. Old sweats appreciate that sort of thing.

Mike was a swine, but a decent swine. He never did anything out of spite or malice; what he did was always necessary – and he never spared himself. Mike was the only major I have ever known who didn't have a batman. He could clean a pair of iron-hard boots and make them as soft as butter in record time. He knew how to clear a trench with a bunch of hand grenades; he knew how to fire the short bursts that gave a flame-thrower the greatest effect. When Mike headed an attack, we knew that we were half safe. Mike, like the rest of us, was a guttersnipe who had landed in the army for want of anything better, in a regiment without battle honours. His greatest pleasure was at roll call to single one of us out and ask:

"Who are the world's best soldiers?"

We knew the answer he wanted: "The United States Marines," but it amused us to give him a different one. The Legionnaire, of course, replied:

"*La Legion Etrangère.*"

To which Mike's comment was always: "Scum from Europe's sewers," which always made the Legionnaire go white in the face with rage.

If 'Barcelona' Blom was asked, he replied:

"*Ingeniero del ejercito español*, the bravest of the brave."

At which Mike laughed scornfully and said: "I've heard that you dream about a bunch of orange trees. How actually did you get into the civil war?"

"I was one of the crew of one of those big barges, on which the rich men's tarts sprawl under an awning and try to forget their impotent keepers."

"Did you get a go with them, Feldwebel?"

"Now and again, Herr Major. I was in Barcelona the day the General popped up in the south. At first people laughed at him and thought it all a joke, but that time it was in earnest."

The Major nodded understandingly.

"But how did you get into the Spanish army, Feldwebel?"

"I was in Barcelona with one of the big pots and before I knew what was happening, I was clinging on to a lorry with a lot of others. They sent us to Madrid, after we had learned by heart a lot about Marx and Engels, but I never found that much help in the trenches. So, one day, a chum and I raised our lids to them. That was during the fighting in the university quarter."

"Were you at the Ebro, Feldwebel? You should have had just one battalion of our marines. They would have got things going."

Barcelona could not be bothered to protest. You could not explain to that sort of fanatic how gruesome the civil war was.

"What was the cost of the Spanish civil war?" Major Mike asked.

"A million dead, Herr Major."

57

Major Mike asked no more questions. A million dead is a lot, even for a big country. He stood in front of the squadron, legs wide apart.

"None of your regiments is a match for the United States Marines," he boasted. Proudly, he banged his fist on his muscular chest. "I, your commander, am proud of having served in the US Marines."

When we were back working on our tanks the Old Man snorted angrily: "Mike is a dangerous chap."

We seated ourselves comfortably. Porta had a surprise for us. A butter-keg full of brown beans. We pulled our folding spoons and forks from the legs of our boots. The keg was placed in such a position that we could all reach it from where we sat. The beans were cold, but that did not matter much.

Barcelona produced a cigarette and broke it in three. The pieces went the round.

Porta dealt.

"Is there anything nicer," said the Old Man with a smile, "than sitting up on a hill on a good bog with a barrel of beans in front of you and a good game of cards, knowing you're more or less safe from shells?"

We agreed that there wasn't. If we could go on sitting there in our private bog, the war could last a hundred years as far as we were concerned. Most of us were not yet twenty-five. We had long since forgotten what civilian life was like. Our greatest luxury was a decent latrine on some mound under the open sky.

IV

*Two squadrons of tanks were standing in readiness in Via di
Porta Labicana.*

*From out of the darkness came hoarse cries: "Sbrigatevi, per
Bacco!" and terrified people leaped out from the covered wagons.
The place swarmed with SD-men and their fascist henchmen;
fierce dogs barked; children cried; a little girl dropped her doll;
an old woman stumbled; hob-nailed boots dealt kicks right and
left; heavy doors were pushed shut and fastened with chains; a
locomotive let off steam.*

*"The swine," exclaimed our minstrel, "Far too many in each
truck to even sit."*

*"Shouldn't we chuck a few grenades at the SD men?" Tiny
suggested, hopefully.*

*"It wouldn't do us or the others any good," the Old Man
muttered angrily.*

*"It was much worse, when they took the Warsaw Jews,"
Porta put in. "They don't use whips here, only their feet."*

*"Why don't they break out?" Barcelona asked, surprised.
More goods wagons rolled up and were filled with silent people.*

*"Are they going to kill them all?" asked the Minstrel who had
been with the SS.*

*"You can take your oath they are," said Heide with a bully's
laugh. "They'll gas them in Poland."*

*"But people can't treat humans that way," the Old Man
murmured naïvely.*

*"Didn't you know," Porta said ironically, "that the crowning
glory of creation is that swine, man?"*

*That was the night the Jews of Rome were deported. Two
squadrons of tanks from the German army safeguarded the
loading of them at Rome's termini.*

The Jews had been rounded up in broad daylight just outside the windows of the Vatican. There had been a brief but violent struggle in Vicola del Campanile, when they had arrested two Jewesses and an old man. One of the women was finally dragged by the feet to the truck parked in Via della Conciliazione.

The round-up was watched by the Gestapo chief in Rome, SS Obersturmbannführer Kappler, in person. The Germans were doing their best to provoke the Pope into making a public protest, which would have been the signal for what Hitler, Himmler and Heydrich had wanted and been dreaming of ever since they came to power: the liquidation of the Holy See.

For the Vatican to have made a protest at that moment would have been to seal its own doom. The people in the RSHA were sitting at a telephone waiting to give the code word "Dog-collar."

PORTA'S GAMBLING DEN

We had a few quiet days during which we did nothing but a little trenching and mine-laying at night. Of course, we lost a few people now and again, but it was a good time, for we did not consider trench-digging anything. There was only one really bad night. We were surprised by violent artillery fire, took the wrong direction and crawled along parallel to our positions. That cost us forty-three dead and twice as many wounded, but all of us old sweats got back with whole skins. What's more we were able to laugh at Heide. He had been scalped by a shell splinter and all the glossy black hair that was his pride was gone from one side of his head. We used two packets of bandages to cover the huge wound. He was so furious, you could hear him cursing and swearing half a mile away. He all but shot Tiny, when he staggered up later with a gigantic mirror that he had brought from the nearby big house, so that Heide would enjoy the sight of himself. But Heide was careful not to break the mirror. That would have meant seven years bad luck. We cursed that mirror. It became a real problem. We tried to get rid of it by giving it away, but nobody would have it, and, in the end, we took it to Palid Ida's whore-house and with considerable difficulty got it fixed to the ceiling in one of the bogs there. Once it was up, we felt that a curse had been lifted from us.

Porta had found a house, standing all by itself among some pines, well hidden from the gaze of the curious. There he had opened a gambling den. Stalin, the cat, sat on a red silken cushion in a parrot cage above Porta's head. The cushion had originally been used under the bottom of one of Ida's girls, and Tiny had removed it one evening, when we had a fight with some Bersaglieri of the 7th Alpino, a regiment we heartily disliked, though nobody knew why.

Porta had "organised" an elegant table. Tiny had taken up position on a bucket placed upside down on another table, from where he had a good view of the players, in case there should be trouble, which there always was. Naturally, the play was not fair, but it was good honest cheating. You were at liberty to examine the dice, if you liked, but people seldom did when they saw the look on Tiny's face, sitting there with a machine pistol on his lap and an American police truncheon nonchalantly swinging from his wrist.

Oberfeldwebel Wolf had been having a run of luck and the pile of money in front of him was growing. He was humming *Three Lilies* out of sheer delight and self-confidence.

"Herr Oberfeldwebel's in luck," Porta said with a crafty smile.

"I'll break the bank," smiled Wolf. He did not hear Tiny's confidential whisper to Porta: "Shall I go after the shit when he leaves and land him one on the napper?"

Porta shook his head. Tiny just didn't have a clue. To his mind it was the simplest thing just to let his truncheon descend on Wolf's head when he was outside and to relieve him of his winnings, but Porta had his own plan on this occasion.

Wolf got to his feet, raked his winnings together and filled his bulging pockets. Then he pulled a pistol from the leg of his boot and spun it round his finger like a wheel.

"You bandits will notice that this is a Colt II, and I should like you to realise that I know how to use it. Anyone who opens the door before I have been gone five minutes will find himself with a hole in his head as well as his arse, and that goes especially for you, Creutzfeldt." Then with a broad grin, he walked backwards to the door, holding the Colt, its safety catch off, in his hand. Outside, he loosed his two big wolf hounds he had tied to a tree. These ferocious brutes were to be found wherever Wolf was. Once they all but killed Tiny, when he had tried to steal a jeep Wolf was intending to flog privately. As he disappeared down the path through the pines, we heard Wolf laughing and his dogs barking.

Tiny leaped down from his table and dashed towards the door. He flung it open and found himself gazing into Wong's yellow face. Wong was one of the two Vlassov soldiers

Wolf had as a bodyguard.

"You no out of door go. Wolf say no. Njet. Njet."

Tiny withdrew before the muzzle of a Russian machine pistol that pointed straight at his midriff. A little further off he could see the figure of Thung, the other guard, among the trees.

Tiny slammed the door shut and clambered back on to his pail.

"That Wolf's not nice," he said indignantly. "Setting murderers on to peaceable people! If only he would go up to the front for a few minutes."

"He certainly won't do that," Porta said in a tone of conviction, "not even Adolf could lure him there."

We took our places again round the gaming table.

"He'll come back," Porta prophesied confidently. "Make your stakes." He rang a little silver bell, and Tiny banged on a horseshoe hanging on a string from the ceiling with his truncheon. Porta rolled the dice across the table. They were rather special dice. Pressure in a certain place caused a weight inside to shift with the result that the dice did as the banker wanted.

"Can I join in?" asked Eagle, who had been sitting despondently in a corner.

Tiny leaped down from his bucket and felled him to the ground with a blow from his truncheon.

"Empty his pockets," Porta ordered. "He's had his game and lost everything. That'll give him a shock."

"The prison-rat's got a couple of gold pegs," Tiny announced, after being through the pockets of the unconscious ex-Haupt. and Stabsfeldwebel.

"Not for long he hasn't," said Porta. "Here with them!"

Tiny resolutely pulled them out.

"What does such a man need spare teeth for?" Porta demanded. The two gold teeth disappeared into his canvas bag.

"How many have you got?" Heide asked curiously.

"What bloody business of yours is that? You're not going to have any of them." He spat at Eagle, who was beginning to move. "Look at that greasy prison-rat. Three months ago he was right up at the top. He kicked me in the arse and threatened all sorts of things."

63

"Let's send him across to the Amis with a cut-off ring finger in his pocket," Marlow suggested.

Eagle got to his feet with difficulty.

"You hit me," he said plaintively to Tiny.

"I did, and what about it?" Tiny grinned, provocatively. "What else did you expect? You tried to steal from the banker when you had lost in fair play."

"Lost?" Eagle muttered in a stifled voice, a crazy look on his face, and began feverishly searching his empty pockets. "You've plundered me! I know I haven't been playing. Everything's gone. My watch!" His cry rose to a heartrending shriek. "And my silver ring with the eagle Gauleiter Lemcke gave me!" He opened his mouth. His fat furred tongue ran searchingly across his top teeth.

"It's impossible," he muttered, refusing to believe what his tongue was telling him. Nervously, he poked a dirty index finger into his mouth. Slowly realisation came: his pride, his two gold eye-teeth were no longer there.

"Where the hell are my gold teeth?" he called wildly and looked round desperately, but everywhere was met by grinning faces delighting in the situation.

"Have you gone mad?" Porta said icily. "What teeth are these you're talking about."

"You know perfectly well," Eagle squeaked, his voice rising. "I had two gold teeth here." He desperately turned to Marlow and Barcelona: "You two are feldwebels. You must back me up against these thieves. I'll take this to court."

"*Caramba*," laughed Barcelona, delightedly. "No one will believe you, if you say they've snitched your gold teeth."

Marlow doubled up in a gale of laughter.

"Tiny! Show the gentleman out," Porta ordered.

Tiny laid truncheon and automatic pistol aside, clambered down from his table and went and opened the door wide. Then he positioned Eagle in the doorway, took a run and dealt him a kick worthy of a soccer international. Eagle soared off into the trees.

We went back to our playing.

Quarter of an hour later, Haupfeldwebel Hoffmann appeared, a glint in his eye.

As no one appeared to be going to order those present to spring to attention, he did so himself, but, to his boundless surprise, no one moved. He had not yet been in the squadron long enough to know to keep well out of Porta's way.

"Didn't you hear the order?" he pointed at Porta. "And take that yellow hat off your head."

"Can't be done, Herr Hauptfeldwebel. I've only two hands and I've got dice in one and my croupier's rake in the other. If I drop either of them, it would be the end."

Hoffmann bellowed: "Mutiny! Insubordination." He cursed us, calling us all sorts of creatures unknown to zoology and wound up: "I forbid you to play games of chance."

Porta pulled a stout notebook from an inside pocket, licked a finger and thoughtfully turned the pages. With a comical movement he placed his chipped monocle in his eye.

"Let me see, now. Incest," he turned a few more pages. "Theft of army property. Falsification of documents, Hauptfeld – no, Oberleutnant Hi . . . Rape, abuse of minors . . ."

Hoffmann opened and shut his mouth several times. He didn't understand.

Porta went on, thoughtfully: "Fraud, false declaration, paternity case – that's Stabsintendant Meissner. What a swine. He'll end in Torgau." Porta turned the pages eagerly. Then he gazed at Hoffmann with a resigned look: "Beg to report that my intelligence service has informed me that Herr Oberst Engel, who passes his time as IIA of the Divisional Staff, a week ago won 10,000 marks at HQ guessing the numbers on 100-mark notes. At the same time, they planned the attack that we are lying here waiting to start. This is confidential, Herr Hauptfeldwebel. The attack is Top Secret. They bandaged the eyes of the regiment's mascot, a nanny goat, which was present during the discussions, and put cotton wool in its ears, so that it wouldn't give things away, if it met a billy. Oberst Engel is a dog at guessing the numbers. He gets them right every time." Porta tugged the lobe of his ear and offered Hauptfeldwebel Hoffmann a pinch of snuff from a silver snuff box.

Hoffmann declined angrily and his face became suffused with purple.

"Incredible the things you hear," Porta went on genially.

"This morning I heard that a certain Hauptfeldwebel in our honourable Special Duties Regiment had sent some parachute silk back home to his wife."

Hoffmann's teeth were chattering as if he was a mule with fever. His complexion changed from yellow to blue and back again. He was no longer capable of coherence.

"Ober- Ober- Obergefreiter Porta," he stuttered, "something's going to happen. By God, it is. This can't go on." He turned round and ran out in a teetering zig-zag. The last thing he heard was Porta saying to the Legionnaire: "Now we'll soon have a new Hauptfeldwebel."

"How did you make all that up?" the Old Man asked, amazed.

"Make up," snorted Porta. "Facts aren't things you make up. Make a note of that, Herr Feldwebel Beier. It's just that I keep my eyes open. If you are to survive in a civilised country, you'd best know something to the detriment of your fellows, then you can rely on them. There's no one who hasn't some shady thing in his past, whether he's emperor or louse. Take yourself, for example, Old Man. Do you believe that everything Adolf does is right? You think him a pretty good bugger, don't you?"

"Of course," said the Old Man.

Porta grinned, fished his black book out of his pocket and made a careful note in it.

"That was a bad mark against you, and only the total defeat of Germany's arms can wash you clean of it. If I was you, I'd go to our padre and get him to help you pray for the speedy entry of the American marines into Berlin." Then he produced his flute and we all sang:

> To Hell with Hitler and all the Nazi baiters
> Wipe your arse with the swastika flag
> And open your arms to all good traitors

"You're crazy," Marlow laughed. "Hoffmann will get his own back."

Porta gave the cat in the parrot cage a piece of sausage.

"If he comes back, it will be to join the game. From now on he'll lick my boots, if I want. Have you seen his green cushion with horns on that he's so fond of? He'll make me a present of that tomorrow."

"Fancy you've never been made feldwebel," Marlow muttered admiringly.

"Idiot! As obergefreiter I'm the army's spinal column. It's me decides whether my immediate superior shall have toothache, lumbago or what. When we were in the Ukraine, we were saddled with a hauptmann called Meyer, an upstart village school master. He died."

"What happened to him?" Gregor Martin asked, curious.

"He happened to put his broad bum on a T-mine," Porta said genially. "Come along, stake your money. One green dollar to a thousand Hitler units."

"Will you take Churchill money?" Gregor Martin asked.

"Of course, as long as it started life in the Bank of England. As far as I am concerned, you can stake yen, roubles, zlotys or kroner. The rate is fixed by me and New York. But beware of marks, they're falling in value every hour. Pearls, gold and like articles are valued in dollars. No proof of ownership required. By the time we've finished, it will be mine anyway."

The dice rolled. Hour after hour. The sun went down. The mosquitoes buzzed and bit our bare arms and necks, but we never noticed, all our attention being concentrated on the dice. The room filled with smoke; the lamp on the table guttered, unable to get enough oxygen; pearls, rings, paintings, dollars, pounds, Danish and Swedish crowns, Polish zloty, Japanese yen, Indian rupees, favourite pistols and close combat weapons changed hands in that ramshackle Italian mountain hut.

Feldwebel Marlow went out for a while shortly before dawn and returned with three rolls of silk. An Italian Bersaglieri lieutenant, a count of the blood, flung a bundle of documents on the table in front of Porta, the deeds of some castle near Venice.

"20,000 dollars," he muttered.

Porta passed the documents to the Legionnaire, who examined them carefully, then whispered something to Porta. Porta glanced up at the Count.

"As you're Italian, I'll give you 17.5. If you had been a

Prussian with two iron crosses and *pour le mérite* round your neck, you'd have got 10."

"18," said the Count, trying to look as if he did not care.

"17," said Porta with a smile.

"You said 17.5 before," the Count protested.

"Too late, my dear Count. World history changes from minute to minute. Your castle may be requisitioned tomorrow by farmer-boys from across the seas, and who the hell can sell a requisitioned castle? Not even a Jew could manage that, even if he had ten Greeks and five Catalans to help him."

The Count gulped.

At that moment an oberjäger threw cameron. With an avid look he scraped a large pile of green banknotes to him.

The Count stared as though hypnotised at Porta's yellow hat, then his gaze moved up to the cat in the parrot's cage, saw the oberjäger win once again. He had no idea that this was arranged, part of Porta's psychological tactics. Suddenly, he made up his mind that his castle was an old ruin, and he shrilly accepted Porta's offer, and crumpled his feathered cap in his hands. The six dice rolled and he was then the late owner of a castle outside Venice. He managed to say a few foul-mouthed things before Tiny chucked him out.

"I am a lieutenant in the Royal Italian Army," he shouted at the dawn.

"You won't get fat on that," was Tiny's parting shot, before he slammed the door shut.

In deep depression, the Count walked off down the path. Just before it joined the road at the three twisted cork oaks, he ran into a joint military police patrol commanded by an Italian fascist captain and a German oberleutnant. As the Count had left his pocketbook with his papers in Porta's hut, the patrol gave him short shrift. The whole country had just been put under military law, because so many were deserting.

"Badoglio swine," the captain shouted vindictively, as they forced the Count to his knees. They kicked his feathered hat, tore the shoulder straps and ribbons from his jacket. Just before they shot him, he called out something about an "illegal gambling den and robbery".

"What a swine," snorted the fascist captain and spat on the

corpse. "Calling Benito's Italy a gambling den."

At three a.m. a staff M.O. appeared. He lost his entire field hospital, but Porta magnanimously gave it him back on loan for the rest of the war.

When the sun was about to set again and Porta announced a three hour interval, there were wild protests from those present, but Tiny made everyone see reason with the help of his truncheon. Porta announced with no little satisfaction that the bank had not lost. Quite the contrary. We felt the need to celebrate and our cat, Stalin, was told that it was his birthday and in record time we had procured the two essentials of any feast: beer and women.

Tiny and Porta had 'found' an overfed pig, which we pronounced oberleutnant and honorary member of the Party. Two men took the feldwebel to the depot and there, with the help of a bottle of brandy and threats of court-martial, Gestapo and military police, got the largest uniform jacket they had. It almost fitted the pig, except that we could not get the collar done up. The pig was loud in its protests against having to wear German uniform. We tied it to a chair which we nailed to the wall and there it sat, the exact image of a dyspeptic overfed German LOC officer. The Old Man laughed so much he put his jaw out of joint and Tiny had to put it in again with a blow of his fist. It was hopeless to try and get boots on the pig, but we gave it trousers and a field cap. Marlow pinned a notice on its chest: "I, Oberleutnant Porker, am the only decent swine in the German army."

"To hell with this," Heide exclaimed. "I know nothing about this, make a note of that."

"Bugger off, then," Porta suggested with a superior air. "Nobody's keeping you here."

"Bugger yourself," Heide replied angrily. "You know perfectly well that I can't do without you."

"Shall I give him one on the napper?" Tiny asked bloodthirstily, swinging his long truncheon.

Heide drew a hand grenade from his boot.

"Hit me, if you dare, you great shit-house."

Tiny began brandishing his arms in a frenzy. The word 'dare' never failed to get him worked up.

69

The M.O. and Oberfeldwebel Wolf rolled in a 20-gallon barrel of beer, helped by the quartermaster-sergeant, Krabbe. Some time before, after reading a book about the soldiers of Charles XII, Krabbe had appointed himself quartermaster. He was a dangerous competitor of Porta's. You could buy anything and everything from Krabbe, even a battle cruiser if you happened to need one. Porta and he hated each other, but were always courteous and polite.

"Well, I'll be damned," Porta exclaimed, when he saw the barrel come rolling in, "Krabbe, you haven't been committing larceny?"

Krabbe drew himself up to his full height, which was no mean one.

"That is a grievous accusation to make against a quarter-master, Obergefreiter Porta. This beer is saved up rations. When I heard you were having a celebration, I thought it was the right occasion to drink it."

"Krabbe, you are our guest this evening; but first bring me Eagle. I have need of an orderly."

"You can soon have him," Tiny put in. "I caught him down by the Regimental HQ, slinking about with a long report in his hand. I've tied him outside there on the midden and had to stuff a pair of dirty pants into his gob because he bawled so unpleasantly when I told him we would make a bonfire of him in the early morning."

"Produce him," Porta ordered.

Eagle was brought in. He rolled like a ball to Porta's feet, impelled by Tiny's boots.

"Stand at attention, you scum," Porta commanded, "and don't blink your peepers so idiotically. Tonight you have been allotted to me as my personal orderly, but first salute our C.O. in the chair there and sit down beside him."

Eagle had to salute the uniformed pig; first, five times doing an eyes right as he marched past him; then facing him. Every time the pig grunted, he was to ask: "Herr Oberleutnant wishes?"

The pig was given a bucket of beer and schnaps, and Eagle was to see that Leutnant Porker got a good gulp of the mixture every quarter of an hour. When the pig had had its drink,

Eagle could take one from the bucket too.

"What's good enough for one pig, will do for another," said Porta and chuckled delightedly. "Between drinks park your arse on a chair in front of the oberleutnant and salute."

Eagle protested, but Tiny soon made him see reason.

"Reminds me of the parish priest in Pistolen strasse who wanted to put in a complaint about Bishop Niedermeyer," Porta put in. "He wrote for three days. . . ."

"Oh, shut up, Porta," the Old Man called. "We can't stand that again today."

Porta nodded understandingly and pointed to Eagle.

"There you see, you moth-eaten prison fart, how little weight people attach to complaints. No complaint has yet found a place in world history. If you're fed to the teeth with us, just regard it as a necessary evil. Behave properly and your life will be more or less tolerable. Otherwise I shall hand you over to Tiny's jurisdiction. He will blaze you off like a rocket on December 31st at five minutes to twelve."

Eagle got to work, pale but composed.

After his third mug of ale, Porta asked one of the girls, why she had knickers on.

After the seventh glass of beer Krabbe proposed a quick game of strip poker. Beer by itself no longer appealed to us. It was too slow to take effect. The big barrel was half empty and we now filled it up with whisky, chianti, vodka, genever and to make it really tasty, we topped it up with a bottle of Worcester sauce. The smart set did that when they made cocktails, Porta said.

Eagle had to trundle the barrel twice up and down the hill to mix it properly. He was weeping by the time he had finished.

Tiny got to his feet, hitched up his trousers, picked a length of rope from the floor, and, as he strode towards Eagle, made a running noose.

"Everything comes to an end," he said genially, placing the loop round Eagle's neck. "Here's a nice bit of rope. Go outside now, find a nice tree and be a man and dangle yourself out of this world."

Eagle shot out of the door with Tiny at his heels. A loud screech came from him, as a well-placed kick sent him

71

sprawling down the slope, the rope's end fluttering behind him.

"When you get to the bottom, you'll find a good tree right on your left."

"That was a sight to gladden my eyes," said Porta laughing. "Tiny has the morale you others lack."

Our young M.O. had got fearfully drunk and was paying court to the quartermaster-sergeant in the mistaken belief that he was Greta Garbo.

"Your knickers are made of very coarse material, Miss Garbo," he said with a loud hiccough.

Krabbe hit him over the fingers with his bayonet:

"Claws off, you enema-specialist!"

The M.O. burst into tears. Then his face suddenly lit up, like at the end of a funeral, and he spat on the floor.

"I shall do you a death certificate," and he wrote on one of the girl's slips: "Ex-Stabsfeldwebel Stahlschmidt is dead. Suicide." Then he fell upon Marlow, who was lying on his back drinking: "You're a corpse," he exclaimed, which was very nearly the truth. "I won't have a corpse lying here boozing. Under the sod with you! Or I'll send for the military police."

"And we won't allow Padre Emanuel to bless Eagle. And he's not to have extreme unction either!" Heide called.

"God have mercy on him, if he has the cheek to come to life again," said Porta threateningly. "Now let's give thanks."

Heide leaped to his feet and began to beat time, while with our arms round each other's shoulders and Tiny weeping emotionally, we sang.

We then began the ritual salutation; the superior inviting the subordinate, or, if both were of the same rank, the one with more decorations, the one with fewer, to drink with him. Porta started. He raised his mug to the M.O.

"You have sneaked into our trade union by the back door from your university stupefying institute. You wear our uniform, but you don't even know the difference between a machine gun and a catapult. You have no idea how to order a flock of hungry cocks to meals. I salute you."

The M.O. got unsteadily to his feet, stood swaying, raised his mug and drained it, as the rules prescribed.

Then Heide saluted the M.O. Then Marlow. By the time it

was the Old Man's turn, the young doctor could take no more. He collapsed like a punctured balloon and was borne out on a stretcher to the strains of a funeral dirge and dumped on the midden.

Wolf wanted to drink with Porta, but was derisively refused. Proudly patting his be-ribboned chest, Porta said:

"You bloody sparking plug, do you think I'm a distributor that you can just tell to make a spark! Go and fetch me a lock of a US marine's hair and you'll have a slight chance of being allowed to drink with a front line obergefreiter."

"You must excuse me," hiccoughed Wolf and tried to bow, but lost his balance and fell at the feet of the uniformed pig, which he mistook for one of the girls. "My dear young lady, your behaviour is scarcely decent," he exclaimed, "Going about in public without knickers." Then he gave the pig a resounding kiss right on its snout, grinned idiotically and cried: "Your lips are cool and irresistible." Then he became coarse; but in the middle of a sentence caught sight of the badges of rank on the pig's jacket: saluted awkwardly with wide-spread fingers. "At your service, Herr Oberleutnant. I'm at your service, Herr Oberleutnant, you're a swine!" He then subsided onto the floor.

A fresh funeral then took place. Raised high above our heads we carried him out to the midden and laid him there beside the corpse of the doctor.

Padre Emanuel appeared. He stood for a moment in the doorway watching us and shaking his head. Marlow invited him inside. Tiny staggered stubbornly after him, but collapsed exhausted on the midden. Seeing the doctor's lifeless body, he was overcome with grief and begged his forgiveness for killing him. He swore he would never do it again. Then he discovered Wolf and began sobbing broken-heartedly.

"Good God, I'm a mass murderer!" Then he began thinking of all the insults Wolf had heaped on him in the past and began spitting on the corpse instead.

Then something happened that almost made him pass out: the corpse sat up! Tiny uttered a screech of terror, grabbed his pistol and emptied the magazine at the ghost, but fortunately all eight shots missed.

73

"What the hell's this!" exclaimed Wolf, pulling a hand grenade from the leg of his boot, which he flung at Tiny, but forgot to pull the fuse cord.

Tiny burst into the hut.

"There's a corpse chucking hand grenades at me!" he cried. "I'm going home now, I've had enough of war."

Wolf staggered in. He pointed an accusing finger at Tiny: "Murderer!"

Tiny seized an automatic pistol, which we had the utmost difficulty in wresting from him. He only calmed down when Wolf invited him to drink with him.

Suddenly Marlow, the ex-paratrooper, leaped to his feet and listened intently. On the floor beside him lay a girl, legs wide spread. Tiny was lying on top of another paying what he liked to call court to her.

"Tanks coming," Marlow bellowed.

That sobered us. We seized our weapons and heard the familiar clanking sound that can freeze the blood in the veins of even the bravest.

"Marines," Porta laughed and tied four hand grenades to a bottle full of petrol.

"*Nom de Dieu*, they've heard of our little celebration," laughed the Legionnaire.

The door was flung open, a steel-helmeted sentry stuck his head inside and gasped: "Alarm. Sound of tank tracks from the valley."

Barcelona swept him aside.

"Bugger off, little boy. We'll deal with this."

Tiny was flat on his face searching for a panzerfaust under the bed. One after the other, we staggered outside where we could hear the sound of the engines. The Old Man went first, a bundle of grenades in either hand. Marlow followed just behind, carrying a T-mine.

"Maybach engines," Oberfeldwebel Wolf announced.

"And Tiger tracks," Porta replied with the assurance of the professional.

"There's something wrong about this," Wolf said. "We haven't any tanks at the repair shops, and we're the only Tiger battalion in this sector."

We peered through the trees down the serpentine road. There were at least five or six of them. We heard voices cursing in German.

"Change gear, you arse-hole!"

A grinding of gears followed; a motor roared; Porta and Wolf looked at each other.

"Amateurs," Wolf muttered.

"They've never learned to drive Tigers," Porta said. "I believe they're gypsies."

"Sinister, anyway," Barcelona put in, swinging a Molotov cocktail. "I'll teach them a lesson."

Porta took up position in the middle of the road, feet wide apart and firmly planted. He rubbed his hairy chest with a hand grenade. In his left hand he had a jug of rice spirit.

The clatter of tank tracks became deafening. Barcelona set up the machine gun behind a fallen tree. He had to do it single handed, for he had no helper. He trod the three legs of the tripod into the ground, checked the level and adjusted the elevation; then he placed three Molotov cocktails beside him.

Marlow and Wolf hung a 7.5 centimetre grenade in a tree, connected various wires to it, thus transforming it in a few seconds into a lethal *baumkrepierer*. Woe to anyone who ran into any of those wires!

The Legionnaire was lying up on the hillside behind two linked flame-throwers. If they tried to withdraw, they would be as good as dead, for they would have to go through a wall of burning oil.

The first tank appeared on the hairpin bend: first, the flash-guard on the long muzzle of the cannon. It was a Tiger II, our latest model, the one with the turret at the side. The hatch was open and in it we could see a black uniformed figure. But they had made a bad mistake in sending them out as commando men. The tank commander in the turret was wearing a Tyrolean cap, which no German panzer man has worn since the beginning of 1942. It was the headgear you stealthily took on leave with you in order to give yourself airs.

Heavy, broad, enormous, the Tiger came lumbering up the serpentine road, another close behind.

Porta remained standing in the middle of the road. He put

75

up a hand to halt the steel monster towering in front of him. He peered into the muzzle of its 8.8 cm cannon and smiled to the commander, who was leaning over the turret.

"Welcome to our joint," he called.

The tank commander had a typical Dresden accent:

"Grüss Gott! We've had a job finding you. I suppose you're No. 5 Squadron of the 27th Special Duties Regiment? I'm Oberfeldwebel Brandt from No. 2 Squadron. We have to report to you. We've the new flame-thrower tanks. Have you been told about us?"

Porta took a draught of his rice spirit and kissed the back of the cat's head.

"He's good, isn't he, Stalin? Bloody good. He could do a fine circus act!"

Tiny began fumbling with the cap of a grenade.

"His arse is going to be hot."

The Old Man shoved Porta and Tiny aside. With heavy tread and swinging arms he went up to the great tank:

"Hallo, chum. What about the password, just to do things properly?"

"Scharnhorst," the other answered with a broad grin.

Marlow nudged Heide.

"Do you see? The pale turd's got SS death's heads on his lapels? If this is Mike's marines, I'll bring up."

"*C'est le bordel*," the Legionnaire murmured. "They're putting their feet right in it."

The first tank was directed forward to the road block, where the eight T-mines hung. We climbed up onto it.

The man in the turret grew nervous, when he caught sight of our Molotov cocktails.

"Like a cigar?" Porta asked, holding out a stick grenade, its porcelain ring dangling dangerously from the opening.

The next tank, a Tiger I, came lumbering up the road and halted right behind the first, which was a dangerous tactical error. We couldn't believe our eyes, when the other four did the same.

"Have you any cunt here," the commander of the first tank asked.

"We've weapons," Porta smiled.

76

"Have you come from Rome?" Marlow asked tossing a hand grenade into the air like a juggler with a burning hoop.

"Why have you got mixed tanks?" Porta asked inquisitively.

"Why are you bringing them to us? We're a training regiment. We know the I's. We got rid of them three months ago. Where were you a recruit?"

"With Panzer 2 in Eisenach."

The Old Man shoved me forward.

"Here's one of yours then."

I smiled.

"I don't remember you. What squadron were you in?"

"No. 4."

"Ah, yes. Hauptmann Krajewski was your boss. Who was the C.O.?"

"Major von Strachwitz."

He was well informed. The panzer count was the unit's commander.

The Old Man nudged me, but I did not quite know what he meant.

"Can you remember the name of the adjutant," I asked. "I always forget it."

"Oberleutnant von Kleist," grinned the oberfeldwebel with the Dresden accent.

"When did you leave the regiment," I asked.

"Just after Ratibor."

"Do you know where Hyazinth Graf von Strachwitz is now?" I asked.

The man could scarcely conceal his nervousness.

"What the hell is this cross-examination?" he exclaimed irritably. "Open that barrier and let us in. We have to report." He held out various documents and pointed to a stamp. "As you see, we've come straight from Army Command. So up with that boom."

"Steady on now," Porta grinned. "This campaign's no express affair. One should never go out onto thin ice. Hop out of those tanks and we'll drive them in. Major Mike prefers to see familiar faces in the turrets."

"Is that the major who was with the US marines?"

"Yes, brother. Shuffield Barracks. Hawaii."

The other gulped.

Tiny went travelling on the cannon's barrel. He put a grenade in the muzzle and toyed casually with the porcelain ring.

"What the hell do you think you're up to?" called the oberfeldwebel. He said something to the crew inside that we didn't catch, but we saw the evil eye of the flame-thrower begin to move.

The Legionnaire who had got himself upon the rear hatch, peered into the turret with interest.

"*On lui coupe les couilles!*" He turned his thumb down and at the same moment his pistol roared.

The man in the turret fell forward, riddled. Molotov cocktails went sailing through the open turret hatches. Wolf swung his arm back and with a masterly throw landed a T-mine under the turret ring of the third Tiger.

There was an ear-splitting explosion and fifteen tons of steel soared upwards. An 8.8 cm long-barrel cannon went sailing into the pine wood, and bits of bodies were scattered on all sides. Burning petrol spurted round us, and explosion followed explosion, like a volcano erupting.

In the middle of this inferno stood the swaying figure of the young doctor holding his first aid bag. He called something unintelligible, his face covered with blood and half his nose missing.

The heat struck us like a clenched fist. Burning oil, petrol and the nauseating stench of burned flesh.

All six tanks were in flames.

"Traitors," muttered the doctor and flung himself down beside Porta.

"German-Americans," Porta corrected. "There are no rules in this war. All foul play and dirty tricks. If these amateurs had tried it on a squadron that had had tanks being repaired and not chosen a Special Service Regiment, it would have come off."

"They should have taken the trouble to get regulation death's heads for their lapels," Tiny muttered. "Everyone knows there are no SS-panzers down here."

Porta got to his feet, glanced indifferently at the blazing tanks.

"Now I want a fuck!" he announced.

We put up 42 birchwood crosses in the pine wood with the names of American tankmen. Each got his deserts.

V

*Monte Cassino, a name, a monastery, a half-forgotten place south
of Rome? No, a hell so indescribable that even the most imaginative would not be able to describe its horrors. It was a place, where
the dead died five times over. A place of hunger and
thirst.*

A graveyard for young men between twenty and thirty.

*The trenches were piled high with bodies. There were so many
of them. we stopped trying to clear them away. We trod on them
and started back, rigid with horror, when they uttered their
'E-e-e-eh!' and then 'E-e-eh!' Sorry, chum, I thought you were
dead.*

*And they were dead. The cry came from wide open mouths
when you trod on their gas-filled bellies.*

*Which was worst? The drum fire? The hunger? The thirst?
The glinting bayonets? The burning oil of the flame-throwers?
Or the naked rats, the size of cats? I don't know. But one thing
that neither I nor any other soldier who was there will ever forget,
was the stench. The sweet stench of corpses mixed with chlorine.
It clung to the wounded in hospital for months afterwards, nauseating doctors and nurses. Their uniforms had been taken and burned,
but the stench had permeated them to the bone. The stench of
Monte Cassino.*

*Nine out of the ten supply columns remained in the gorge of
death, unrecognisable bloody lumps. You can eat bark, leaves,
even earth to help your hunger, but thirst! We fought like wild
animals over a puddle. We discovered a shell hole full of water
out in no-man's-land. A horde of rats was drinking avidly at it.
We flung a hand grenade at them, then heedless of the bursting
shells, we flung ourselves down there and drank, drank,
drank!*

By the afternoon bursting shells had emptied the hole. On the bottom were some distended corpses. They had been there a long time. We spewed our guts up. But the next day, we found another shell hole and drank again.

That was Monte Cassino, the holy mountain.

SECRET MISSION

The crest of the ridge was veiled in dense, blue mist. We kept marching into patches of low mist. A flock of crows wheeled down delightedly upon a forgotten corpse. A big herring gull drove them away.

We were bad-tempered and tired after a night's digging that had cost us twelve men.

The first shells fell. They were evil 10.5's. They sounded like a huge door being slammed. Fortunately for us, they were not fitted with contact fuses. If they had, most of us would have been done for there and then.

Porta and I were unrolling a coil of barbed wire, when they started coming over. For the next two hours we lay out there in no-man's land. Then they attacked. Shoals of infantry. We had only light arms with us, as we were digging, and so we had to use barbed wire and stanchions as weapons. One of our pointed steel stanchions was just as good as a bayonet. Most of our losses were incurred when we returned after the attack, for our own infantry shot at us, firing low, thinking we were the English. When we reached their positions, Mike hit the company commander in the trench and knocked him out, and Leutnant Ludwig collapsed at the feet of his C.O. with half his guts hanging out of a gaping hole in his belly. Ludwig was only eighteen and that was his first action. The C.O. vomited.

Trenching and wiring was not reckoned as anything. It was on a par with guard duty. Nobody was particularly keen for it, but it had to be done. There were always casualties. It was the units in rest positions, who were given the job.

We could hear violent gunfire in the North. It sounded as though something were going to start at Forti. But we didn't care. It never moved us, when we heard of a whole division being wiped out. They weren't people we knew. We were out-

and-out egoists. War had made us indifferent to other peoples' pain.

When we reached the road, where the trucks should have been waiting for us, there were none. We flung our helmets on the ground angrily and cursed the service corps to hell and back again. We couldn't stand them and regarded them as spongers, like the cookhouse men.

Leutnant Frick emerged from the mist together with two strange Luftwaffe officers. They walked slowly along the squadron picking out various people, who were told to fall in on the lefthand side of the road.

The Old Man nodded: "More dirty work in the offing. This stinks of special mission."

Almost all of No. 2 Troop were selected. Seventeen in all.

"La merde aux yeux," cursed the Legionnaire, shuddering with cold. "There goes our morning coffee."

Leutnant Frick beckoned to the Old Man. They whispered together. Then Gregor Martin and Marlow were called out and sent across to us.

"So you couldn't do without us," Marlow said, grinning, as he sat down beside the Legionnaire.

The Luftwaffe officers had a good look at each of us. Some trucks came jolting up.

"No. 5 Company, board. Those picked out to the left," Mike ordered.

The delighted lucky ones clambered up on to the trucks and waved to us. We spat at them. That wasn't enough for Tiny. He threw a great stone at them.

"Pick up your arms. Single file. Follow me!" ordered Leutnant Frick.

Luftwaffe trucks drove us to Teano. There we lay all day behind the station, waiting. Half of a soldier's time is spent waiting.

We played pontoon. When dinner time came we broke into a supply wagon standing on a siding. Two cases of cognac made us take a somewhat brighter view of life. Porta found four sucking pigs which we roasted on a spit.

"That's plundering," the Old Man muttered. "You could be hanged for that."

Porta said: "At least I'd go out with a full belly."

It was midnight when they woke us and marched us to a thick wood, where fifteen SS trucks stood waiting. That was a surprise. The trucks all belonged to the 20th SS Grenadiers, a division that consisted largely of men from the border states. We had met the division once, in White Russia. In the trucks, at the back, were SS greatcoats and helmets.

"What the hell's this?" the Old Man growled, amazed. "Are they going to try and shove us into the SS?"

Barcelona and Tiny were already delightedly trying on great-coats. Tiny had put on an unterscharführer's and was walking around in it, showing off. He pointed contemptuously at the Old Man, who gaped at him.

"Pull your old bones together, you antique, when an unter-scharführer passes! Or would you like a spell in a concentra-tion camp to learn manners? I'm a big wig. I once kissed the Führer's arse. Remember that!"

Leutnant Frick appeared from behind one of the trucks.

"Take that greatcoat off, Creutzfeldt, and keep your mouth shut!"

"Jawohl, Untersturmführer, SS Unterscharführer Creutz-feldt begs to report his departure." He chucked the greatcoat and helmet into the depths of the truck, walked up to Leutnant Frick again, banged his heels together. "Herr Leutnant, Obergefreiter Creutzfeldt, reporting back."

Leutnant Frick waved him away with a gesture of irritation.

"Get into the back of that truck and do me the favour of going to sleep there."

Shortly before daybreak we swung into the open space in front of the monastery of Monte Cassino, where a number of heavy Luftwaffe trucks were already standing. Some young officers from the Hermann Göring Panzerdivision were bust-ling about. They ordered us to camouflage our trucks and take cover. Some men were already obliterating our trucks' tracks.

Tiny could not contain himself. He again put on a SS great-coat and helmet. A Luftwaffe major ticked him off roundly and threatened all sorts of disasters, if he let himself be seen in that uniform again.

We waited all morning without anything else happening, but Allied bombers flying overhead leaving vapour trails in the sky. We had had the foresight to supply ourselves from the railway truck and Porta had a quarter of a sucking pig in the pocket of his greatcoat.

"We've to blow the whole shitting place up," Tiny told us, his face beaming.

"Blast them," Porta exclaimed angrily. "They could let the engineers do that. This is gala night at Palid Ida's. She's got a lot of fine tarts coming from Rome, all fragrant with rose water."

Tiny let his prurient imagination have full rein. He dribbled at the mouth.

"There are nuns in this holy building."

Heide's eyes narrowed.

"Freedom to loot would suit you nicely, wouldn't it?"

Tiny swallowed, then licked his lips.

"Don't talk about it. I'm almost bursting out of my trousers."

Porta took a mouthful of sucking pig. His face glistened with fat.

"Have I ever told you about the time I was gardener to a nunnery?"

We laughed and edged closer together under the lorry, settled our gasmasks comfortably under our heads.

"Was that down on the river Dubovila?" the Old Man asked.

"No, no! It was when I was on loan to the 2nd Panzer Regiment."

"I certainly don't remember you being that," laughed the Old Man with a sideways glance at us.

"Your memory has never been anything to boast of," retorted Porta. "But we, No. 2 Regiment and I, that is, were somewhere down among the Black Sea farmers. I was wandering about on my own looking for something important."

"Cunt?" Tiny asked, suddenly interested.

"That's the only idea you've got in that thick head of yours," Porta said. "I was looking for defeat."

"Was it supposed to be found round the Black Sea?" the Old Man asked, amazed.

"I had just heard that morning on the Tommy radio that

defeat was imminent. The fighting in the Struma valley was going to be decisive. So I was searching with my magnifying glass behind every stone. All at once, I heard women screaming. Aha, I thought, there are some who have found defeat. But judging by the sounds it was knickers rather than flags that were being hauled down. The screams came from a nunnery. I swung myself up onto the wall and stuck my tomato inside. Imagine what I saw. Our faithful allies were busy helping the nuns. I can't remember what I said to them, but they withdrew at some considerable speed. I landed in a bed of tulips and received an excellent reception."

Porta's absorbing tale was here interrupted by Leutnant Frick ordering us to fall in.

An oberleutnant with the white collar tabs of the Hermann Göring Panzerdivision, looked us over.

An observer 'plane was circling over the monastery.

"Artillery observer," Heide said. "If he catches sight of us . . ."

Some monks brought us hot tea. We tipped half of it away and filled the cups up with rum. We still did not know what we were there for. We could hear hammering and sawing inside the monastery and in the distance the gunfire was unceasing.

"They're hard at it beyond the hills there," said the Old Man thoughtfully. "There's something brewing. I can feel it in my bones."

Whenever the Old Man said that, it was so. He was an old sweat and as such could smell dirty work a mile away.

"What are we here for?" Heide asked, addressing himself to no one in particular, and gave himself a shake.

"No idea," muttered the Old Man, giving his nose a tug. "I don't like all these people with the white tabs and the SS uniforms in the trucks. It stinks of hanky-panky. They've threatened us a hundred times with God knows what, if we go near the monastery, and now here we are at it, and armed to the teeth. I wonder if the Catholic hunt hasn't perhaps started?"

"God preserve us, if that's the case," Barcelona said. "We'll be wading up to our chins in blood, if it is."

The Old Man slowly lit his pipe.

When night sank over the mountains hiding them, we backed

the trucks to the monastery door. No lights were to be used in any circumstances. An elderly Luftwaffe leutnant ordered us to put our weapons in the driver's cab. No one was to enter the monastery armed. Somewhat reluctant, we chucked our automatic pistols into the cab. We felt naked without our arms.

"Take off your equipment and arms," the strange leutnant ordered heatedly.

Tiny tried to dart inside with a P.38 sticking out of his trousers pocket. The leutnant called to him hectoringly:

"War without shooting irons is crazy," Tiny could not help saying.

"Shut that mouth of yours, obergefreiter," the leutnant fumed.

The Legionnaire came gliding up with a cigarette dangling from the corner of his mouth. He laughed openly at the leutnant. He had his heavy Russian pistol hanging provocatively on his chest.

"Court martial, Herr Leutnant? *Merde alors!* You must be joking."

"What's this behaviour, man," the leutnant exclaimed indignantly.

"That's what I would ask you, Herr Leutnant. I would be most interested to know what a court martial would say to these goings-on." Casually, the Legionnaire lit a fresh cigarette and puffed the smoke into the Luftwaffe officer's face. "We refuse to hand over our arms, Herr Leutnant, and we will not take part in sabotaging orders. You and your colleagues have more reason to fear a court martial than we."

"Have you gone off your head," the leutnant cried in a voice that had a nervous quaver in it. "What's this nonsense of yours?"

The Legionnaire grinned impertinently. He turned to the rest of us, who were listening with intense interest.

"*Il nouse casse les couilles!*"

"I understand French, you lout." The leutnant was almost beside himself with rage.

"*Je m'emmerde!*" laughed the Legionnaire.

We thought for a moment that the leutnant was going to go for the Legionnaire, who continued unconcernedly to examine the magazine of his heavy pistol.

We were open-mouthed with amazement. We could not understand it. The Legionnaire was hundred per cent a soldier. He never went too far. He could be more impudent than most, but he never took risks. He must have been onto something big. Without quite knowing how, we had got hold of our arms again and had closed up behind the Legionnaire.

The leutnant turned and rushed up the steps.

"Now the balloon'll go up," Rudolph Kleber whispered. "This is like the Florian Geyer* mutiny."

"Nothing's going to happen," the Legionnaire said with calm assurance. "If they become impertinent, we'll shoot them down. We'd get medals for doing it."

"What's happening?" Heide asked. "You might at least tell us. I'm almost pissing my pants with excitement." Greedily he flourished his automatic pistol, an Italian Biretta.

Porta heaved the container of his flame-thrower on to his back and pulled the straps tight.

"Let's singe the hair off their balls," he said and put the setting to close range.

"*Hamdoulla*" (slowly) said the Legionnaire. "If we're to shoot this *bande de funistes*, I shall shoot first."

"Well, for Christ's sake explain," Marlow said irritably.

"*C'est le bourdel*. They're sabotaging a special order from Adolf himself and Kaltenbrunner."

A group of officers came hurrying down the steps. Our Leutnant Frick came sauntering along behind, smiling. He knew us. He obviously wouldn't have any funny stuff.

The little Luftwaffe leutnant was cackling like an old hen. A broad-shouldered major shut him up. None of them was armed. They did not even have their belts on.

Some of us took cover behind the pillars in the cloisters. The Legionnaire seated himself provocatively on the parapet of the well in the central court. He had one finger on the trigger. He was as assured as a Russian commissar who had Josef Stalin behind him.

The broad-shouldered major took up position in front of

* Famous SS cavalry regiment.

him. He was twice the Legionnaire's size. His greatcoat was open. There was no doubt that he was unarmed.

They regarded each other in silence.

Porta toyed thoughtfully with his flame-thrower.

"Bon, mon Commandant? What now? Court martial! Drum head perhaps?"

"I would like a word with you in private."

The Legionnaire smiled enigmatically.

"Non, mon Commandant. I don't aspire to a bullet in the back of my head in some dark cellar. I have heard of so-called officers' special courts. I am not an officer. I am only a *caporal-chef*, an unknown without name or honour, from La Legion Étrangère."

A hauptmann took a couple of steps forward, but was halted by the major.

"I give you my word of honour, unteroffizier, that nothing will happen to you."

"An officer's word to a lousy soldier?" The Legionnaire shrugged his shoulders.

The major took a deep breath. His face was suffused.

Tiny opened his mouth to give his contribution, but Porta gave him a warning kick on the shin.

Unconcernedly the Legionnaire lit a fresh cigarette.

"What is it you want, unteroffizier? Do you think we should destroy a thousand-year old culture, because a madman has ordered it?"

"Madman? That remark could cost you your head, mon Commandant."

The major took a step forward and made as though to set his hand confidentially on the Legionnaire's shoulder; but the Legionnaire avoided it with a twist of his body and thrust him back with the barrel of his pistol.

"A subordinate must stand three paces from his superior, mon Commandant."

Again the hauptmann wanted to intervene.

"I have told you to keep quiet," said the major angrily; then, turning to the Legionnaire, he said: "Unteroffizier, do you know what Monte Cassino is? Do you know that it is the oldest cultural centre in Europe? It is the Benedictine's original monastery, and in it are Christianity's most sacred relics? Do you want a library of 70,000 irreplaceable volumes to go up in flames? A library it has taken the Benedictine monks many centuries to collect. To say nothing of paintings by famous masters, age-old crucifixes, historic carvings in wood and wonderful goldsmith's work. Will you with a clear conscience let all that be destroyed because of a crazy order? You are a hard and a good soldier, unteroffizier, that I know. You are proud of having served in a famous corps of brave men under the French flag, but don't forget that that same French army throughout the centuries has protected the Christian faith. Will you now, a French soldier, for that is what you are, prevent us saving all that? You and your comrades can kill all of us here in the monastery. You can start with me and end with the arch-abbot Diamaré. Nothing will happen to you, if you do. You might even be decorated for doing it; but I can assure you that the French army will have nothing more to do with you. They will deprive you of the red ribbon you wear over your breast pocket. I am not afraid of dying, unteroffizier. Nor are my officers. We know that we are staking our lives in doing this, but we do not intend to let all this be destroyed. We are merely people. We can be replaced, but not one splinter, not one document in there could ever be replaced. The Benedictine order has had its home here since the year 529. In a short time Monte Cassino will be the centre of desperate fighting. Its walls, statues, the basilica, all these lovely buildings," he raised his hands in a desperate gesture, while the wind tugged at his greatcoat and ruffled his grey hair, "these we cannot save from destruction. They will be razed to the ground, and thousands of young men will be killed and maimed. But the unique, irreplaceable treasures that the holy monastery contains can all be taken to safety in Rome in two or three nights."

"And if we are caught, mon Commandant?" asked the Legionnaire with a smile. "We would gladly help you, if it means so much to you, but we are not going to let ourselves be tricked and threatened by your officers. As you said, we are soldiers. We have been soldiers a long time. That is all we are good for. Our job is to burn, plunder and kill. We were born on the army midden and there we'll peg out, but we know the sentence a court martial will pass for sabotaging the Führer's orders. We're not idiots. We are to be shoved into SS greatcoats and undertake illegal transport that will use up a thousand gallons of precious petrol. Petrol, mon Commandant, that is badly needed for our heavy Tigers. Misuse of just a few litres can cost one's head. We don't want to be broken on the wheel by the Gestapo in Via Tasso. I have heard quite a lot about Sturmbannführer Kappler, who resides in the former cultural section. We don't intend to let ourselves be slaughtered at the eleventh hour for any amount of sacred trash. If you can give us the all clear in the shape of a regulation order, we are with you."

"Here, here," came Porta's voice from the background.

"If all goes well," Tiny said dreamily, "they might put up a statue to us. I wouldn't mind standing here looking out over the Lire valley."

"You can be the weather cock on the church," said Porta.

"Shut up!" the Legionnaire snarled angrily.

"If you like, I will give you a written order. You are properly attached to my unit. No one can hold you and your companions responsible, if things go wrong."

"Let's hope so," the Legionnaire muttered. "Though I'm not so sure. All right, we'll do it."

The officers disappeared up the steps to the basilica.

The Legionnaire swung his machine pistol. We held our breath, thinking he was going to mow them down. He laughed maliciously.

"We're crazy. If we had riddled them and reported the business, we would all have been promoted and perhaps got away from the front. I never liked this business," he explained. "Then I came across a chap in a monk's cowl. He was an SS man. One of the gang Heydrich got to enter the religious orders so as to undermine them from within. He told me about a special order, one of the absolute top secret ones."

"How on earth did you get him to talk?" the Old Man asked.

The Legionnaire laughed slyly and held up a Party book. We nodded, recognising it. It was the one we had taken from the

SS man sent to us for cowardice whom we had thrown down the cliff.

"He hasn't been here very long. He came with some refugees, but he knows all that's going on. According to this special order, nothing must be removed from the monastery. Everything has to go up with it, be destroyed. Not by us, but by the other side."

Porta whistled appreciatively.

"Far from stupid. The decisive battle will be fought here on the top of the holy mountain. We are to protect the monastery, while the other side blows it to smithereens. And Goebbels will have a long story ready about the atrocities of those barbarians from across the sea, who have destroyed the oldest and finest cultural objects Europe possesses. We would have tried to move the treasure, but their beastly artillery prevented us. And every naïve soul will swallow it raw. Goebbels just has to say: was it our shells smashed the monastery? No, sir, it was the other side's. I should be surprised if it wasn't the Vatican's turn after Monte Cassino. I do believe this here is a try out. If it comes off, the Pope will have had it."

The Legionnaire rubbed his chin, then went on.

"This is a bloody dangerous business. I don't think those officers realise how dangerous. They think that the worst that can happen to them is a court martial and up against the wall. But it wouldn't be like that. We would be screaming, begging for death. We would beseech them to shoot us. Man is incredibly long-lived in the hands of experts. The idea with the monastery is Kaltenbrunner's. He is an even greater hater of Catholics than Heydrich. The boys in the Via Tasso will break us on the wheel."

"I once saw a leutnant's stomach burst with compressed air during interrogation. They use water, too." Tiny put in.

"Another time, Tiny," the Old Man waved him silent.

"I suggest," the Legionnaire went on, "that Tiny and I lay that SD man stiff. I have promised to alert the SD in Rome and am to meet him shortly by the old crucifix outside. Tiny can come up on him from behind and put the sling round his neck. Then we'll put him under a truck and drive over him, so nobody will have any suspicions, and then, I think, we should hop it from here as fast as we can. We won't get anything out of handling this red-hot shit. Nobody will thank us. The officers will be lauded to the skies and we'll be forgotten."

"On the other hand," Porta said with a sly grin, "I think it is idiotic to let such valuable things be destroyed. Lots of people are crazy about old things. Suppose some of them disappeared between here and Rome? Do you see the idea?"

"We could get into the hell of a lot of trouble, once the war's over," the Old Man remarked dryly. "Don't think this war will end just when a couple of generals sign on the dotted line. That's when the fun will really begin. Everybody will be in the hell of a hurry then to clear themselves. And we coolies will be the ones who will pay for it."

"*Tu as raison, mon sergent,*" said the Legionnaire with a nod of agreement.

"Bloody funks, you are," Gregor Martin said. "My general and I left the museums we visited with lots of nice pieces."

"Hear, hear," Marlow and Porta cried simultaneously.

The Legionnaire nodded to Tiny.

Tiny with a murderous glint in his eye, waggled his steel sling. Then the two walked out of the gate and disappeared into the dark down the narrow path.

VI

We were sitting on the bare earth. The tanks were dug in, so we
were hidden from the enemy's eyes. Now and again a shell came
over. When trucks passed on the road above, they raised a cloud
of dust that settled on our black uniforms and made everything
white.

The river twined along at the foot of the mountain, its water
dark blue like the sky, and through it the stones on the bottom
shone whitely like diamonds. Our mess tins were full of spaghetti.
The experts could roll it round their forks. Heide was one, but
he did everything perfectly. Porta held up his fork, the loose
ends of spaghetti dangling free and sucked them into his mouth
with great sounds of relish.

Tiny had nothing to eat with but his fingers.

Every time a shell dropped near us, we flung ourselves flat,
grasping our mess tins, and laughed heartily when we found
ourselves unhurt.

Porta pointed to a couple of disintegrating corpses sailing down
the river. We could smell the stench of them.

Barcelona laughed.

"It doesn't matter who one eats with, as long as one eats well!"

Porta sucked a lump of pork clean of tomato sauce and oil and
put it into his pocket as a reserve. Porta always thought of the
rainy day.

None of us counted for anything, so we hated the war. On the
other hand, we had forgotten life before the war. The only one who
pretended he could remember things, was Porta, but he was a
heaven-inspired liar.

We had a carboy filled with wine, that tasted a little of acid,
but what did that matter. If you held your nose, when you drank,
you could scarcely taste it.

A series of shells lashed into the river. The water-splash almost reached us.

Tiny licked the mess tins clean, which saved us the bother of washing them. He always licked the big mess tins clean at the mess-truck. He was never satisfied. But then he was pretty big.

We had been sitting there all morning and most of the afternoon. It was a good place. They must have been searching for us for a couple of hours already. We didn't care. It wasn't us who would win the war – we were of no account.

SS-UNTERSTURMFUHRER . JULIUS HEIDE

Tiny and Porta were in the first truck, Tiny clasping an ancient crucifix as they openly discussed how much a rich collector might be prepared to give for such an object. Between them sat a nun, ignorant of their language, so when they became lewd, she laughed with them, not understanding.

As we reached Cassino itself, we were stopped by the military police, the beams of their torches shining on the SS signs on our uniforms.

"Are you out having a lark?" Porta laughed to the brutal face beneath the steel helmet.

"Special Unit?" growled the M.P.

"That's what we are," Porta twittered, carefree. "Special assignment from the SS Reichsführer direct."

Heide came striding along the column, the skirts of his SS untersturmfuhrer's greatcoat flapping, a machine pistol dangling on his chest.

"Who the hell's daring to stop us?" he bellowed with a swagger.

The military police feldwebel became nervous, banged his heels together and rattled off a report: "Beg to report, Herr Untersturmführer, all vehicles have to be searched. Army Command order."

"I shit on all army commanders," Heide bellowed. "I have only one commander: the Reichsführer SS." He brandished his pistol. "Make way for my column, damn it, unless you want to dangle, feldwebel. And this transport is 'Top Secret,' remember that."

"Jawohl, Herr Untersturmführer," the military policeman stammered nervously.

"You can stick that 'Herr' up your arse. We dispensed with that in the SS long ago." Heide held up his hand in an arrogant gesture and bellowed a 'Heil Hitler' into the darkness.

The boom was raised. The column rolled on.

There we unloaded in the fortress of San Angelo, or rather, others unloaded for us, while we lay in the shade, drinking. Porta got hold of a whole bucket of food. Some service corps men tried to ingratiate themselves, but were brutally refused, and a stabsgefreiter got uppish, which cost him two of his front teeth.

When the sun was setting, we drove back to Cassino. A hauptmann from the Hermann Göring Panzer Division brought us our movement orders.

On the next journey we were not stopped until near Vala-montone, some twenty kilometres from Rome. This too Heide dealt with SS fashion, but not so easily, because here we had to deal with a police leutnant, a mountain of a man with hand grenades stuffed in his belt.

"Movement order," he demanded, a gallows with rope dangling in his eye.

Heide was oblivious of danger, for he was possessed by his SS uniform. He went close up to the man, flexed his knees, shoved his SS cap back onto his head.

"What the bloody hell do you cold-arsed buggers imagine you're doing? This is the second time I have been delayed on this Top Secret transport. I'd like to hear what the Reichs-führer has to say, when he learns about it."

But the mountainous leutnant was not one to be intimidated by the first roar.

"Your orders, untersturmführer? The Reichsführer SS would not approve of my letting a column pass unchallenged."

"If there's anything you want to know, leutnant," Heide's voice rang over the houses in blacked-out Valmonte, "apply to the boys in Via Tasso. They'll teach you to sabotage the Reichsführer's orders. I'll give you ten seconds to remove that piss-box you've blocked the road with! Otherwise there'll be bullets and bodies flying."

The leutnant seemed to diminish a little in bulk. He made a nervous gesture, that presumably was meant to be a salute, then turned on his oberfeldwebel, who was nonchalantly leaning against the truck: "Get that thing out of the way, man! Don't

stand there gaping! Do you want to sabotage the Reichsführer's orders? Got a yearning for the snows of the Eastern
front?"

The oberfeldwebel became busy, snarling and slanging the
driver sitting up in the cab.

Heide demonstratively took a pull at his flask without
offering it to the leutnant. There he stood legs wide apart, his
SS cap on the back of his head and his finger on the trigger of
his pistol, watching the laden trucks drive past the police
leutnant and his eager men. He began a carefree whistling,
with a scornful look at the leutnant.

The leutnant squinted at the armlet that Heide had put
round his arm, his own idea. Reichssicherheitshauptamt, it
said.

Heide thrust his arm under the leutnant's nose:

"Don't you like my armlet, leutnant?"

"If you'd said straightaway that you were from RSHA, you
could have gone through without discussion, but there are so
many shits drifting about with the most incredible papers
signed by some lousy general or other. But it's different with
you Heinrich lads."

A ten-ton Krupp drove past slowly. Leutnant Frick,
wearing an SS helmet, looked down from the window of the
driver's cab. In his confusion he saluted, which could have
been a fatal mistake, if Heide had not reacted instantly.

"What the devil do you think you're doing? Do you imagine
you're still an oberleutnant in the army? Haven't you yet got
it into your head that in our lot we use the German salute and
none of your junker gestures!" With a broad grin he turned to
the police leutnant: "An inheritance from the Luftwaffe.
What are we to do with the filth? We took on ten thousand of
them at Charkov. That was General Hausser. He should
never have been our C.O. No, Papa Eike or Sepp-Dietrich.
That would have been something."

"What unit are you actually?" the leutnant asked.

"1st Latvian SS Grenadier Division."

The leutnant gave a long whistle.

"Then there *is* something brewing. It was you boys did all
the transports of Jews. I was with one to Auschwitz, on which

your boys from the 1st Latvian provided the guards. It took a bit of stomaching and I've seen more than most. I was in that big shooting at Kiev, when we laid several thousand flat in a couple of hours."

"The Reichsführer likes us," Heide said proudly. "We do what we are told to do and no nonsense."

The leutnant bent confidentially closer:

"Unterstormführer, is Pius coming out of the bushes? Has the time come? It's being said the action against the Jews here is only to provoke the old fox and his bloody cardinals."

Heide gave a loud laugh that could have been taken either way. The leutnant nodded and clapped his pistol.

"They promised us at the secret party meetings in '34 that the pest of Christianity would be rooted out."

"I know. There isn't room for both the crows and us in this world," snarled Heide. "And we're not giving way."

"That's what I like to hear," grinned the leutnant, rubbing his vast hands delightedly.

"I should hope so," Heide hissed, "otherwise I might have wanted to take you with me."

The leutnant gave a rather forced laugh. "Don't misunderstand me, untersturmführer. I understand your transport is Top Secret, but are you heading for Rome?"

Heide drew himself up.

"Of course, I'm going to Rome."

The leutnant drew his hand confusedly over his square chin. Then he said: "Do you know that you have two more road-blocks to pass? We set them up twenty minutes ago. Orders from Via Tasso."

Heide bit his underlip, tightened his chin strap.

"What devil's nonsense is this? Those chaps will get an arseful, if I'm delayed any more. The Reichsführer's last words to me were: 'Don't hesitate to shoot, untersturmführer, if you run into hindrances!' But, perhaps, it would be better to let me have the pass word."

"I don't quite know . . . . It's a great risk, untersturmführer." The mountain of flesh was visibly agitated. "My orders from Via Tasso were also marked Top Secret!"

Heide let the muzzle of his pistol drop until it was pointing straight at the leutnant's belt buckle.

"The Reichsführer's orders were to shoot, if I was delayed."

"Waterloo," whispered the leutnant, staring as though hypnotised at the muzzle of the Mpi.

Heide's face lit up with satisfaction.

"And the response?"

"Blücher."

Heide let the pistol muzzle sink.

"Thanks, comrade. I hate plugging a fellow officer unless it's absolutely necessary."

The leutnant became suddenly busy. He dashed to a wooden hut at the roadside.

"What a buggering collection of nitwits!" He flung an unteroffizier aside to get to the telephone quicker. Frenziedly he wound the handle, hissed a string of code words into the mouthpiece, cursed and swore: "Oberfeld," he bellowed at the man at the other end of the wire. "If the column that's on its way now does not get through the barrier like a rocket, you'll loose your bloody head! Orders of the Reichsführer."

Heide's little SS amphibian was standing with its lights out by the side of the road.

"Follow me," bawled the leutnant and flung himself into his big Kübel that was standing in the cover of some trees. A great roar came from its heavy engine as it shot off in the direction of Rome with mud spurting on either side.

Heide jumped into his amphibian and gave Gregor Martin a grin of encouragement.

"After him, Gregor! Show us what a van driver can do! He mustn't get away from us. If he once starts thinking, we've had it!"

Five minutes later Gregor swore, braked frantically and just managed to avoid a big halted truck. The light amphibian slithered sideways up the line of trucks, spun round twice and landed in a field.

Cursing and swearing, the two crawled unhurt out of the wrecked car. The big leutnant came running up with two of his MPs. Servilely he began dusting Heide down, but was shoved aside with a gesture of irritation.

"What in hot hell is this, leutnant? Have you stopped my

vehicles again? Get me through to SD, so that I can have a word with Gruppenführer Müller in Berlin. It's high time you lot had a rocket up your arses."

"Everything's all right, untersturmführer. The column can go straight on. I'll deal with the snotty oberfeldwebel in charge here."

An oberfeldwebel of the military police, standing just behind the nervous leutnant, stammered an explanation.

"Kindly shut your mouth, oberfeld'." the leutnant shouted hysterically. "You're a dirty saboteur. You'll soon be a private footslogging in Russia. You'll see. And now, vanish! Out of my sight!"

The oberfeldwebel muttered something we couldn't hear.

The leutnant tore his pistol from its yellow leather holster.

"Shut your mouth, you ersatz soldier, or I'll drill a hole in you for insubordination."

Heide grinned all over his face. He stood there in the middle of the road, feet planted wide apart, his pistol across his chest. Even Himmler would have approved of him. Heide played his part beautifully, as if he was born to it – which, in a way, he was.

"Why not do it now, leutnant? We've no place for half-soldiers in our ranks. In that man's face I can see a nice bit of rope dangling over a bough."

The oberfeldwebel disappeared hurriedly into the darkness, in his own mind wishing all SS officers at the bottom of hell's hottest part. A few seconds had turned his admiration for the German system into hatred.

"An ugly customer," one of his subordinates whispered.

"He'll grow wiser, when the Americans come, the shit," the oberfeldwebel growled. "I'll volunteer for the new military police our present enemies will organise in the Third Reich after their victory, and I'll spend all my time catching SS officers!"

The amphibian car was blazing merrily. The leutnant magnanimously offered Heide his own big car, Heide graciously accepted the offer and promised to leave it at the control-post on his way back.

Leutnant Frick was shaking with nervousness. He praised

and cursed Heide. If the police leutnant began to suspect he had been made a fool of, the consequence would be incalculable.

Porta laughed heedlessly.

"They'd search for the culprits in the 1st Latvian Division."

"And when they find that it isn't even in Italy?" Leutnant Frick asked, shaking his head.

"Then they'll suspect the partisans in the mountains, Herr Leutnant," Porta said and swung a heavy case on to his shoulder. "They'll never think of looking in the 27th Special Duties. Remember, there are not many at Army HQ South who know about us.

"Our being in Italy is so bloody secret," Tiny shouted from one of the cellars of San Angelo, where he was wrestling with a heavy packing case, "that we scarcely know we're here ourselves."

Then Barcelona stumbled, dropped a case of altar reliquaries which slithered down the stairs and crushed two of Tiny's fingers. Tiny gave vent to a fierce bellow, tugged his hand away, leaving two fingers under the sharp edge of the heavy case, and in a couple of mighty bounds reached the top and went for Barcelona, blood spurting from his injured hand.

"You Spanish cunt thief, you did that on purpose!" He snatched an ancient crucifix from Porta, and, with it murderously poised above his head, rushed at Barcelona who fled from the courtyard.

Padre Emanuel, who was standing in the gateway with two monks, took in the situation in a trice. Whether it was to save Barcelona or the crucifix, we never learned, but he thrust out a leg, tripping Tiny and sending him slithering along on his front for several yards. The monks had the crucifix off him quickly.

Tiny got to his feet, fuming and swearing. Then he sighted Heide, who was swaggering about with his hands on his back in his SS officer's uniform, but he didn't get out of his way quick enough.

"You tripped me, you swine," Tiny shouted and went for him like a hurricane.

Heide took to flight, but Tiny caught him up in the middle of

Ponte San Angelo and sent him flying like a mortar bomb into the river. Heide did the crawl to the bank like a speedboat, climbed up in a zigzag, swept Leutnant Frick aside, when he tried to hold him back, and went for Tiny.

Tiny picked up a thick balk and wielded it like a flail. We exulted. This was just what we needed: a good stand-up fight!

Leutnant Frick threatened to court martial us if we did not continue unloading, but no one took any notice of him. We were not going to miss a fight between Tiny and Heide.

"Tiny," Gregor shouted provocatively. "Julius says you couldn't thrash him."

Tiny snarled savagely and wiped his face with his crushed hand, covering it with blood.

"He's bleeding a lot," Padre Emanuel observed.

"That's nothing," Porta grinned. "He's got plenty of that stuff. Julius'll be done for, long before he's shed the last drop."

Heide circled, arms wide-spread, round Tiny, who held his great balk aloft, ready.

"Jew-hater. I shall kill you."

"Your time's come, puke-bag," hissed Heide; then he picked up a piece of wood and flung it at Tiny.

Tiny charged, the balk held in front of him, like a battering ram. Heide was sent flying through the gateway, but Tiny's impetus was too great, for him to be able to follow up this success. There was a splintering of wood and tinkle of breaking glass, as Tiny's ram went through a shutter and the window behind it. He stumbled, was again up in an instant, the balk above his head, like a great mace.

We thought Heide's last moment had come, but a second before the balk struck, he rolled to one side and drew his close-combat dagger from the leg of his boot. Tiny had just time to dart behind the door before the dagger came whizzing. He seized Heide by the ankles and swung him round. If Heide had not had a steel helmet on, his head would have been crushed against the stone wall.

Tiny jumped with both feet on his stomach, aimed a kick at his head, blind with rage. For a few moments he was quite beside himself, but Heide managed to roll away in safety under one of the trucks. He seized hold of a fire extinguisher, banged the knob on the ground and directed the jet of foam at Tiny, turning him in a second into a snowman with wildly flailing arms. Blinded, half-suffocated, he ran screeching in a circle and by mistake got hold of Gregor Martin.

"Let go of me, Tiny. It's Gregor."

The next instant they had both been knocked out by Heide's empty fire extinguisher.

VII

Death! What is that? It comes like lightning. We were always expecting it and it had become a companion, a habit. None of us was religious. We had never had time. Sometimes, in a shell hole, we might discuss death, but none of us knew if there was any hereafter. How could we?

It is best to regard death as an unending dreamless sleep. We were so often threatened with court martial and execution, that it no longer made any impression. When one is to be killed anyway, it makes little difference who does the killing. Nor did we care, where or how we were buried. In the ditch under a rusty steel helmet or in a pompous graveyard with an everlasting flame burning.

The only thing we considered important was that death should be swift and painless. A firing squad in many ways was preferable to slow death in a burning tank.

Most of the old lot had gone. There, before Monte Cassino, at Christmas time 1943 there remained only 33 of the 5,000 we had started with in 1939. Most had died in flames, the classic death of the tank-man. A few were limping about minus legs and arms, some were blind. Some we had visited in hospital on our way through: Schröder, for example, the feldwebel par excellence. He had eaten sand in despair at losing both his eyes. It had been one of those shells that exploded twice. His whole face had gone.

None of us who visited him in hospital will forget the sight. He, the smart, elegant Feldwebel Schröder, did not want us to see him. He chucked bottles of medicine at us.

We sat on the steps outside the hospital and ate the chocolate and drank the red wine we had brought for him. They hounded us away. We were not allowed to sit on those steps. We weren't maimed yet.

That same night Tiny rammed his great head into some Staff M.O.'s belly. That made us feel better.

VATICAN TRANSPORT

We were sitting on the stone parapet outside the Roman theatre. The monastery towered above us and we looked down on Cassino at our feet, where people walked about in blissful ignorance of the fact that the village would soon be razed to the ground. Some German and Italian officers were sitting outside Hotel Excelsior chatting over a glass of chianti.

"Porta, I've seen a really fine piece," Gregor Martin said, thoughtfully swinging his legs. "We're taking the next lot to the Vatican, and this is our chance. Remember, the workshop company of the Hermann Göring Division has most transport, and they're scarcely aware of our existence. As Tiny says, we're so top secret, we scarcely know ourselves that we're here." He spat at a lizard that bustled busily across the road. "Let's get some benefit out of this war. We can hide the shit at Palid Ida's until things are quiet again. She's a smart girl."

Barcelona and Tiny came up.

"What're you two plotting?" Tiny called in a voice that echoed through the mountains. "Discovered a way of pinching some of the stuff yet?"

"Don't shout so, you idiot!" Gregor said.

We walked slowly up to the monastery. In the south we could hear the rumble of artillery. A well-disciplined unit of the Hermann Göring Panzerregiment marched into the monastery yard. Swiftly they loaded up some trucks. We watched them in silence. They were men who obeyed their orders to the letter. The white tabs on their collars shone. They worked in stubborn silence, just the right number for lifting and carrying in each gang. What a different lot to us!

An unteroffizier with cold, fishy eyes and an incredibly clean uniform came striding self-assuredly up to us.

"Think you're ruddy tourists," he bellowed. "Get inside. You're needed. Hurry now or your backsides'll smart."

The Legionnaire appeared. He had a field wireless receiver in his hand.

"Shut up, comrade, and listen to what our friends on the other side are bawling into the ether today!" He turned the receiver up as loud as it would go:

"This is the Allied transmitter for Southern Italy. We repeat our previous message to patriotic Italians: unite against the bandits who are desecrating your churches and graves. At this moment the Hermann Göring Panzer Division is plundering the treasures of the monastery of Monte Cassino! Fight and stop them! We repeat: under command of a staff officer the Herman Göring Panzer Division is plundering Monte Cassino monastery. One transport has already got away successfully with treasure of untold value. Italian patriots, protect your property. Don't let these bandits rob you."

The Legionnaire switched off.

"Now the fat's in the fire, *mes amis!* I wouldn't wear a white tab for the next few days, if I wanted to stay alive."

"We are here in accordance with orders," the unteroffizier protested, but now his fat-headed arrogance had gone.

"Orders?" Porta laughed. "Adolf's?"

"I'll bet a thousand to one," Gregor Martin said, "that at least a company of MP's is speeding towards us at this moment."

"Our C.O. will deal with them," the unteroffizier said desperately. "You're a lot of cowards, sticking your tail between your legs already."

A hand grenade went past close to his face and at least ten pistol muzzles were pointing at him.

"You buggering Hermann-turd, repeat that and I'll lay you cold," Porta hissed. "We have more iron crosses and bars in our lot than you have hairs in your arse. If anyone's a coward, it's you white-tabbed haemorrhoids!"

"Oh, kill him," Tiny said. "Then we can tell the MP's when they come: we happened to be passing, dressed for the occasion, and saved the treasures."

The unteroffizier turned on his heel and walked away. His

men glanced about nervously. They didn't quite know where they stood.

An obergefreiter mechanic asked cautiously: "What is all this, fellows? It appears to be very secret."

"You may well say," Porta laughed. "It's so bloody secret that not even Adolf knows it. But our colleagues on the other side of Naples appear to be busy telling him. Hermann's proud Panzer Division has become a lot of highwaymen. Pah! Tomorrow they'll be accusing you of raping the nuns. I'd take your white tabs off. I've a pair of pink ones I could sell you. They'll hang you after the liberation."

A Kübel pulled up before the monastery with squealing brakes. Five trucks followed close behind. Two platoons of MPs commanded by an oberleutnant poured in through the gateway, their half-moon badges glinting. Hoarse commands echoed among the ancient walls.

The head-hunters were grinning delightedly. This was something that just suited them.

"Well, plundering are you, you shits? That'll cost you your heads! We're well practised in drumhead court martials. You won't see the sun go down!"

We dived into cover behind some rose bushes.

"Look what you're doing, you idiot," Porta hissed, as I fumbled getting the cartridge belt into the breech of my LMG. "Unless there's a miracle, we won't be alive in an hour's time."

I loaded, shoved the safety catch forward, pressed the butt into my shoulder, and glanced across at the Old Man, who was lying behind a big stone with his SMG.

"Shoot, bugger you," Porta whispered, screwing the cap off a hand grenade. "If we're going to peg out, we'll each take one of those bloodhounds with us. Sweep the yard clean from left to right."

"I'm not shooting till the Old Man orders it," I said.

"Bloody fool, you!" said Porta and gave me a kick in the side that sent me rolling away from my machine gun. Then he pressed the butt into his own shoulder. I scarcely dared breathe. At such short range he would have killed every one of them, including the white-tabbed soldiers.

The Legionnaire was kneeling behind a tree clutching a

108

panzerfaust. Its long high explosive rocket looked evilly out of its stovepipe-mouth. He was evidently quite prepared to send the devilish projectile into the huddle of MPs.

In the monastery windows we could see the faces of nuns and monks anxiously watching what was going on.

A Luftwaffe major appeared.

"What's going on here?" he asked the MPs' officer. "Your blustering behaviour is making my men nervous. I have given orders that my people are to be on the alert for partisans."

"Herr Major," the police oberleutnant's face glowed with enthusiasm. "I'm here on the direct orders of GOC South. The allies' transmitter is reporting that German troops are plundering the monastery and it is my duty to investigate. I must ask you, Herr Major, to come with me now to the GOC. Seeing what's going on here, I can only conclude that the Allies are right."

"I have no time to go anywhere just now," said the major smiling. "Archbishop Diamare can assure you that there is no plundering. If any soldier pockets as much as a splinter, he'll be shot on the spot."

Tiny nudged Porta.

"Herr Oberleutnant," the Major went on. "You can tell them at HQ that I am assuring the safety of the monastery. Within the next few hours I shall make a detailed report in person. Now, get yourselves away from here, before your migration attracts the attention of the enemy's 'planes."

The oberleutnant withdrew with his men.

We spent the next few hours sweating with heavy packing cases. Even before it was dark, the first column got under way and went to the monastery of Vulgata in San Girolamo. Shortly after dark a second column drove off, heading for Sao Paola.

Then our peace was shattered by a whining in the air and a roar as the first Jabos came sweeping over the monastery. Bombs hailed round us.

Porta, who was sitting under a truck trying to empty a bottle of rice spirit, suddenly found himself without cover as the heavy vehicle was sent flying up into the air like a tennis ball and went rolling down the mountainside. A paratrooper who was asleep in the driver's seat was chucked through the roof and fell on to a stack of rifles, spitting himself.

Then the next wave came roaring; they had their throttles wide open and tracer bullets spattered from their noses.

A paratroop oberfeldwebel was sawn in two as he ran across the open space in front of the monastery. The lower half ran on a few steps without its top.

Porta sat in the middle of the space brandishing his empty bottle.

"Good old Charlie, back again, are you?" he shouted at the attacking machines. "We've been missing you. We were afraid you'd suffocated in spaghetti."

A Jabo swept past a few yards above his head. The slip-stream sent him flying. He dusted his yellow top hat that had dropped off, got to his knees and shook his fist at the Jabos. Shells from the Jabo's guns were bursting round him, but nothing touched him.

There he sat, all by himself, while flares turned night into day.

"He's mad," one of the monks said to Leutnant Frick. "Get him away."

Porta got to his feet with a LMG in his arms. He fumbled a bit with the cartridge belt, put his top hat carefully down on the ground beside him and screwed his chipped monocle into his eye.

"Select own targets," he ordered himself, "fire!" He swayed under the tremendous recoil from the LMG as it spat glowing steel at the attacking Jabos. Cursing and swearing because it was so hot and burned his fingers, he changed barrels. His eyes were laughing. He was crazy or drunk, or both. He had put in a new cartridge belt and now leaned back against the remains of a smashed driver's cab. A flare thrown by a Halifax flooded everything in brilliant white light, that surrounded the mountains like a halo.

The open space was spattered with bullets and shells from the swooping, diving Jabos and Mustangs.

"Porta," the Old Man shouted desperately. "They'll kill you."

"Get him in," a Luftwaffe officer ordered. "Three days

leave to the man who gets him in! He's mad."

A fresh flare burst out of the dark sky. To the north a 'Christmas tree' lit up.

Porta took a pull at his field bottle, and lit a cigarette. Then he spread out the LMG's legs, adjusted the air sight and laughed a tipsy laugh.

"Come on, Charlie, now I'm ready to ram you up the arse!"

You would have thought that he and the enemy pilots were in direct communication, for the moment he had shouted the words, the first 'plane came swishing into the area of light. A bomb exploded with a thunderous roar. The 'plane wobbled, swung away. Long flames were streaming from its lefthand wing.

Two machines came roaring in one after the other. Bombs crashed. A sea of flame hid Porta from us, but he emerged unscathed out of the smoke, doubled-up with laughter and his LMG in his arms.

He swung round. In a few seconds the muzzle was pointing at an attacking Mustang. Porta blazed away at its fire-spewing exhaust. There was a gigantic explosion. Pieces of wreckage came hurtling down. Porta must have hit the bomb underneath the 'plane, which was pulverised into millions of pieces, literally turned to dust.

"Good night, Charlie," he shouted. "I'll send your mother a postcard!"

"This is fantastic," exclaimed a paratroop officer. "Who is he? A phantom?"

A gigantic figure emerged from the pine trees dragging a searchlight, a job that usually calls for a crane. In the shadows were two men busy with the cables. It was Tiny come to help. Heedless of the shells exploding round them, the two saluted each other with outstretched hand and raised their hats.

"They can't work that searchlight by themselves," Heide shouted. "I must go and help. Joseph! Mary! Holy Jesus, hold your hand over me!" Bent double he zigzagged across the brilliantly lit open space. He lay down under the searchlight to act as a live turntable. The beam of light shot into the sky, a beam that would burn out a pilot's eyes.

"I've got him, the devil," Tiny jubilated. "He's staring into my fire. Now you're for it, Charlie."

The first fighter died in a sea of spurting petrol flames. The searchlight went out. Tiny banged his fists on the ground exultantly.

"It was me got him. I got him." The hair on his head suddenly caught fire. Heide put it out with his greatcoat.

The searchlight's beam stabbed out again. Millions of candle-power pointing at the lowering clouds.

A Mustang with shark's teeth painted on it dived.

"I have him. I'll burn the peepers out of his ugly mug."

The flying shark went into a spin as it tried to get out of the mortal beam.

Tiny switched off and listened to the roar of the motor. Was it chance or devilish calculation by a brain that had never been taught mathematics, that he switched on again at exactly the right instant, hitting the machine in its mad dive and blinding the pilot for the rest of his life? Heide was on all fours under the searchlight, thrusting his shoulder from one side to the other as the 'plane desperately attempted to escape the beam; then it struck the ground at 300 mph.

Two Halifaxes and four Mustangs roared down across the open space. A string of bombs sent flames shooting up from the monastery. Phosphorus seemed to be bubbling and spluttering everywhere.

The roar of aeroplane engines died away into the night. The Californian killers had dropped their load. Their ammunition was all used up. The last few gallons of petrol would just get them back to base.

* * *

Just before the column moved off, the sound of pick and shovel could be heard from the flat ground below the monastery, where a couple of months later General Ander's Polish Division was to find a resting place. That was Porta, Tiny and Heide digging a grave for the burned-out remains of the Charlies.

When the grave was ready, they laid them in it side by side, each with an American cap between the bones of their hands.

Then the rest of No. 2 Squadron with Padre Emanuel arrived.

The Old Man shovelled the first spadeful of earth, saying something that sounded stupid to us:

"For your mothers and God!"

Leutnant Frick was next. The last was our padre, Emanuel. He spoke about God. A whole lot of stuff we didn't understand. We sang an Ave Maria. The graves were quickly filled in and five minutes later, we drove off.

It was the toughest trip we'd made. Two of us lay on the roof of each driver's cab with a machine gun on its air defence stand. Swarms of Jabos came sweeping up from behind us. The Via Appia was at times carpeted with light.

Endless streams of trucks were coming towards us from the other direction: artillery, sappers, tanks, bridging material, ammunition trains and ambulances.

Bombs struck the ammunition trucks which went up, flinging their loads in all directions.

A big Mercedes with a general's banner in front and escorted by military police on motorcycles wound its way in and out among the heavy vehicles.

"Keep to the right. Keep to the right," bellowed a military police major. He was the kind that would ruthlessly go for anyone who got in his way.

At that moment four Jabos attacked. Tiny saw them as they appeared out of the clouds and came for us. I jumped down on to the bonnet to get better support. Tiny held on to me so that the recoil would not throw me off.

Heide opened fire first. He was behind the machine gun on the truck just behind us.

"Move over, damn you. I can't see anything," shouted Porta from the driver's seat.

There was a scream, a crash and a bump, and the police major and his motorcycle were crushed beneath our heavy dual-wheeler.

"To hell with him!" Tiny grinned. "We'll send Charlie a postcard of thanks."

The general's car was in flames. A figure in furs rose up, tried to get out, but fell back into the sea of fire. The car skidded, turned a somersault and exploded. An ambulance went slap into a 28 cm cannon. Its rear door was flung open and eight stretchers went hurtling into the road.

A wounded feldwebel tried to roll clear of the crushing wheels of the heavy trucks. He was wearing a mudded tunic. His midriff was covered with bandage. One foot had been amputated. A caterpillar tractor went over his head.

A military policeman jumped forward and tried to halt the column, but collapsed as a salvo from a diving Jabo hit him.

The whole Via Appia was bathed in brilliant light. Two marker 'Christmas trees' glowed over the middle of the column. A Halifax was spewing flames.

"Hold tight," Porta called. "I'm going off the road into the fields." The heavy truck bumped down into the ditch, crushing a little amphibian into a shapeless crumple of iron.

All the other four trucks followed Porta. The two monks we carried in each, kneeled on the floor praying. We battered our way through the wall of a graveyard, toppling gravestones and tearing up new graves with our mighty wheels. A little chapel was razed to the ground. We drove on with a crucifix dangling from the bumper.

Then Barcelona's engine cut out. The first towing wire broke as if it had been thread. The next held for a couple of minutes. A twenty-ton truck with a tired engine is not easily hauled out of the soft earth of a graveyard. Porta jumped cursing from his cab, threw a steel helmet at Marlow and demanded a steel hawser.

The winch on Barcelona's truck unwound, and Gregor took hold of the thick wire. Porta went quite savage, when he discovered that Gregor was wearing gauntlets.

"Who the hell do you think you are? Take those bloody things off!"

Gregor answered back and lashed at Porta with a piece of broken wire. In a moment we were tumbling among the graves in a savage fight. A flare lit up the scene. A fighter came roaring out of the clouds. A paratrooper toppled off a truck with blood trickling from a line of holes in his chest. A monk doubled up like a pocket knife. The tarpaulin of our truck went up in flames. A monk tackled it with a fire extinguisher.

Leutnant Frick blew his whistle and threatened us with

every sort of disaster: court martial, Torgau, execution,

I spat out two teeth that landed in Heide's lap. A bloody flap of skin was hanging over Porta's left eye. Heide had a long gash in a buttock, and Tiny's mouth was torn up to one ear. It had been a nasty fight. It took our medical orderly and Padre Emanuel, cursing us, an hour and a half to patch us up.

We got the steel hawser round the tired truck. Gregor and Porta righted each other's bandages and shared the contents of a field bottle.

"Now I'm going to start," Porta called from his cab. "Away from the wire. If it parts, it'll have your nuts off."

Slowly, incredibly slowly, the heavy truck began to move. The flares had gone out. Five maimed corpses remained. The fire in the truck had been put out and none of our precious cargo had suffered.

All hell was loose on the Via Appia. It appeared to be in flames for at least seventy miles.

The Old Man and Leutnant Frick drove first in the Kübel. Intently they studied the map to see if they could find a cross country way. At San Cesarea we had a fight with a group of partisans, in which we lost three men, including Frey, our medical orderly. A hand grenade blew both his legs off, and he bled to death in a moment.

The sun was about to rise as we reached Rome. A house standing on its own was burning merrily.

Two men in long greatcoats with machine pistols at the ready emerged from behind a halted car.

The Legionnaire began humming:

"Come now death, just come!"

He rested the barrel of his Russian machine pistol on the top of the door. A tongue of flame shot out into the darkness. A wicked rat-tat-tat echoed among the houses. The two men crumpled. One's steel helmet rolled cluttering into the gutter. A pool of blood formed quickly, mixing with the pouring rain.

"What was that?" one of the monks in the back asked.

"A couple of bandits wanted to talk to us."

The monk crossed himself.

As we were driving along the Tiber, we met a column of SS grenadiers. They were from the Moslem Division and wore red fezes with silver death's heads on them.

At Piazza di Roma Porta took a wrong turning and we ended up in Piazza Ragusa. An ordinary sentry stopped us. We exchanged cigarettes and schnaps. An infantry feldwebel, in command of the guard, warned us against partisans wearing German uniform. Some said they were in military police uniforms.

"Shoot at the least suspicion," he advised. "If you should make a mistake and shoot a few bloodhounds, it won't be all that of a disaster."

"We'll shoot as soon as we see a half-moon badge," Porta said with a grin. "I'd love to lay a few of them flat."

"Look out for the spaghetti-eaters," the feldwebel warned. "They're beginning to make life difficult for us. Shoot every one you meet. They're getting pretty bold these days. The other day we had to liquidate a village north of here. They had started celebrating the Allied victory!"

We drove on following the railway line. Again Porta went wrong and the whole column followed him. We drove round in circles, unable to find the way. We enlisted the help of a couple of tarts standing at the corner of Via La Spezia and Via Taranto. They got up into the cab beside us. The police turned them off in Via Noazional.

All at once we were in St. Peter's Square. Tiny gaped.

"This is a bit of something! Is this where the Pope has his cave?"

No one answered him.

"I don't like it," he went on thoughtfully. "Suppose he's got second sight, like God!"

"But you don't believe in God," said the Legionnaire smiling.

"I'm not going to discuss that, while we're anywhere near here."

We swung back again, drove down Borgo Vitterio to Via di Porta Anglica.

A broad gate was opened. We were evidently expected. We drove up a narrow street and through another gateway. A couple of Swiss guardsmen showed us the way. We were nervous. This was something new. Even Porta's flow of words dried up. You didn't hear an oath or a swear word, though normally we couldn't say three consecutive words without one. That was part of war.

The tarpaulins were flung back. A few orders issued in quiet voices and we began unloading: swiftly and intently.

We had breakfast in the Swiss guards' barracks. Porta and Tiny gaped, when they saw a guard come in with his halberd.

"Is this the papal antitank weapon?" Tiny laughed.

An officer hushed him, but there was no restraining him.

"Are you proper soldiers?" Porta asked.

Tiny was enchanted, when they allowed him to put on a helmet with a red plume and hold a halberd. He looked ridiculous in it. It hardly went with his modern camouflage uniform. He offered his machine pistol and steel helmet in exchange for the Swiss helmet, but it wasn't for sale.

Porta held up a halberd.

"The marines would goggle, if I hacked their heads with this."

On the way back, Porta and Tiny made another attempt to buy a helmet and halberd, but the Swiss just shook their heads.

Then Porta produced his trump: he held out a fistful of opium cigarettes. But the guard was incorruptible. Tiny added three gold teeth and a box of snow. No normal person could resist that, but the Pope's soldiers would not sell. Porta and Tiny were dumbfounded. They would have sold each other for that amount. Then Tiny pointed to his boots. American airman's boots. The loveliest soft leather. The Swiss was not interested.

When the trucks were unloaded, we sat down on the coping stones.

A Nobel officer had come for Padre Emanuel and Leutnant Frick. A quarter of an hour later, the Old Man was sent for. The best part of an hour passed.

"As long as they don't piddle on us," Porta growled. "Perhaps they're doing something to those three. If they don't turn up in an hour at the latest, we'll go and fetch them. All our irons are up in No. 5. We'll soon overrun the Guards."

"You must have been bitten by a blind ape," Marlow protested. "Suppose there really is a God. He'd never forgive it!"

"I'll take over command," Porta decided, "then you'll be out of it and can plead not guilty before God's court martial."

Marlow shook his head.

"If there is a God, he'll know I'm a feldwebel, and he'll know too that no normal feldwebel lets himself be ordered about by a rotten obergefreiter."

"Then pretend you're not," Tiny suggested facetiously.

"God won't go for that," Marlow shook his head. "When he sees all my metal, he'll give me short shrift. 'That won't do with us, Marlow,' he'll say, and I'll go tumbling into the Devil's lap. And I'm not keen on that. This has to be taken diplomatically. Let's send Tiny in to have a word with them."

"Not on your life," Tiny protested, edging away. "I'll roll up any American trench you like alone, but they're dangerous in there."

Two hours passed, and we were jumpy and on edge. Most of us had already fetched our pistols from No. 5 and tucked them into our boots. Porta sat playing with an egg-shaped hand grenade.

"Let's do a bunk," Heide suggested, squinting up at the big library building.

"Shut up, you Nazi tough! Do you think we'd leave the Old Man here?"

"To say nothing of the padre," Barcelona put in. He had a tremendous respect for everything Roman Catholic, which dated from his time in the Tercio during the Civil War. We never discovered what was the cause of it all. He always brushed our questions aside, saying: "One doesn't talk about this! And, anyway, you wouldn't understand."

"Padre Emanuel can look after himself," Porta said. "He's in direct communication with the heavenly HQ group. But the outlook's not so good for the Old Man and Leutnant Frick."

"*Tu as raison, camarade,*" said the little Legionnaire nodding assent. "You have to stand alone before God's court martial and have no one to defend you. Your files lie open there. Allah knows everything including the reason for one's damned escapades. Hard, clean justice is the only thing that matters. It's not easy to get an acquittal there."

"That's all a lot of shit," Tiny decided. "I'd never get an acquittal."

"You never know," the Legionnaire replied convincingly. "With Allah the most remarkable things turn out to one's advantage. Are you really so great a bandit?"

Tiny wagged his great head and shoved his cap onto the back of his head.

"I don't really know. But they have given me a sock on the jaw once or twice. I'm not one of the best. Most of us sitting here do so of our own free will. They've looked after us well here. But anyone who says I have shot anyone except on orders, is a bloody liar. I haven't enough grey matter. That's why we have officers to think for us. Is there any obergefreiter in the Prussian army with so much tin on him as I?" He thumped his chest. "Who was it saved the whole regiment at Stalino? Who got the fuses out at Kiev? Yours truly! Do you remember counting the seconds that time at Kertz, when I crawled through the hole. You cheered when I blew the whole tractor factory up."

Barcelona laughed scornfully. "You pale-arsed lot! Three days ago you used a roadside crucifix as a target. Now your blubber's trembling because you're in His Holiness's city."

The Old Man returned. He was strangely quiet.

"I've met the Pope."

"Have you seen him?" Tiny whispered, awestruck. The Old Man nodded and lit his pipe.

"Did you touch him?" Barcelona asked, looking at the Old Man with a new respect.

"I didn't touch him, but I was so close to him that I could have."

"What uniform was he wearing?" Porta asked, unwilling to capitulate. "Did he have the knight's cross?"

"He was magnificent," the Old Man muttered still under the influence of his tremendous experience.

"What did he say?" Heide asked.

"That I was to salute you. He blessed me."

"Did he, by Jove?" Heide exclaimed. "Blessed you, did he?"

"Did you see a real cardinal?" Rudolph Kleber asked. "In a red hat?"

Questions rained over the Old Man.

"Had he been told about me?" Tiny asked.

"Not specially about you or any of us individually, but he had been told about No. 2 Squadron as a whole. He gave me a ring." The Old Man raised his hand out for us to see.

"Is the ring for the Squadron?" Barcelona asked.

"Yes, he gave it to me, as a general is given the knight's cross. I wear it for the squadron."

"Can I try it?" Heide asked, a strange look in his eye that ought to have warned the Old Man, but he had not yet fully returned to our brutal reality. Trustingly he gave Heide the ring.

Heide held his finger out for us to admire the ring. When Tiny tried to touch it, he got a smack on his finger from Heide's bayonet.

The Old Man held out his hand:

"Give it back."

"To you?" Heide smiled slyly. "Why should you have it?"

The Old Man was so astounded he just opened and shut his mouth.

"It's my ring. I was given it. The Pope gave it to me."

"Gave *you* it? He gave it to the Squadron. The ring belongs to No. 2 Squadron, like the American boots Tiny's wearing for the time being. You aren't the squadron, any more than Tiny is. I, Sven, Porta, our pistols, our 8.8s, the No. 5 and all the rest of it, that's the squadron."

Heide rubbed the ring on his sleeve, breathed on it, rubbed it again, held it up to his eyes and regarded it proudly.

"Now that I've seen this gift from His Holiness Pius the Twelfth, I'm not sure I don't believe in God."

"Give me that ring," the Old Man said, his voice quivering with indignation, and took a step towards Heide.

"Keep your paws away," Heide snarled, "or you'll get one on the skull. I shall wear it for the squadron. But if I kick the bucket, you can be ring-wearer instead of me. We can draw up a document as we did over Tiny's boots."

"Not on your life," Porta cried. "When you get your deserts, it will be my turn to wear it. The Old Man's seen the Pope. That must do him. He isn't entitled to any more."

Barcelona pulled his close-combat knife from his boot and began cleaning his nails with it. It was not because his dirty nails worried him, but more as emphasis to what he now said:

"Take care, Julius, that you don't die young."

Heide scowled and stuck the hand with the ring into his pocket.

"Who do you think you are, you ersatz Spaniard?"

The Old Man was puce in the face with anger. He tried to threaten Heide into giving the ring back, but Heide paid no attention to him. He was not handing it over.

He went into the Swiss guards and proudly showed them the ring. It was while he was there the first attack came. A halberd blade swished past his head only an inch away. No one saw where it came from, but Tiny was under strong suspicion.

Heide dashed to the truck and thrust two pistols, safety catches undone, into his belt. The holy ring had caused bad blood between us. It was dangerous to have it, yet everyone wanted it.

The second attack came twenty minutes later. Heide was lying out in the middle of the yard with two paratroopers admiring the ring. Something made him turn his head, the next moment a 20-ton truck rolled across the exact spot where he and the two paratroopers had been lying, and pulled up with a bump against a tree. Muffled laughter sounded from the corner of Via Pio and Via di Belvedere, where the rest of the squadron sat dicing.

"Queer, how a truck can drive off on its own like that," Porta said thoughtfully.

Heide mopped his brow and shoved his cap onto the back of his head. With both hands deep in his pockets, he sauntered across to us.

"Band of murderers," he said. "But you're not getting the ring. I'm not so easy to kill."

"That remains to be seen," Barcelona said and, smiling, threw the dice.

*   *   *

We lost three trucks and seven men on the way back along Via Appia. Marlow was badly wounded, and we put him in an ambulance on its way back to Rome. His skin was already like parchment; his lips blue and his teeth showed. He whispered a protest, when Barcelona drew his Nagan and his holster off his belt.

"That's mine. Leave it with me."

"You'll get it when you come back," the Old Man promised.

"Give me my Nagan. I can look after it. They won't steal it."

But we knew better. We knew the significance of that yellow skin. We knew when the man with the scythe had put his stamp on one and that an orderly would steal that Nagan even before Marlow was dead. Why should an orderly have it, when it would do us good service?

Tough Marlow wept. Then Tiny did a clumsy thing. Just before the ambulance drove off, he took Marlow's greatcoat, which lay rolled up beside him. It was one of the good waterproof kind paratroopers had issued to them. They were in great demand and Tiny and Marlow were roughly of a size. Marlow tried to get out of the ambulance. He shouted curses at us, as the ambulance men shoved him back and slammed the doors shut, swearing. As we stood in the roadway watching the ambulance drive off, we heard Marlow shouting:

"Let me stay with you. I don't want to die. Bring me my Nagan!"

"He'll be dead before they reach hospital," the Old Man said quietly.

We nodded, knowing that he was right. And Marlow knew it too. Twenty minutes before he had been with us laughing over Tiny and his helmet.

As Porta speeded up, he muttered almost to himself.

"A good thing, he won those last few throws."

The Legionnaire was examining the Nagan, which he had already swapped with Barcelona. Then he slammed the magazine into place and thrust the heavy pistol into its splendid yellow leather holster that had been Marlow's most cherished possession. He stood up in the cab, patted the holster and said: "It sits well."

We could see how he revelled in the weight of it. It would give him a sense of security, as it had Marlow.

It is most important for a front line soldier to be aware of his pistol. It should feel like a friend's protecting hand, and that's how a Nagan always felt. We thought a lot of them. All the ones we possessed, we had got from the Russians at the risk of our lives. We had five in No. 2 Squadron and took good care not to lose one. We always took a dying man's pistol. Once dead, others were entitled to his possessions; but, as long as he was alive, he and all his possessions belonged to No. 2 Squadron. The unpleasant thing was that the dying man almost always knew that we had taken it. His pistol was his assurance of life and when it went, life's flame flickered frantically. But we couldn't afford to be sloppy, where a Nagan was concerned.

The next morning we left the monastery. Just before we were to go, we were all taken into the basilica. There, Archbishop Diamare appeared. He raised his hands and chanted:

Gloria deus in excelsio!

Then, for the next ten minutes, he conducted a service so gripping that even we heathens in the front rank were spellbound. Then the monks, nuns and children from the children's home sang a choral that rang out between those venerable walls most magnificently.

Silent and somewhat awed, we marched out and drove away.

Barcelona and I looked at each other. We had a secret that we could not tell to the others. They would have laughed at us. We had been on guard together. Just before daybreak, we were down at the end of the line of vehicles. The clouds were scurrying across the heavens and the moon shining through every now and again. We leaned against the wall, our machine pistols under our greatcoats to protect them from the frost, looking in silence down the slope of the mountain and enjoying the secure feeling that really good comrades give each other. I don't know which of us saw it first. It appeared down below behind some trees, a figure enveloped in an enormous cloak and looking rather like a shadow. A bent, hurrying figure.

"One of the monks?" Barcelona queried.

All at once, the figure halted in the open space, where later they buried the Polish Division. It brandished its fist at the monastery. Then, for a second or so, the moon came out through a hole in the scudding clouds, and we saw the figure distinctly. Our hearts stopped beating, as the wind took hold of the cloak and blew it out and back. That figure was Death with a scythe on its shoulder!

The blood froze in our veins. Then we heard a laugh, a long, triumphant laugh. Then the figure was swallowed up by a roll of mist.

We stumbled over each other's feet as we ran for the guard hut. The Old Man, Porta and the others were asleep inside it. Our teeth were chattering, and I had dropped my pistol.

"You must go and get it," Barcelona said. I refused. Instead, I stole one from a sleeping paratrooper. When it was light, Barcelona and I went to look for mine, but we never found it.

The others saw that something had happened, but we did not dare tell them about it. We thought for a moment of going to the Padre, but then agreed that it would be best to keep quiet about it altogether. As Barcelona rightly said: "You don't have to tell everything you see."

We ended by acting to each other, as if we had forgotten all about it. But Death had visited the holy mountain to view the scene of his approaching harvest, and by chance Barcelona and I had seen him and heard his jubilant laugh.

VIII

*Joseph Grapa was a Jew. We met him one evening, when we paid
a visit to a group of deserters in the attic of a house behind Termini.
You got up to it through a camouflaged trapdoor. One of Ida's
girls who had had to go underground, was there.*

*Heide got the hell of a surprise, when he found himself standing
face to face with Grapa.*

*"Ground not getting too hot under your paws, Schmaus?" he
said provocatively. "I could get a fine price for you. What would
you say to a single ticket to Via Tasso?"*

*Porta started cleaning his nails with his close-combat dagger
and Tiny rattled his steel sling. That checked Heide and from
then on he and the Jew just slung accusations at each other.*

*"All my family, all my friends have been dragged off to
Poland," Grapa said quietly.*

*"Don't squeal, Schmaus," Heide grinned. "Those of you Jews
who survive will get your revenge. You'll be sacred cows, and
preserved. I shouldn't be surprised if it was forbidden to call you
Jews. Adolf's really doing you a good turn. You'll get your revenge
on the Catholics, whom you hate as much as Heydrich and
Himmler do. I can see that you are going to accuse the Pope of
gassing the Jews."*

"No honest Jew would do that," Grapa protested.

*"There are no honest Jews," Heide said and laughed. He
pointed an accusing finger at Grapa. "There are lots of documents
that can be used against the Pope. The Vatican is a louse between
two fingernails. Don't misunderstand me. I have no love for the
Pope's black crows. Do them in tomorrow and I'll gladly help."
He rubbed his hands at the very thought.*

*"Why doesn't the Vatican protest?" Grapa cried. "The de-
portations would stop, if it did. They wouldn't dare go on with
them."*

Heide guffawed.

"Not dare! You are blue-eyed! Do you think we're afraid of a few dirty saints? If only the crows would protest! Then you'd see something. Perhaps Hitler and Stalin would find each other. You know who should have protested? The president of the U.S.A., the king of England and all the others with armies at their beck and call. But they didn't so much as let out a fart, when they heard we had begun slaughtering you. The whole world knew what we were doing in '35, to say nothing of '38. But they just put plugs in their ears."

"Do you think all that would have prevented the killings?" Grapa asked.

"One protest, no," Heide said. "But an economic boycott as late as '38 would have done it, but no Pope or umbrella carrying prime minister will frighten Adolf. And, anyway, who says our opponents don't like us gassing you? They would not even ransom you with a few trucks and lorries. Stalin in Moscow certainly won't miss you. I don't know what the Pope has to say, but I should think he's the only one who would stand up for you, if he had a strong enough army behind him. But for him to protest now will do as little good as a white dove standing up in front of the Doge's palace and making a fuss. You Jews are bust and you always will be. You can be up for a short time, but then some idiot among you will throw his weight about too much, and then you'll be dropped again. You should have your own state. That would be best."

Porta spat contemptuously onto the floor.

"Man is the stupidest of all animals."

OPERATION DOG-COLLAR

The rumours of what we had been doing at Monte Cassino reached Berlin. In fact, a stream of reports flooded in to Prins Albrecht Strasse 8, with the result that one sunny morning a Heinkel bomber landed at Aeroporto dell' Ube outside Rome. Out of the 'plane stepped General Wilhelm Burgdorf, chief of the army personnel section, a slim black document case under his arm. He brushed some imaginary specks of dust from his blood red general's tabs and smiled his usual kindly smile. The General was a man who regarded the whole world as a gigantic joke, who promoted a colonel to general with the same smile with which he handed a field marshal a cyanide pill. He nodded pleasantly to the open-mouthed commander of the airport and enquired about his health, with the immediate result that the major in question went deathly pale. General Burgdorf grinned.

"Get me a car, Herr Major, with a driver who can drive. I don't care whether he's a convict or a field marshal, as long as he can drive. I am in a hurry to get to the Army Commander South."

The major was obviously agitated. Burgdorf's sudden appearances always entailed a number of suicides.

"Herr General," the major clicked his heels together twice, "we have a Special Duties Tank Unit at the barracks in Via de Castro Pretorio. We can get a first class driver from it."

They walked together to the airport commander's private office. All other officers seemed to have vanished. Some people said, and not without justice, that he was the most powerful man in the army. One word from him and a general was no longer a general. Another word and a young leutnant could exchange his silver shoulder straps for a pair with braided gold, in record time. One thing was certain: no one was promoted without General Burgdorf's approval.

The airport commander got the office-wallahs moving. It was as if a hurricane had swept through the building. Ten telephones began ringing simultaneously in the barracks in Via de Castro Pretorio. Ten men scribbled down the same order.

People whispered the name 'General Burgdorf' in alarm, and an oberleutnant and a major went and reported sick without waiting for further details. There was a general sigh of relief when it was realised that the general only wanted a car and driver.

Hauptfeldwebel Hoffmann nearly swallowed a rollmop the wrong way when, after baying some impertinence into the 'phone in his arrogant way, he discovered that he was speaking to the Depot Commander in person. His arrogant bark became a faint-hearted miaow. Fearing the worst, he listened to the strange order; then carefully he replaced the receiver and for a moment gaped in silence at the black instrument. Then he suddenly came to life:

"You wet bugger," he bawled at the clerk, "haven't you yet grasped the fact that General Wilhelm Burgdorf is here and requires transport? Pull yourselves together and get a move on, else you'll be on your way to the Eastern front before you can say bloody Robinson."

At that moment Major Mike and Leutnant Frick came in. Hoffmann bawled out his report.

"Burgdorf! Phew!" Mike exclaimed. "Wants a car, does he? He shall have one and a driver. We'll give him more, the arrogant shit, because he's going through a dangerous area, where the little spaghetti boys might get the bloody good idea of blowing him up." He smiled satanically to Leutnant Frick: "What do you say, Frick, shall we give him my Kübel?"

Leutnant Frick laughed maliciously: "Splendid idea, Mike. And Porta to drive it."

Major Mike nodded enthusiastic agreement: "And Tiny as escort."

Hauptfeldwebel Hoffmann blenched. Twice he asked for the wrong number. Somehow his tongue would not obey him. Major Mike and Leutnant Frick sat down on his desk and watched him with obvious enjoyment. Finally, he managed to get hold of the garage. Ten minutes later he retired to bed with a violent headache and dancing specks in front of his eyes. But before he went, he drew the sergeant clerk's attention to the fact that he had no knowledge of what had been ordered. Major Mike and Leutnant Frick preferred to get drunk and go underground till the danger was over.

Fifty men were out looking for Porta and Tiny. Both should have been in the garage servicing their vehicles, but in some mysterious way they had seemed to have got themselves transferred to other duties. Porta was discovered in the armoury where he was playing housey-housey with the quarter-master and Padre Emanuel, in the act of pulling in a jackpot. Tiny was traced to a backroom behind the canteen, where he had been hobnobbing with the canteen unteroffizier and two girls from the kitchen. He was just buttoning his trousers, when they found him. He set off at a slow trot for the garage with an ammunition pannier on his shoulder. Catching sight of Porta in the distance, he shouted:

"We're to take a general for a drive. Visit a field marshal."

You could scarcely have called them fit for the parade ground as they drove off to fetch the general, and the airport commander got a shock when they reported to him. But General Burgdorf was amused. They were a type he liked. He gave them each a handful of cigars and did not even bother to look at the major.

They sped through Rome at a good seventy, Burgdorf's adjutant, a hauptmann, sitting with his eyes closed, wishing he could get out, but the general enjoyed the speed. He had seen at once that Porta knew his job, but even so he paled slightly when he heard Porta tell Tiny that the front axle was still dicky, so he must keep a look out for potholes. With less than an inch to spare they squeezed through between two trams in a shower of oaths and curses from the two drivers and passengers. They spattered a policeman with mud and made him jump for his life and convinced him that he should join the partisans that night.

The general listened with interest to Porta's and Tiny's conversation, admitting to himself that they were the toughest couple of drivers he'd ever had. He could hardly say that they seemed in any way impressed by driving a general. As far as he could understand they were planning the theft of a pig, which apparently was at Army HQ. That did not concern the general. He had not come to Italy to deal with petty misdemeanours.

Porta gave Tiny a detailed description of his favourite way of cooking black pudding. Once he even took both hands off the wheel to demonstrate what he meant.

With squealing brakes they pulled up before Army HQ in Frascata. A Luftwaffe leutnant almost fell down the steps in his eagerness, tore the door open and helped the general and his adjutant out. The general glanced at Porta and Tiny who had remained in their seats – most undisciplined! – then shrugged resignedly and began to mount the steps. They were too small game for him. The leutnant could not see what it was the general was laughing at, as they walked inside.

The Army Commander was in conference when Burgdorf arrived. Three officers and two feldwebels sprang to their feet and rushed to help him off with his dusty overcoat, but Burgdorf waved them away.

"Would you like me to complain of the undisciplined behaviour of the two obergefreiters in your car?" the Leutnant asked servilely.

General Burgdorf smiled his dangerous smile.

"Leutnant, if I wish to criticise I would start with you. Your right breastpocket button is undone. And since when, leutnant, have infantry leutnants been allowed to wear spurs? Am I, an infantry general, wearing spurs? Kindly give my adjutant a report on your irregular dress before I leave. Have you been very long on the general staff?"

The leutnant stammered something incomprehensible. Before the war he had been a schoolmaster in some dreadful little village in the Eger mountains, where he was the terror of the twelve-year-olds. Burgdorf looked at him with a sneering smile.

"Have you a pistol?" he asked in an interested voice.

"Jawohl, Herr General," the leutnant bayed, banging his irregularly spurred heels together.

"Splendid," Burgdorf smiled. "I'm sure you know what use to make of it. Good-bye, Herr Leutnant."

Those present were a shade paler in the face now. Burgdorf tapped a rittmeister on the shoulder with his cane.

"Will you tell the Army Commander that I want a talk with him in private."

"Herr General, unfortunately that cannot be done. Herr Generalfeldmarschall is in conference and not to be disturbed. We're planning the next attack and the defence of the Gustav line," the rittmeister added.

General Wilhelm Burgdorf laughed heartily and remarked that the rittmeister evidently did not realise that he was dealing with the most powerful man in the Germany Army. He then turned to an oberfeldwebel.

"Fetch my two men from my car."

"Jawohl, Herr General!" bawled the oberfeldwebel.

"And," Burgdorf added thoughtfully, "tell them to bring their pistols."

Three minutes later Porta with Tiny at his heels rushed into the room with no little commotion.

Burgdorf smiled wryly.

"Until further notice, you two brigands are my personal bodyguard. If I throw down my gloves, you shoot at everything and everyone."

"Ah, we know this, Herr General," Tiny said. "We did a trip once with a generaloberst and he gave the same orders. Only it was his cap he was to throw down."

Burgdorf preferred not to hear Tiny's remark. He turned to the rittmeister:

"Herr Rittmeister, I am in a hurry. I imagine it will not have escaped you that we are waging a war. The army in Italy is only a tiny part of this war. Go to the Army Commander and report my arrival."

The rittmeister vanished hastily. Burgdorf paced up and down the floor, his hands on his back, his long leather coat flapping round his legs. He was no longer smiling. Porta and Tiny stood like statues one on either side of the double doors. They held their machine pistols under their arms; their ammunition pouches were open.

A moment later the double doors flew open with a bang and Generalfeldmarschall Kesselring stood in the doorway, tall, broadshouldered, dressed in grey Luftwaffe uniform.

"My dear Burgdorf, this is a surprise! I am at your service."

General Burgdorf smiled and gazed intently at the glowing end of his cigarette.

"Herr Feldmarschall, I am delighted to hear it. Then, we can soon be finished. Send your men away."

The officers present hurried out. But Porta and Tiny remained.

"Herr Feldmarschall, there are the craziest rumours in Berlin about what is going on here. Are you negotiating with the Americans? For example, about the withdrawal of the German troops in Rome? I mean, have you taken it into your head to make Rome an open city? We know that there is an American general in Rome."

"Impossible, Herr Burgdorf. If it were so, I should have known of it."

"It is not impossible, feldmarschall. But the question is, whether you know it and whether you have perhaps met this general?"

"I give you my word of honour, Herr Burgdorf, I have not."

"I believe you; but what about contact men?"

Generalfeldmarschall Kesselring shook his head. His face had lost its healthy red colour.

"Is it true that the sacred relics have been removed from Monte Cassino? You must know what General Conrad is doing. The Allied broadcasting stations have been proclaiming from the housetops that a few days ago the Hermann Göring Panzerdivision was busy plundering the monastery. It is certainly plundering of which the Reichsmarschall is entirely ignorant, but perhaps your intelligence officers are asleep. In that case, I would suggest a drumhead court martial within the next half hour. We know in Berlin that Oberleutnant Schlegel from the Panzerdivision's HQ has conferred with Conrad, who has given the all clear for sabotage of the Führer's order. The Führer wishes that all that stuff in the monastery should be destroyed by the American bombardment. General Freyberg, the New Zealander, is demanding that American bombers smash the monastery, but our colleagues on the other side are not particularly keen on the idea. However, our New Zealand friend is a stubborn brute and no doubt in the end he'll succeed in getting that bit of rock split for him; in the meantime your damned general and an idiotic oberstleutnant have spoilt our entire game. Can't you understand what we're aiming at, man? Just imagine the headlines in the gutterpress all over the world; Anglo-American gangsters destroy West's most precious Catholic relics! We even have commando troops ready to liquidate that old idiot Diamare. We can get them to smash the monastery, but the important thing for us is that the art treasures in it should go up in smoke at the same time. Freyberg is quite convinced that our agents are telling the truth, when they report that the monastery is being turned into an impregnable fortress, so just before they raze it to the ground, we shall see that we get a statement from the lot of black crows up there that there has never been a single German soldier inside it. From the point of view of our propaganda that will be of tremendous importance for us. The only good thing Schlegel's transport has done, is that the trucks have been photographed by Allied reconnaissance 'planes, which is grist to Freyberg's mill. Now we must ensure that every one of the relics is safe and sound. The Führer is furious. Obergruppenführer Müller is already in Rome. You have one foot in front of a court martial, Herr Marschall. The whole business has to be twisted so that you have known all about the damned transport; otherwise the entire world will accuse us of plundering. We cannot at this moment take too much of that sort of thing."

The Generalfeldmarschall's face was deathly pale.

"I don't understand you, Herr Burgdorf."

Burgdorf smiled a dangerous smile.

"I thought I had made myself quite clear. Do you wish to appear before a Court of Honour for High Treason, or will you yourself pluck these chestnuts out of the fire? Gruppenführer Müller is in Via Tasso. He has no objection to landing a marshal in his net."

"This is slander, Herr General, the nastiest slander!" Kesselring exclaimed angrily.

"I believe you have got your ideas of the new age somewhat

confused, Marschall. Germany is no longer imperial Germany. We are a national-socialist state. We shrink from nothing in order to reach our goal."

"The Führer wishes this damned question of the Jews solved. I personally do not sympathise with all his political ideas, but I am a soldier and have taken an oath of loyalty just as you have." He banged his fist on the table top of Venetian mosaic. "If I am given an order, I obey it to the letter. I love children, especially babies, but if tomorrow I receive an order to kill all children under two in Europe, they will be killed without consideration for my personal feelings, and any of my subordinates who do not obey my orders exactly will be court martialled. We are aware of your religious convictions."

"Do you not believe in God, General Burgdorf?"

"What I believe in should not interest you. I am a soldier. I have been one since I was sixteen. A soldier's job is to wage war and war means killing. I have a suspicion that you are not fully aware of that. I warn you. At this moment, there are 36 generals in Torgau. We are shooting two of them early to-morrow. I have as you see, two obergefreiters with me. I got them an hour and a half ago from a Special Duties Panzer regiment in your army. These are men who would crucify Christ a second time, if they were ordered to do it and happened to lay their hands on him." Burgdorf went close up to Kesselring and menacingly brandished his fieldservice cap in front of the Generalfeldmarschall's pale face. "They would not hesitate to drag a Generalfeldmarschall behind the garbage bins and shoot him."

"Herr Burgdorf, I must give you notice that I intend to complain to the Reichsmarschall of your unheard of behaviour."

Burgdorf laughed, flexed his knees, thoroughly sure of himself.

"You don't think, surely, that I am here of my own volition? I came here on direct orders from the Führer, and I am not alone. As for the Reichsmarschall, I would not reckon on help from that quarter. He fell out of favour some time ago. Between ourselves, the Führer can't stand him. The Luftwaffe is altogether in the background these days. The Führer regards it rather as a dud."

"My paratroopers are fighting like devils here in Italy. If they go on as they are, there won't be any survivors."

"The Führer will shed no tears on that account," Burgdorf said drily. "I can take you back to Berlin with me and put you in Torgau, where you'll slip quietly into eternity early one morning, for not preventing that business with Monte Cassino. At eleven o'clock tomorrow morning I have an important conference with two divisional commanders and a couple of regimental commanders concerning Operation Dog Collar, and woe betide you, Herr Marschall, if a single word gets to the Vatican. Oberführer Müller has been stirring up the security service. We have agents in the Vatican who report everything to us. We want to provoke Pius into protesting against the persecution of the Jews, and we'll get him to open his big mouth, be sure of that."

"Are you planning to arrest the Pope? That would be a crazy thing to do. You must be joking, Herr General!"

"It is deadly earnest. Do you think I have time to joke?"

"One cannot do it," the feldmarschall whispered hoarsely, nervously fingering his knight's cross.

"One can do much more," Burgdorf jeered. "It wouldn't be the first time in history the Pope has been taken prisoner."

"What do you hope to achieve by it?"

"The same as by liquidating the synagogues and Jews. Your job is to see that the orders issued by Berlin are carried out." Burgdorf rested his clenched fists on the Venetian table. "And you will shoot the Pope in the back of his head, if you are ordered to do so."

"But this is devilish," the marschall whispered.

"Am I to inform the Führer of your opinion, when I make my report? Don't you know that the Führer is beyond criticism? We have plenty of people who can take your place. The point, General, is this: Do you intend to fulfill your oath of loyalty or not? You are a believer. You swore it on the Bible?"

"Herr General, I do not break an oath."

"We did not expect you would, Herr Marschall. Berlin will be able to justify any liquidation of the Pope all right. Catholicism is the most dangerous obstacle in our path."

135

"One would think you came from Stalin, Herr General."

Burgdorf banged his shining boots with his long cane. The red stripes on his trousers glowed like blood.

"Our war is not a national war. If we lose, our role of great nation will be at an end, perhaps our very existence. That is why the war must be waged with a brutality and hardness, the like of which the world has never seen. We shrink from nothing. If there are officers in our ranks, who will not carry out Berlin's orders regardless, they and their families will be liquidated. When Berlin sends out the code word Dog Collar, your duty as commander-in-chief here is to ensure that it is carried out." Burgdorf looked thoughtfully out of the window. " 'Dog Collar' is veiled in darkness. It doesn't exist on paper." He smiled and struck his boot a powerful blow. "One thing the Kremlin and Prinz Albrecht Strasse have in common: both reckon on the bourgeois lack of imaginative judgement. A thing can be so huge that it appears quite incredible. It does not matter if a few sharp intelligences believe it, if the vast, stupid bourgeoisie fail to grasp it. When the truth does filter out, it will at once be dubbed a lie and so give the executants the glamour of persecuted innocence."

The generalfeldmarschall stared at Burgdorf with an expression as though he believed him sick in mind or else Satan's own adjutant.

"If we lose the war," he said with a break in his voice, "we shall be condemned by the historic truth in all its cruelty."

Burgdorf shook his head.

"Berlin will be able to do it so efficiently that it will exceed your wildest imaginings. First, the world will be shocked. Then doubts will arise, and before ten years have passed, the bourgeoisie will be refusing to accept the facts. The Pope is afraid of both Stalin and Hitler, as he has good reason to be. We shall take him to Berlin, officially, to protect him.

"After the Vatican has been occupied by German troops?" the feldmarschall asked doubtfully. "You won't get anyone to believe it."

"Do you think that we in Berlin are so clumsy?" Burgdorf laughed scornfully. "German troops will occupy the Vatican after it has been attacked by a band of partisans under Jewish-communist leadership. Why do you think we have brought a battalion of Dirlewanger Special Duties to Rome?"

"Won't they talk eventually?" the feldmarschall asked thoughtfully.

"None will survive to do so. The Special Duties Panzer regiment will see to that."

"Will Germans shoot at Germans?"

"The Panzer regiment will not be shooting at Germans, but at bandits in Italian uniform."

"The world will never relish extermination of Catholicism," the marschall insisted stubbornly. "It will rouse a storm of indignation."

"The liquidation has already begun," Burgdorf began. "In Dachau we have executed twelve hundred priests. There are several sitting in Plötzensee waiting to be strangled. Have you heard of anyone protesting? I haven't."

"What about the Concordat? Doesn't that come into it?"

"Quite without significance," Burgdorf said. "It's like our promises to the Jews. If you want to avoid panic among cattle due to be slaughtered, you have to pacify them first. On June 12, 1933 the Führer said: 'The Concordat does not interest me at all, but it will let us get on with our struggle against the Jews in peace, and after that it will let us get on and do other things'."

"I can't understand how the Vatican entered into this Concordat with the Reich. There was always a risk of it being used against them."

"A risk the Vatican were compelled to take," Burgdorf replied in an irritated tone. "In order to avoid worse things than the death of a couple of million Jews."

"There are thirty million Catholics in Germany," the marschall put in. "And think of all those in other countries."

"A bagatelle to the Reichsführer. We have ten million fanatical non-believers who would be delighted to cut the throat of every Catholic they can lay their hands on, if the Reichsführer SS gave the word tomorrow."

"I do not see, Herr Burgdorf, why Berlin is so interested in getting the Pope to protest against persecution of the Jews?"

Burgdorf smiled condescendingly.

"I should have thought it was obvious enough and, I am

afraid, they are beginning to smell a rat in the Vatican. If the Pope protests against persecution of the Jews now that we have occupied Italy and declared a state of emergency, he would be in conflict with the security regulations and we would have definite grounds for securing his person, as he then will have given public expression to a hostile attitude towards us. Having once got him away from Rome, we shall certainly manage the rest."

"That would mean war against 400 million believing Catholics. Too enormous an undertaking."

"Everything can be done, if one disregards mistaken humanism. At the moment, we are just in the experimental stage of extermination of unwanted elements; and this would be an action that enjoyed Marshal Stalin's entire sympathy. Who knows, perhaps Berlin and Moscow will find each other through this very action. Both Berlin and Moscow realise that we cannot reach our goals without first rooting out Christianity altogether."

"The world will rise in protest," the marschall cried despairingly, "when this comes out."

Burgdorf shook his head.

"The numbers are altogether too great for them really to shock anyone. The ordinary person will be incapable of grasping them. At Kiev in two days we shot 34,000 Jews and gypsies. There are plenty of towns with populations smaller than that. In Poland we are daily executing 4 to 6,000 people. In Oswiecim we have liquidated 600,000. In Auschwitz not quite 300,000. Since 1940 we have killed two million Jews. If we had had time, we would have killed six, ten or twenty million. The world has heard of these ghastly figures long ago. To the average person, the journalists who have written about them are liars. But if, instead, we had executed 800 children and not 135,000 the world would have raised an outcry; because 800 is a figure people can grasp." Burgdorf tucked his cane under his arm, buttoned his gloves, set his cap jauntily on the side of his head. "Herr Marschall," he went on, "if your conscience forbids you to keep your oath of loyalty, drop us a note and you shall at once be relieved of your command." He looked the marschall straight in the face. "But I am sure I do

138

not need to tell you the consequences that would entail. A soldier should never think about the whys and wherefores of the orders he receives, but just carry them out. Some things that he does stink! All that matters to us, is what the Führer orders. His will is our will. His faith in victory is our faith in victory." Burgdorf raised his cane in brief salutation and left the room.

The marschall stood alone in the middle of the floor, gazing after the elegant figure.

IX

Porta drew the bow. The long arrow sped on its way, bored into the neck and appeared out on the other side. The tall, lanky American captain swayed, fell forward and the arrow broke.

Porta was proud.

"They'll make me an honorary chief. If this goes on, I'll adopt the name of 'Red Flame'."

During the next two days he had eight similar hits. The Americans called across to us wanting to know who our bowman was. One of their negroes who was a good shot with a bow had deserted and they thought it was he. They offered us God knows what if we would hand him over.

"We've no niggers here," Heide called. "Nor any damned Schmauses either."

Then we waved a white cloth on the end of a bayonet and Porta climbed up onto the parapet.

"Keep your officers away," Heide shouted. "Red Flame only shoots officers."

Porta swung his yellow hat over his head. His red hair flamed in the sunlight.

"Salutation Pale Faces," he shouted.

The Americans tossed their helmets in the air and jubilated. A gigantic sergeant with battle dress flapping round him clambered up onto the Americans' parapet.

"Here's Grey Bear from Alaska. How many years' service have you, Red Flame?"

"Eight."

"Child, you are. I've done 24. I shot your lousy father at Verdun."

"That's a lie, you filthy Yankee," Porta yelled. "My old man's doing his third year in Moabit, cell 840. An A-prisoner, one of the tough ones."

The American put a forage cap on top of his helmet.

"You miserable kraut, you have appropriated an Indian name. I represent my tribe here. Shoot this cap off my helmet and we will bow to you. There are three of us Indians here. If you miss, you'll be fetched tonight and we'll cut your prick off."

Porta pulled an arrow from the quiver he had on his back, drew the bow and took careful aim.

"Don't try it," the Old Man advised. "If you kill him, they'll avenge it."

"The Holy Virgin guide your hand," muttered Padre Emanuel, crossing himself.

Hundreds of pairs of field glasses were trained on the American's cap. There was a deathly silence. Then with a whine the arrow sped, transfixed the cap and swept it away. A great roar of enthusiastic applause rose from both lines. Helmets and rifles were tossed into the air. We chaired Porta along the parapet. The American sergeant raised his hands in homage to the victor, and at that moment One-Eye appeared.

"What the bloody hell is this? Have you all been bitten by mad monkeys! You deserve to be court martialled!"

The war continued.

MAJOR MIKE'S PRIVATE WAR

The sleet lashed our faces, ran from our helmets down our necks, caught in the stubble on our faces and formed a painful guttering on our lips.

"And this is supposed to be sunny Italy," came Porta's voice from the rear.

We were marching in double file up the mountain side. The monastery lay perched high above us. It was not there we were going, but right across to the other side by Monte Caira. The engineers had told us that there were Japanese holding that sector.

"Close up," Major Mike commanded. "And don't let your tongues wag so much."

Darkness enveloped us. Guns were rumbling away to the south-west. Star shells went shooting up. Incendiary shells traced their course like peacocks' tails across the sky. It was so lovely a sight, you could almost have enjoyed it, if it had not been so damned dangerous.

We were a special task force. That was nothing new for us. Before we left our rest quarters, we had dug three big common graves. None of us believed that they were for us, so the job had left us unmoved. But Porta had made one specially nice place which he said was for Eagle, whom Hauptfeldwebel Hoffmann had chucked out of the office. Mike had welcomed him to the ranks with a grin.

"You're too fat, Stahlschmidt. You need to lose weight. You had better be my runner." That was the toughest job in the squadron.

Porta and Tiny at once began instructing Eagle in his duties.

"You just have to use your flat feet," Porta said, "zigzag

between the bursting shells and don't shove your fat fizz in front of a sniper's rifle."

Eagle was just in time to see the runner he was replacing. Half his skull had been torn away. He was still alive, but died before we left. Eagle took his message bag.

A shell spattered down near us. In a second the squadron had scattered. We had heard it coming. Mike almost swallowed his great cigar.

"*Hombre*," Barcelona Blom exclaimed, "those bloody shells always come so suddenly!"

We marched on. Nobody had been hurt. Porta and Tiny went up alongside Eagle and forced him into No. 3 section.

"Nasty world this you've come to, eh, Stahlschmidt? Shells, incendiaries, saw-edged bayonets and nasty samurai swords. They're out to tear your balls off now. Flame-throwers that shave you in a flash. Pah! It was better in your cage in Altona, wasn't it? But war is like the cinema, the best seats are at the back and the front is all flicker. But, take comfort, we have made a nice soft place for you in the common grave."

"Shut your mouth," Eagle snarled. "The laugh may be on you in the end."

"What's the longest a squadron runner's survived?" Tiny crowed maliciously.

"With the engineers a week," Heide said with a satanic chuckle. "In the infantry five to ten days, and with us never more than two."

Tiny made the sign of the cross in front of Eagle's face.

"Are you a Catholic?" he asked.

"What business of yours is that?" Eagle snarled.

"I think you ought to go to the Padre and get your mug rubbed with the last unction before we reach our positions." Tiny whinnied delightedly, thinking himself the wit of all time. He laughed for a good fifteen minutes.

"It really is cruel that such promising officer material should die in his prime," Barcelona remarked.

"That's the harsh rule of war," Porta said and looked searchingly at Eagle. "Are you afraid to squeeze your arse together, Stahlschmidt?"

Tiny demonstratively took hold of the seat of Eagle's trousers.

"Not yet," he announced. "But it's coming."

Eagle hit at him furiously with his message bag.

"I've been a soldier longer than you, you great bog."

"Cardboard soldier," Tiny scoffed. "If Walt Disney had known you, he would have made you the villain in Donald Duck." He collapsed with laughing and rolled about on the ground. He was one of the fortunates who can be amazed by one thing for hours on end.

We had found an old film projector, a great heavy monster, but we carted it everywhere with us. There was only one film with it, or rather half a film, a Pop-eye film. Whenever there was an opportunity, we ran the film through, over and over again, finding it just as funny each time we saw it. Four times already Tiny had dislocated his jaw with laughing at one of the scenes, where Pop-eye drives an old Ford through a band saw.

We came to a wood, where all the trees had been split and splintered by shells. Until you see such a sight, you cannot believe it is possible. Dead trees everywhere pointing accusingly to Heaven. We joked as we marched through it, again at Eagle's expense.

Some shells dropped some distance behind us.

"I don't like this," muttered the Old Man.

We were approaching the death ravine, the most feared sector on the Cassino front, and the air was full of whistles and whines and howls. This was a narrow sector under enemy observation. Hundreds of blown-up bodies of men and horses lay there. Only five per cent of our supply columns came through.

"Distance, distance!" the order was passed down. "No smoking."

A fresh salvo of shells dropped. We began to run. Breathing heavily we toiled along. One of the men dropped a mortar. Shirker-Brandt it was. He was always trying to get out of things. The Old Man threatened to shoot him if he did not pick it up again. A 75 mm whizzed into the ground. Brandt dropped to his knees, a fountain of blood spurting from the place where his head had been. Then he collapsed over the mortar. The Old Man and I flung his body aside and carted the mortar along between us. Brandt was forgotten.

Shells hammered down among us. People screamed. We thought only of ourselves. Our legs worked automatically. We had only one thought: to get out of there and into cover. We did not notice the machine gun banging against our helmets, the straps cutting into our shoulders. On, on! There was no need to urge us now.

A feldwebel running beside me had both feet shot off.

Unteroffizier Schrank from No. 1 troop stopped abruptly, gazing in amazement at the machine gun and his severed arm lying together on the ground in front of him. Gefreiter Lazio was sitting in the middle of the path trying to stuff his guts back into his riven belly.

Then we were through, having left a quarter of our number among the piles of dead. Eagle was not the only one who had filled his trousers during that ten minutes run.

We had a breather, our faces were very different now that we were through. The man with the scythe had laid his hand on our shoulders and we were no longer the same. We were killers now; deadly dangerous. You can take cover from a shell, but it is difficult to hide from a scared soldier thirsting to kill.

Snipers sit up in trees with rifles with telescopic sights. They always place their bullets between the eyes. That kills you. Down goes the curtain. A stray bullet or shell splinter can pierce your helmet. At the best you will merely be scalped, but if it should lodge in the soft part at the back, friend, the stretcher bearers must drag you away. You have a chance; but not a big one. If they aren't too busy at the field hospital, they will get it out all right, but it will mean months and months in hospital afterwards. And you will have to learn everything all over again: talking, walking, moving. You won't even be able to smell any more. You will have forgotten everything. Perhaps you will go mad before you have relearned it all.

> Die blauen Dragoner sie reiten
> mit klingendem Spiel durch das Tor . . .

What German soldier has not sung it in the garrison? It is

such a glad gay song about the poacher who makes a fool of the warder. But you won't sing it the day you find yourself sitting in a muddy fox hole holding your fingers to an open artery in your thigh, for your life will be in your own hand, quite literally. You will shout desperately for the stretcher bearers, the front line soldier's friend with the red cross armlet, but he won't come. He has other things to do. He will be busy helping those whose lives can be saved. You are doomed, though you don't realise it. Your wound does not look anything in particular, but one cannot put a ligature on it. Surprised, you see the blood trickling out from under your fingers. In half an hour you will be dead. You will have quietly bled to death.

> Auprès de ma blonde,
> qu'il fait bon dormir. . . .

There are no fifes and drums up at the front. You beseech alternately God and the Devil to help you. But they don't. In a war, both are so busy. Why does God let it happen? you ask. You want to reproach him for it. But it was not God let it happen. He gave man freewill, the liberty even to wage war. A thief or a murderer cannot reproach the police because he is a thief, or a murderer. Nor can you reproach God, because there is a war.

We took over from the paratroopers. They were done. They did not even say goodbye as they marched away. They had only one thought in their heads: to get away. An hour later, we had the first attack. It was the Japs. In a moment we were all rolling about in a savage hand to hand.

The Legionnaire and I got a SMG into position and swept the length of the position. That caused casualties on both sides, but what else could we do? The yellow ones had to be got out and that's what happened. It was the Legionnaire did it. He wrenched the gun off its stand, clasped it to his hip and bawled his '*Allah el akbar! Vive la legion! Avant, avant!*' and we followed him, as so often before in Russia. Even Mike joined in.

Tiny was wielding a sharpened trenching tool. He seized a Jap by the ankles and crushed his head against a stone. In a

146

matter of minutes, they had withdrawn in panic.

We found Barcelona in a bunker with a knife wound in his belly. The man who had given it to him was lying in a corner with a cloven head. We sent Barcelona back to the dressing station. It cost us six cigars, a watch, three opium sticks and twelve French pictures to get him there. It was a stiff price, but Barcelona was a good pal.

The doctor gave him a big shot of morphia.

We were now one fewer in the troop. Just before they took him off, he gave the Old Man the shrivelled orange he had brought from Spain. He had got it into his head that nothing could happen to him as long as the orange was with No. 5 Squadron. The Old Man had to swear on a crucifix borrowed from Padre Emanuel that he would keep it in his righthand trouser pocket until Barcelona returned. Then he waved to us from the improvised stretcher, a greatcoat between two rifles. We watched him until they disappeared up by the ravine of death.

It was that night we captured the boy. He was on his way across the river and ran right into the arms of a patrol. We could not get a word out of him. When they searched him, they found various kinds of seeds in his pockets. Nothing else. When they asked his name, he gave one that tens of thousands of Italian boys of ten have.

The Divisional intelligence officer came up, but he could not get anything out of him either. They sent him back with a patrol, and that evening we heard they had shot him. They had discovered the significance of the seeds: the white ones were tanks; maize was guns, sunflower seeds machine guns; apple pips regiments. He was only ten years old, but a brilliant spy. He had seen his father and mother shot in some sidestreet in Rome and that had made him hate us so much, he had himself cut the throat of a military policeman.

Two days later the Americans made enquiries about him. We told them what we knew. They cursed us and shot five of ours in reprisal.

There was a tree in the ravine of death with a peasant girl strung from one of its branches. She had been caught red-handed burying mines. By the river's bank were two commando soldiers sitting tied together with barbed wire. They had been caught far behind HKL. The headhunters had brought them up, killed them with a shot in the back of the neck and placed their bodies there, right in front of the Americans' noses as an awful warning. They were already beginning to disintegrate, but we were forbidden to remove them under pain of severe punishment. Soon we no longer saw them. They were part of the landscape, like the old willow tree that was trying to drown itself in the river.

It was our instinct told us, the sure instinct of the front line soldier, and so, without anyone ordering us, we began digging one-man fox holes, the infantry's best defence against tanks.

The grenadiers from the 134th laughed at us.

"There aren't any tanks here. You panzer-boys have tanks on the brain."

"*Va te faire cuir un oeuf*," said the Legionnaire. "They'll come. Just wait and see."

And they came. At a time of day we least expected: just after midnight.

We ran back from our positions into our fox holes, from which we mowed down the infantry following the tanks and destroyed tank after tank. Thirty six reeking bonfires we lit. Only ten tanks got back.

Porta and Tiny were out hunting for gold teeth, even before the attack was over. They had been told that the Japanese were usually well supplied with them. Loud was their disappointment when an energetic search yielded only nine. They decided that they would examine the corpses again by daylight. They could have overlooked some in the dark. For at least the twentieth time Major Mike threatened to court martial them, but they remained unmoved. Nothing could overcome their hunger for gold. Tiny proudly displayed a magnificent eye tooth.

We were moved to new positions by Hill 593, on the other side of which lay the 34th Texas Division. We could see as far as Rocca Janula, on which shells were raining. Mike spent hours with the glasses glued to his eyes searching for faces he knew, for 133 US Infantry regiment was slightly to one side of us and Mike had been in it as a recruit.

We could see that he was concocting some dirty trick to play on them. He had a grudge against them. Suddenly he saw a few he recognised. He shoved the artillery observer aside, seized the field telephone and demanded to be put through to the major in command of the unit. Leutnant Frick tried to stop him:

"Don't, Mike. They'll smash us."

Mike grinned evilly and stuck one of his big cigars into his mouth.

"Bugger off! This is my private war. I've looked forward to this for many years." He summoned Porta, who was going about with a seven foot bow he had found lying beside a dead American. Mike pointed out a target for him. "Can you see those three bushes just beside that five-sided rock?"

Porta nodded.

"Slightly to the right, three fingers about, there's an opening," Mike went on. "Can you see it?"

Porta peered through the glasses, then gave a long whistle.

"I've got it. An observation post."

Mike grinned and chewed at his cigar.

"Not it! It's their command post. There's a turd there, who was in F Company with me. Can you get an arrow across with a note?"

"Could do," said Porta.

Major Mike tore a leaf from his message book and wrote swiftly:

"Joe Dunnawan can you remember Michael Braun? We were in Shuffield Barracks together. You split on me, Dunnawan. It was your fault I was chucked out. Now I'm a major.

"We're coming across to pull your arse hole over your face. There's a lot of interest on our account to be paid, Joe, and Joe, I'm going to get you even if you hide in General Clarke's HQ!

"In exactly three minutes I'm sending a bunch of shells across. Take cover, Joe, or your head will go flying, and I wouldn't like that. I want to get you alive. By Jesus, Joe, you're going to yell, as we slaves in the garrison jail used to when Major One-Leg beat us up.

> Be seeing you, Joe!
> Mike Braun.
> Major Company Commander"

Porta tied the paper to a long arrow, drew the bow, took careful aim and with a whine the message sped away.

Mike started his stop watch, rushed to the field telephone, snatched the observer's calculations and, a satanic smile on his face, gave his orders to the heavy howitzer battery. Then he asked for the rocket battery.

Exactly three minutes after Porta shot his arrow, there was a roar as if a hundred runaway express locomotives were rushing past overhead. Involuntarily we dropped to our knees. A wall of fire, earth and stone rose above the enemy positions. That was the howitzers. Ten salvoes they fired. Five seconds later the rocket battery joined in. The howitzers were nasty, but they were nothing compared to the 30 cm rockets which then came sweeping with long tails of fire behind them. We had experienced it many times, yet it never failed to send us cowering in terror at the bottom of the trench. We knew that the rocket battery had three projectors, but each projector had ten tubes. That made thirty of those terrifying things, and all because Major Mike bore a grudge against a man. There he sat on the bottom of the trench, legs wide apart, an evil smile on his face.

The silence was uncanny after that rain of shells.

"Look out," Leutnant Frick said. "They're bound to answer."

And they did. For a whole quarter of an hour they pounded away with every gun they had. Then peace returned.

Mike was sitting in his dug-out concocting some fresh devilry. Soon after darkness fell there was a call for volunteers, for a storming party we were told. But everyone knew of Major Mike's private war and no one volunteered. Mike jeered and called us sissies, but we didn't care. "I'm leading it myself," Mike said, as if that meant anything. We had no confidence in Mike as leader of a night storming party. He did not dare order us out. It could have had very nasty consequences for him, if he had and things had gone wrong. They weren't amateurs on

150

the other side. So, there was no storming party that night. Mike even promised Porta and Tiny 60 opium sticks and as much gold teeth plundering as they liked, if they could get a group together. They did what they could with threats and wonderful promises, but we just weren't having any.

The next morning the Americans began jeering at Mike. They flung an old infantry boot with a dead rat inside it across to us. The message was obvious. Then they began using an amplifier:

"We haven't forgotten you, Braun. You're the nastiest renegade ever wore American uniform. You fit in well with the krauts. I'm here waiting for you; but don't keep me waiting too long. I don't want a corn on my bum because of you. Ersatz-Major Mike Braun. We promise 20,000 dollars and as many cigarettes as two men can carry, if your squadron will cut your head off and chuck it across to us. And if they don't cut your turnip off, we'll slaughter the lot, when we come to fetch you."

Their snipers were busy all day and killed eleven of us. Just after midnight they killed our sentries, and it was only due to the Legionnaire that they didn't clear the trench. He had gone out of his dug-out to pee and saw them running up. He at once opened fire from his LMG, and it took ten minutes hard fighting to turn them out. That cost us another dozen men. But now we had had enough. They had gone too far.

Mike rubbed his hands delightedly when the Legionnaire came up and reported that the storming party was ready. We were going to slip down and fetch Mike's friend just after 19 hours, when they would be in the middle of issuing rations. They would be intent on their food, and as we had ours doled out at roughly the same time, they would never in their wildest dreams imagine that we would come across at such a time. It was the Legionnaire's idea and met with considerable opposition from the foodhogs like Porta. Mike did not like it much either, but the Legionnaire had his way. Tiny and Heide cut a way through the wire and we crawled through at lightning speed. We assembled in a couple of shell holes in front of the enemy position. We unscrewed the caps of our grenades, undid the safety catches of our pistols. We were so close we could hear them joking about the contents of the mess kids. One said it was a stew of dead German telephone girls. Two were squabbling over a bottle of whisky.

Mike picked out the way through his infra-red glasses. Whispering, he told Tiny to come with him and help bring Joe Dunnawan back. The Americans seemed to have forgotten everything but their food. Mike let his hand fall, the signal to attack.

We rushed forward. One mess kid flew high into the air when a hand grenade landed in it. We flung mines and hand grenades into their dug-outs and swept the trench clear with our machine pistols.

There was enormous confusion. Within a few minutes we were on our way back. We had just had time to destroy their mortars and heavy machine guns before we went. We landed back in our own trenches thoroughly out of breath.

Mike was almost speechless with fury. Tiny had been too rough with Dunnawan and throttled him, so all Mike could do was kick his dead body. What angered him even more, perhaps, was the fact that he could not even punish Tiny for his ham-handedness, as the whole undertaking was quite irregular.

During the next few days we amused ourselves shooting with bow and arrow and blow pipe.

It began to rain. We froze in our camouflage dress. We could look across at the monastery that was like a menacing clenched fist. Early one morning, the entire south-westerly horizon seemed to go up in flames. The heavens opened and we found ourselves staring into a line of enormous blast furnaces. The mountains trembled. The whole Lire Valley quaked with terror, as eight thousand tons of steel fell thundering over us. The greatest artillery battle in history had begun. In one single day as many shells fell on our positions as were fired during the whole of the fighting for Verdun. It went on implacably, hour after hour.

Our dugouts kept collapsing and we had to dig ourselves out with hands, feet and teeth. We became moles. We squeezed against the trench walls, or rather what was left of them. It was the worst shelling hell we had experienced. We saw a 38 ton tank go soaring through the air. Scarcely had it landed, tracks in the air, balancing on its turret, when blast sent it hurling back to where it had come from.

An entire company making its way along a communication trench was buried alive in a couple of seconds. All that remained of them was the barrel of a rifle poking up here and there.

That night the shelling began to drive people mad. We had to knock them down and beat them to restore them to their senses. But we did not always manage to get hold of them in time to prevent their running out into the rain of shells, where no one survived long. The whole place was an inferno of red-hot flying steel.

Leutnant Sorg had both legs blown off and bled to death. Our two medical orderlies were killed. One was crushed by a balk falling on him. The other was cut in half, when a shell landed just in front of him as he was going to Leutnant Sorg. Tiny's nose was cut off and the Legionnaire and Heide held him, while Porta sewed it on again. This was done under cover of a pile of corpses. So it went on all night and all the next day. Our own field batteries had long ago been silenced, and our tanks had been burned where they stood.

Suddenly the barrage lifted, moved on behind us. Then they came, emerging out of craters and holes. They were devils. They shouted and screamed. Confident of victory they stormed forward, sure that none of us could be left alive. But we lay crouched behind our machine guns and flame-throwers in shell holes and between rocks. The first ran on past us, as we shammed dead. More and more came. One of them kicked my steel helmet and made my head ring. Wait, you swine, I thought. You won't get back alive. Through my lashes I could see running feet, long American laced boots, white French gaiters, English puttees. They were all mixed up. Then some negroes came, quite grey in the face with fear.

A hoarse voice commanded:

"For-ward. For-ward!"

A machine gun began to bark. I rolled on to my face, heaved the machine gun and stand out of the mud. Tiny shoved a belt in. I loaded, fired. Tracer went hissing into the backs of the khaki clad soldiers, mowing them down. They tried to surrender, but Death just harvested them.

We went at them with bayonets and spades. We trampled bodies, scattered and slipped in spilled guts, throttled our fellow humans with our bare hands.

Kill, soldier, kill for your country and the freedom you will never enjoy!

I swung my spade and sliced off the face of an American negro sergeant. His blood spurted over me. I leaped into the cover of a three-foot hole. Something moved beneath the mire. A face appeared beneath a flat helmet. I gave a cry of fear, clasped my spade, emptied my pistol without even hitting him. He rose up, dripping mud. I dealt him a kick in the belly. He came at me with a bayonet. I stood up, knocked the bayonet from his hand and hacked him again and again in the face with my knife-sharp spade.

Pro patria! Forward, my hero, on with your bayonet and spade.

X

It was Carl's idea to block Via del Capoci and a traffic policeman
helped us to place a rack across the street at either end. Mario
fetched the bowls and we began playing Petanque. Some people
made a fuss, but the policeman just roared at them. The entire
street joined in. It was wonderful, except for a few slanging
matches with drivers who could not understand why the street was
blocked.

The quiet was broken only by the pleasant click of the bowls
striking each other. We knelt and aimed, measured and argued.
We played all day and only stopped when it began to rain.

We did not remove the blocks before we left. We might want the
street again the next day.

Then we set out for the brothels in Mario de' Fiori, but before
we got so far, we became involved in a fight with some Italian
mountain troops. That was outside the big confectioners in Via
del Corso. We went through one of the glass windows. Then the
carabinieri arrived, but it was only Italians they caught. The rest
of us took up position in a brothel.

"It's lovely here in Rome," Carl said.

IN ROME ON LEAVE

Several times the truck felt as though it would go over, as it lurched over the countless shell holes. My leave pass rustled in the breast pocket of my stiff camouflage jacket, promising me a fortnight's oblivion in Hamburg. The adjutant had whispered something about a chance of getting it stamped to allow me across into Denmark. The regiment could not do that for me, but if I could get it done in Hamburg, I could go on to Copenhagen. But what should I do there? Hop across to Sweden and be handed back by the Swedes? That was routine with them. Three days before we had provided the firing squad for a couple of airmen who had deserted from Rome and got as far as Stockholm. They had travelled back in handcuffs. The Swedish police had escorted them to Hälsingborg, where they were handed over to the military police. And eventually we had shot them. One of them died cursing the Swedes.

"Where are you off to?" an elderly obergefreiter with the red braid of the Grenadiers on his shoulderstraps, asked.

I gazed at him in silence. I could not answer.

"I asked, where you were off to?" he said with peasant stubbornness.

"What bloody business is that of yours, you stupid swine? Have I asked where you are going?"

"You seem to want a bash in the face, you young bugger. I'm old enough to be your father."

"Come on then. I'm ready." I whipped off my belt and wound it round my fist, ready to fight.

He hesitated, unable to understand why I was so angry. But I had to take it out of someone or other, and the old chap would have done very well. If he would just hit me, I'd kill him. I didn't care what would happen to me. I just felt I had

156

to do something desperate after 62 maddening hours in the stinking turret of a tank.

I seemed to be surrounded by Service Corps men, but away at the back I caught sight of two sailors in crumpled, oil-smeared uniforms. The buttons on their jackets were green with verdigris. One had lost his capband and even with the best will in the world, you could not read what was on the other's. The badges on their sleeves told me they were in submarines. I felt that I would not mind a chat with them and imagined that they would be glad of a chat with me. But, like me, they were no doubt afraid to make the first move. Perhaps we would never exchange a word throughout the 100 miles we had to go in that lumbering truck.

We got to Rome in time for me to catch the express north, but first I had to go to No. 12 Hospital to deliver a packet for One-Eye, a packet addressed to a woman doctor. It was incredible, but our General One-Eye was in love. I was eager to see the girl. If she was One-Eye's equal in looks, she would not be up to much. But the girl turned out to be amazingly pretty and I hopped into bed with her as One-Eye's deputy.

My pockets were stuffed with letters that I was taking so that they did not go through the field censor, a nice collection of highly treasonable missives. The worst, no doubt, was Porta's. It was to a friend of his, a deserter spending his fifth year in hiding, who had started a sort of 'illegal group' along with a policeman, giving help to those who could pay for it. But woe betide you if you got into their clutches without being able to pay. Porta had some sort of business agreement with them; what it was, was a bit of a mystery, but it was undoubtedly something on a grandiose scale. After the war Porta's friend became chief of police in a well-known town in Germany. I won't say which, in case he brings a libel action against me.

The truck rattled into Rome. A couple of mangy dogs ran barking after us for quite a long way. We stopped outside a barracks, a stinking place with peeling walls. You could see that it was not occupied by its rightful owners. They, in fact, were far away, buried in the African sand or rotting in POW camps in Libya.

A feldwebel began bawling at us.

"Bugger off," shouted one of the sailors, as he jumped down. Close together, their kitbags on their shoulders, the two sailors rolled out through the barrack gates. I ran after them deaf to the feldwebel's shouts. They stank of oil and salt water. We walked on and on. When we got to the Spanish Steps, we stopped for a rest. Then we came to Via Mario de' Fiori and dived into a bar, a narrow gut of a place with a long counter. A traffic policeman, goggles hanging round his neck, cigarette dangling from a corner of his mouth, was talking big. His uniform was all spattered. He stopped talking as he caught sight of us.

A couple of whores were lounging across the bar looking as if they had their apprenticeship well behind them.

The bartender, a tall, fat giant of a man wearing a short sleeved pullover, a sweat rag round his neck, was lazily polishing a glass. The policeman said in a loud whisper:

"Attenzione! Rotten Germans!"

The smaller of the two sailors went straight towards him, one hand resting on his bayonet.

"Comrade," he began, "You are a Roman. We are Germans. We are decent chaps, we won't harm anyone, if we aren't provoked. I believe our friend behind the bar takes things the same way. He only wants what he is entitled to receive. These two ladies are nice ladies, as long as they get what they are entitled to have." He paused briefly, drew his bayonet and picked his teeth with the point of it, then bent right over to the policeman, in doing which his neck stretched forward revealing red, scalded skin, such as you see on survivors, those who have got out of a steam-filled room at the last moment. "But, and please remember this, policeman, none of us is rotten. You know your streets and roads, I my sea. I have been lying out submerged waiting for the big convoys, as you have been hiding behind a stone waiting for a drunken sot to come along." He let go of his bayonet and slammed the flat of his hand down on the bar. "Here with some beer. Three quarters beer and the rest slibowitz. Followed by poor man's champagne," (half beer, half champagne).

The barman grinned understandingly. Wiped his belly with his sweat cloth.

"You're in a hurry to get tight, eh?" He scratched his behind and bit the cork out of a champagne bottle.

We studied the pictures on the wall behind the barman. Fly-spotted pictures of naked girls, which only new customers even noticed.

We three had not yet said a word to each other. We couldn't until we had drunk our first glass, a ritual that had to be scrupulously followed. They did not concern me, nor I them, until we had drunk a glass of slibowitz and beer together. The barman took a lot of trouble over our beer. It took him a quarter of an hour.

"Do you want sticks?" he asked.

Our silence told him that we did.

He shoved a litre mug in front of each of us and put a semi-clean stick in each, the dirty black end up. He took some juniper berries from a big earthenware pot and put some into each mug. Then he pushed a bowl of olives and anchovies across to us. They had no sticks in them as they do in smart places. We just used our fingers.

We clinked mugs and drank in long thirsty gulps. The taller of the sailors, a long thin beanpole, offered us cigarettes. Camel. He scratched his crutch and stared at the two whores, weighing them up.

"We're on the way to hospital," he explained. "Carl burst something inside, when a torpedo fell on him. And my old syph's playing me up, and we both have burns to be anointed." By way of amplification he opened his fall so that I could see the red, burned flesh. "That's the result of a hammering we got off Cyprus. We had been lying on the bottom for 48 hours, then the skipper lost patience. He wouldn't listen to our No. 2, but went up to periscope depth. He was young and inexperienced. Only 21. No. 2 was 47 and had plenty of experience. He had been in a tramp before coming to U boats. When we dragged him out of the command room, his flesh was smouldering on his bones. Boiling oil. We never found the CO. He had vanished. He was after a knight's cross, had been all the time. Thirty-seven of the crew went with them. But we got the old tub home. We had the first engineer to thank for that."

"Fancy bothering to tell him all that," said the smaller of the two, who was called Carl. "Let's whet our whistles."

We each stood a round. Then the barman did. The policeman was taken into favour and had one. We poured the dregs into the v's of the girls' dresses.

Another girl came in.

"Oho," growled Carl sticking a long finger into the tall sailor's ribs, "I want to fuck that one. Wonder what she costs? I'd give 500 for a night." He discussed the price with the girl and they agreed on 500 marks and 10 packets of Lucky Strike. She lived on the second floor over the bar. Otto and I went up with them. The barman stuck a few bottles under our arms as we left.

"I'll look up in half an hour, when I close here," he called.

We clambered up a steep flight of stairs. The girl led the way and we could see far up her legs. She wore red knickers with black lace. Her stockings were long and exciting and had dark-coloured tops.

Carl sniggered hungrily and took hold of her thigh:

"Lovely rigging you've got!"

We followed the girl down a long, pitch dark corridor, stumbling into things, and laughing sillily and taking it in turns to strike matches. Every now and again we stopped for a mouthful of beer.

A woman was groaning behind one of the doors. From another room came a man's lewd laugh. A bed creaked protestingly. Something fell. It must have been a bottle, because it went rolling on across the floor.

Otto bent down to look through the keyhole.

"*Sbrigatevi*!" the girl whispered impatiently. "What the hell are you hanging about there for?"

"Take it easy," Otto said. "We're on our way into dock. There's no hurry."

"If you don't come, I'll get myself another lout. The night's short. I'm busy." She tossed her head, jerking her long blue-black hair behind her. "What's the idea? Do you want a fuck or don't you?"

"We're coming," Otto growled. "We're just having a glass of beer. Have you ever wondered, Carl, why whores are always in a hurry? They are the most industrious business people in the world. Do you remember that tall thin one at Saloniki, who took two clients at a time? She was so busy, she didn't keep an eye on Obermaat Grant. He went off with four night's earnings, and when she went after him, she fell into the water, cutting her forehead on a bollard."

"Don't you call me a whore," exclaimed the girl, who understood a little German, "For you, sailor, I'm a girl, hag, witch, wench, what you like, but not whore."

"That's all right," said Otto soothingly. "Let's go in and adjust compasses. What were you called by the way, when you were still with mum?"

"Lolita."

"Lolita," Otto savoured the name, "Lolita. Have you ever been under the clothes with a girl called Lolita before, Carl?"

"Can't remember, if I have. Come on, Lolita, show us your bunk."

A bottle of beer slipped from Otto's grasp, rolled along the corridor and down the steps. He made a dive for it, dropping the other bottles he had under his arm, lost his balance and went slithering down the stairs making the most appalling racket.

Carl and I hurried to help, thundering down the quiet stairs. Doors were flung open. Men and women cursed us, as only Italians can. A titch standing beside an enormous girl promised to box our ears, but when he caught sight of Otto he withdrew hurriedly and barricaded the door with a commode and a bidet.

The barman appeared at the bottom of the stairs, his body glistening with sweat, a cudgel in his hand.

"*Per Bacco! Accidenti!* If there's anyone after you boys, I'll deal with him."

"It's just that I dropped my beer," Otto explained.

"Did it break?" the fat barman asked anxiously.

"No, praise be. But what bloody awful stairs you have. They remind me of Nagasaki. I went on my arse there too. That was the night I scrounged my syph. A Japanese she was, and only had three toes on her right foot."

"Syph," shouted Lolita. "Then there's nothing doing with

me!" She darted off down the passage, and a door slammed.
Carl began to grumble.

"You flaming idiot! What the devil did you want to open
your big mouth about your syph for? Don't you understand,
Otto, that sort of thing is Top Secret. Have you ever heard
me blabbing about the clap I got when we bunkered in
Piraeus. And that was your fault, Otto. You insisted on going
into that damned cafe. If we had gone to the girls in the telephone exchange, as I suggested, it wouldn't have happened."

"Who says the telephone girls were immaculate?" Otto
said, defensively. "If you've got it coming to you, you'll get it
even if you stalk into the royal palace and hop into bed with a
princess."

We sat down on the stairs and opened a couple of bottles;
then slowly we toiled back up again, pausing for beer on every
landing.

"Beer isn't what it was," Otto said querulously. "It smells
like beer, it's called beer, and they charge for it as if it was beer,
but the muck tastes like water. Once beer starts getting bad,
it's time to stop the war. Nobody can stand a war without
decent beer."

"Are you two regulars," I asked.

"Yes, what else?" Carl snapped. He spat on the wall. "We
went to school together, Otto and I. We got fed up together
and we joined the navy together in '24. That was the only
permanent job they could offer us. We signed on for twelve
years straightaway. What the hell's the use of dividing life
into little bits? And we've stayed in ever since."

"And you're still only mates?" I asked surprised.

"We could have been stabsfeldwebels long ago," Otto
grinned. "We've been reduced five times now. Too much
cunt and beer. And too many idiotic officers. But it was fun,
until this filthy war started. Now, we're the only ones left
out of 375 from the old U boat school in Kiel."

"What'll you do, when we've lost the war and they do away
with the navy?"

"You talk about things you know, son," Carl said with a
disapproving shake of his head. "The navy can't be abolished
just like that. They'll send you others to hell. They may take

the sharks away from us for a bit, but we'll be put on sweeping mines."

Otto had now got as far as Lolita's door and was threatening to shoot the lock, if she didn't open up. He rattled his rifle so that she could hear he meant business.

"Move away from the door. I'm going to shoot," he bellowed.

Two bolts were shot into place on the far side and a stream of oaths and curses poured through. She threatened to send Mussolini, Badaglio, Churchill and the Pope after him, if he didn't go away.

A door opened at the end of the corridor and a hospitable girl invited us in. Otto shouldered his kitbag and carbine, Lolita forgotten.

We shook hands and introduced ourselves. She was called Isabella. She had a whole keg of beer standing beside the washbasin and mugs dangled on strings from the ceiling.

Otto shed his clothes at once. He had big holes in his socks and mould on his trousers. He pointed to his boots.

"Can't get those damned dice-boxes dry," he said. "We had to wade the last bit. The duty boat couldn't get right in. It's a dog's life being a sailor."

Isabella stepped out of her skirt. She had a short black petticoat, which we admired. Carl and I seated ourselves on the edge of the bed, each with a mug of beer. Otto and Isabella squabbled amiably about which position to use. In the end she gave in and knelt on the bed. Carl and I were a bit in the way and had to move over. That was soon done. Then it was the f.l. which was wrong and I had to get another from a packet in the bottom drawer of the chest of drawers. Isabella saw to it that it was put on properly.

"Now we're ready," she said.

"Fine," growled Otto, "Let's get to work then."

Carl gave me a description of life in the depot ships to which they delivered the prisoners they took.

"It was on one of them I had the best fuck of my life," he said. "A black girl, she was, and wild as the devil. The African jungle in person. She moved her undercarriage like the fly-wheel on a steam roller."

Otto sat up, a satisfied expression on his face. Then it was Carl's turn. He went on with his story about the African girl, while taking his trousers off.

Isabella swung her legs round his thighs.

"And while I was on her," Carl went on, "I ate caviar out of a tin with a spoon. I'll give you a hundred extra if you do it French," he said to Isabella.

"As you like. Here with the dough."

"I tried to smuggle her back aboard our shark, but the Old Man saw her just as we were diving into the stern fo'c'sle. I got twelve days, but she was worth it ten times over. You've got a lovely bum," he said with a sigh, pinching Isabella's broad backside.

Otto flung his used f.l. out of the window and put his boots by the radiator to dry.

"You, Sven, what would you say to joining forces with us for a couple of days? The hospital can wait. I think we three ought to have a look at this hole all the fine people seem to want to see. It's part of your education to know Rome."

I agreed, though it meant sacrificing a couple of precious days.

"Our first officer told me of a good hostelry. I have the address. He told me all about it, when we were in a lifeboat in Biscay."

"Were you torpedoed?"

"No, it was a bloody plane. We were up charging our batteries. It came right out of the sun and hammered away at us with its machine cannon. The CO and chief engineer who were sitting smoking forward were killed with the first burst. The next swept the entire gun crew away. They did a crash-dive, of course. The first officer and I were on deck aft. We tugged at the hatch but it was already locked from inside. The first officer just managed to get a life belt loose and in we went with boots, pistols and the lot. We had to get away from the ruddy thing, before we were sucked down. The buggers swung her and darned nearly made pulp of us with the conning tower. A T-boat picked us up two days later. You should have seen Carl's face, when we ran into each other in No. 3 Flotilla's canteen in Bordeaux."

Carl raised himself on his elbows off Isabella's chest

164

and paused long enough to say:

"Jesus is my witness. I had the fright of my life. When that flying bastard had gone, we surfaced to look for you. We searched all night. We even used a searchlight though it's forbidden. The next day, we gathered all your gear together and had a funeral. So, when I saw you in Bordeaux, I nearly peed my bags with fright."

Isabella and he resumed operations.

There was a wild hammering on the door.

"Who is it now," Isabella called in a voice of irritation. *"Via di qua!"*

"Don't shout so. It's me, Mario," came the beery voice of the barman.

Otto opened the door and Mario staggered in, a case of beer on his shoulders.

"I've brought you a few bottles, in case you get thirsty," he explained, dumping the beer down in the middle of the floor. He patted Isabella's turned-up backside. "You're busy," he said and laughed. Then he put his head back and emptied a bottle at one draught.

Carl had finished. Otto said he would like another turn and took up position between Isabella's strong thighs.

"This is what keeps a tired hero going," he said. He set the girl's heels on his shoulders. "We get it seldom enough at sea."

"Not without a f.l.," said Isabella freeing herself. I had to rummage in the bottom drawer again.

"Your papers are all in order, I suppose," Mario said. "The MPs will be here in an hour."

"I've nothing to fear," I said and laughed happily.

"Your leave's for Rome is it?"

"No, Hamburg."

"They'll have you then. Don't let them find you here. But, shit take it, you've time enough. There's a blind old thing lives in the basement. She's got ears like a weasel and as soon as she hears anything, she'll smash a bottle against the wall in the courtyard."

Otto was tired out, and Isabella was sitting straddled over the bidet. The sight of her made Mario lust. They couldn't be bothered to get into bed, but did it on the floor like a couple of dogs. Mario had his beer within reach and did not even stop while he was drinking. None of us took exception to them. Why should we? Isabella was in business and we were her clients. It was just the same as going to the stores and having a beer in the back of the shop.

Mario was sweating.

"Poof, ugh," he groaned. "I've got out of training. I really must do this more often."

"You can do it here as often as you like," Isabella said, "as long as you pay. Otherwise, the shop's shut."

"Haven't you got a fellow?" Otto asked.

"Not now. They took him a week ago. Sent him away with the Jews."

"Wonder what they are doing with all the beaks," Carl said.

"Snuffing them out," Otto said. "I've heard they try out chemical warfare stuff on them."

"People say they're gassed in big camps in Poland," Mario put in.

"Aren't you coming too?" Isabella asked, pointing to me. "If you are, let's do it now, while I'm in form."

I tried to get out of it, but the others thought it was just being embarrassed and helped me. Why describe it? Anyway, we were interrupted in the middle of it all by Carl suddenly saying:

"Let me see your armpit. You haven't a blood group marking have you?"

I was so surprised that without thinking, I raised my upper arm, then I lost my temper.

"You two moth-eaten salt-herring sailors have no right to try and throw your weight about here!" I seized a pot that was half full, and heaved it at Carl. He ducked like lightning and it sailed on to hit Mario as he was draining a bottle of beer.

He wiped the stinking stuff from his face at the same time letting out a flow of sulphurous oaths. The next moment Isabella and I were flung apart.

"You lousy German petrol-yokel," he shouted. "Here you're

getting Italian cunt at sale price and you fling piss at decent people!" He tried to jump on my belly, but I managed to roll away in time.

Carl and Otto leaped at him and managed to get him down. Tall Otto seated himself astride his chest, while Isabella supplied first aid in the shape of beer and schnaps which she poured down his throat in vast quantities to quieten him. Slowly his equanimity returned, but before he would agree to be sensible Isabella had to promise him a sympathetic fuck, and while he had it we sang "Oh, Tannenbaum!" as a part song.

"I could tell you were one of us," Carl began, his face serious.

At the foot of the air-shaft outside a bottle smashed against a pipe. Hurried footsteps sounded on the narrow stairs. Iron-shod boots trying to tread quietly. The military police, blasted headhunters.

Mario jerked himself free of Isabella.

"Hell, boys, they're here. The blind woman's heard them. Out onto the roof! *Sbrigatevi!*"

I tried to crawl under the bed, but was pulled out by my legs.

"Are you crazy?" Isabella hissed. "That's the first place they look."

Mario shoved us out of the window.

"Out, you buggers! And no fuss! If they find you here they'll close the bar and all this business. The devil take you Germans. As far as I am concerned, you can shoot each other as much as you like, only leave us Romans in peace."

I had my pistol in my mouth and two hand grenades strung round my neck. My head swam as I looked down.

Carl came just behind me. He had forgotten his trousers and was grinning sheepishly. They chucked the two sailors' kitbags and my pack into the well of the air-shaft. The sailors' carbines were the worst. They stuck them up the chimney and hoped the cartridges would not explode. We were not the only ones at it in the building. We clung to the house wall like grapes. I had my toes on a jutting brick and my fingers bored into the eaves.

"Don't look down," Isabella said warningly.

God, I was afraid! Why should we have been hunted by our own lot? What had we done? One night's freedom. That was all. We were soldiers in need of a let up. Damn all police.

"My holster and cap are still in there," I whispered agitatedly.

"Idiot," Carl whispered back and kicked on the glass. Mario looked out.

"*Per Bacco!* You Germans are the idiots of all time," he said, handing the things out.

A few minutes later, we heard the door being flung open. They treated Isabella like dirt, struck Mario and jeered at Italy. Then the window was flung open. We squeezed flat against the wall, transformed into silent brick. If we were discovered, it would mean death. No explanation could have saved us.

I pushed the safety catch of my .8 forward. Carl had the cord of a hand grenade between his teeth. In the glow of light from the window I saw a stony face under a steel helmet. The beam of a torch plunged down into the well shaft. Christ, help us. Just this once. Let them disappear and we'll go to Mass tomorrow. You can't object to our amusing ourselves just once!

We could hear the MPs shouting and the sound of wood splintering. Someone shrieked. Sound of truncheon falling on flesh. A pistol shot. Tinkle of glass. Oaths and curses.

"After that swine," ordered a beery voice.

Iron-shod boots clattered down the stairs. Wonder if they caught him. Must have been desperate to shoot. They would break every bone in his body. You don't shoot at MPs with impunity. A heavy engine sprang to life in the quiet street. A couple of BMW motorcycles added their noise.

Now they were going. With the night's catch.

Bit by bit we edged our way along the narrow coping. Just before we climbed in through the window, Otto said:

"Look out. Perhaps they're doing the old dodge of pretending to go, just to entice us out."

I took a deep breath. It was as though my brain lay bared. I had torn a nail and it was hanging by a thread, hurting like the devil, if I just moved my finger.

A window was flung open and a steel helmet looked out. An MP peered down into the well, the beam of a torch played across the opposite wall, a blind was pulled hurriedly.

We could hear someone up on the roof. A skylight banged a give-away. We held our breath.

Finally the window opened and Mario and Isabella put their heads out.

"You damned Germans will be the death of me*," Mario said. "That was a near thing." His dirty pullover was wet with the sweat of his anxiety. "If I ever get my hands on one of that lot, I'll strangle him myself. Tomorrow I shall go to mass. Not that I believe in God, but all the same!" He wiped his forehead with his sweat-rag. "Rita, the silly fool, had one in her cupboard. A deserter from the Luftwaffe. He's been on the run for three months. I've kicked him out once. And he had Italian papers. He could have got away with it, if they hadn't found him in the cupboard. Even a cow would suspect someone found in a cupboard."

"They found the Italian deserter and the Englishman," Isabella put in. "The one who escaped from Campo Concentramento Prigioneri di Guerra 304."

The room filled with people speaking a cocktail of languages. We sat on top of each other on the broad bed. Most were laughing with the relief, but in one corner of the room sat a pretty young girl with a set face. The Englishman had been her friend.

"They pulled him down the stairs, by his feet," she whispered. "His head bumped goodbye on every tread."

The traffic policeman we had met earlier that evening held out a bottle of schnaps, but she pushed it away, muttering something I did not hear.

"They got them, did they? Blast them," Mario said. "They were to have gone to the mountains tomorrow. The partisans were expecting them."

"It's stupid to be in Rome without papers," the traffic policeman said with professional assurance. "You cannot hide here."

* When I visited Mario after the war, he told me that he had had exactly the same trouble with the Americans.

"Where did they find Heinz?" asked a man with a pointed nose, who did an act in a nearby restaurant.

"Under the washbasin in the lav.," replied a girl with a face puffy from weeping. "Just as they were going, one of them turned and shone his torch under the basin. It wasn't even one of the bullies. Only a gefreiter. He wasn't angry. He just laughed and said to Heinz: 'Better come out, little one. It must be dull sitting in there.' Heinz must have been crazy. He pulled his pistol and shot at him. He only hit him in the arm. That brought the others and they beat him to death with the butts of their rifles. They kicked him down the stairs like a football. He lay on each landing until they came down and kicked him off it."

"Are you sure Heinz was dead?" Mario asked between two gulps of beer.

The plump girl nodded.

"How I hate the military police," Otto exclaimed fiercely. "They are the real butchers." He unbuttoned his coat, undid the toggles of his overalls and seemed about to embark on a lengthy exposition, but Carl cut him off short.

"Shut up! Shit on the MPs. Enjoy the war. The peace will be long and dreadful. Haven't you as much cunt and booze as you want? Aren't you with pals? And the bloodhounds have gone. So what the hell are you grumbling about? What more do you want? Isn't God good to us?"

Isabella put a record on the gramophone and each of us danced his or her favourite dance without regard to the music. One girl got a black eye. Mario broke a bottle over the head of the traffic policeman. We relieved ourselves out of the window. It wasn't too easy for the girls. We had to hold them to prevent them losing their balance. None of them would leave the room in case something interesting happened, while she was gone.

Mario and an Italian sailor had got hold of accordions, and from somewhere we got hold of a man with a barrel organ. The whole house began to shake with the ghastly noise. The partition between Isabella's and the next room collapsed.

The traffic policeman and one of the girls took the grave decision that they would together leave this world. They got themselves ready to commit suicide. We helped them fill the bath, but after we had held them under for a short while, they changed their minds. Carl got furious and banged their heads together and cursed them for characterless idiots who didn't know their own minds.

Copulating couples lay about the corridor and out on the stairs. Mario put his dirty feet up on the small of my labouring back. It wasn't that he wanted to impede me and Anna, but there was no where else to put them, if he leaned back with his head between Luisa's lush breasts. He drew his concertina out to its full length, spat a mouthful of regurgitated beer into a flower vase, at which the yellow flowers in it shook their heads in protest.

> Du hast Glück bei den Frauen, bel ami,
> Gar nicht elegant, gar nicht charmant ...

You could not call it singing. It was a savage, enthusiastic bellow. He paused for breath between every line. His sweater was half way up his chest revealing a large expanse of hairy belly.

Otto and a girl emerged from under the bed, where they had spent quite a long time. Then with a foot that was far from clean Otto shoved her back under it again. The girl came from Warsaw and had landed in Rome with a lot of other flotsam and jetsam of the war. She never tired telling one about her noble father's estates.

"Now shut up, Zosia," Otto called. "I cannot be bothered to listen to those stories of your ruddy nags and landaus. I'm never going to drive behind white horses." He swivelled round with his back to the bed and a girl let her bare legs dangle over his shoulders. He took hold of the back of her knees and sang:

> Wir lagen vor Madagaskar
> und hatten die Pest au Bord. ...

He sang of the hard lot of the sardine fisher, who, after a whole night on a stormy sea, hauls in his nets with aching muscles and counts the one fish in them, all he has to feed his flock of children.

A couple of upperclass girls with swing-silly friends joined us. They were tired of antiques and fine crystal and wanted to see dirty nails, hear dirty oaths and smell sour beer. One of them told us that her mother and her lover had taken poison together.

"My mother was a whore. But shit. Wouldn't you like to fuck me?" she said to Carl and flung her arms round his neck. They took up position in the corridor.

Otto came staggering up, supported by two naked girls.

"Don't trust the gentry," he shouted pointing an accusing finger at one of the boys. "They're all liars. Sometime or other in their rotten lives, they play at being communists and talk us honest coolies into hoisting the red flag."

The other upperclass girl laughed, hanging round my neck. Otto tried to help her with her zip fastener, with the result that her skirt tore to the hem.

"Black knickers, short petticoat!" he shouted, seized the girl by the arm and flung her against the bed. "Ought to have their arses kicked, bloody ersatz-proletariats. Aren't you a communist at the moment, pretty boy?" he shouted at her companion.

Carl sang:

> Die Neger in Afrika sie rufen alle laut:
> Wir wollen heim ins Reich!

"You a communist?" Otto bawled belligerently.

The youth nodded. He clenched his fist and crowed something like 'Red Front'.

"Child's play," Otto scoffed. Then he fished a .38 out of his coat and chucked it to the boy. "Go out in the streets, find a Gestapo man or military bloodhound and plug them with that, then. Only you don't dare, of course. You filthy little drawing room turd. I know you upper-class buggers. Ensigns, officer-cadets, champagne-lieutenants, pah! None of you has the courage of an old Roman tomcat."

The accordions fell silent. People's interest had suddenly been caught. Otto nagged on. He was a typical old U-boat sailor, and hated everything connected with the upper classes and to whom the word intellectual acted as a red rag to a bull.

An academic-looking girl wearing glasses tried to intervene

and Otto glared at her furiously, then, suddenly, she found herself sitting at the other end of the corridor.

The young man whose hair needed cutting disappeared through the door with the pistol in his pocket. One or two tried to keep him back.

The other girl came back to me. "Throw your uniform away and come with me," she proposed. "The war will soon be over."

I ran my hand up her thigh. She flung herself on her back on the bed, legs hanging over the edge, and I flung myself on her.

Otto was still grumbling away:

"Communists! Not a bit of it! They'd capitulate as soon as they see a reserve policeman with a swastika on his arse."

The traffic policeman came in with a colleague.

"God damn it, what luck!" he exclaimed angrily. "Two punctures, a front wheel each time. Bruno and I were on the tails of a couple of girls in a sports car. They strewed nails behind them. You only expect that of tough youths. Bruno was driving and we went straight into a tree. But I know who one of the girls is: Her old man will have to fork out!" He poured a bottle of beer down his throat. "I was at Cyrenaica," he told Otto. "I got a bloody bullet in my leg there, so I could get back to traffic work again."

"What concern of mine is that?" Otto growled. "I'm in the navy. It's we sailors bear the brunt of this ruddy war."

"Don't know anything about that," the dirty traffic policeman said good-humouredly and proffered a bottle of beer. "For generations all my family have been in the police. My father was shot in Naples. A bloody ponce got him. They laid my grandfather cold too. He was a sergeant in the carabinieri. They chucked his body into the ditch."

"That doesn't worry me," Otto said. "Never have been able to stand the police. They're the same in all countries."

"I don't wrong anybody," the traffic policeman protested. "But the kid who chucked those nails out – let her wait! Tomorrow."

"If she's upper-class," Carl hiccoughed, "then down with her head. Perhaps I and my two pals here had better come too and help deal with her."

Everything was dripping with beer. One of the girls vomited. She had on a pair of light blue knickers. Mario planted a yellow flower in her bum, but she was feeling too awful to notice.

Then Mario and the two policemen staggered downstairs, each singing a different song. It was time to open the bar. When they got to the first floor they started quarrelling, accusing each other of stealing the other's beer; then Mario's good nature got the better of him and he began to sob. He tried to wipe his eyes on the policeman's holster. Then they couldn't get the door of the bar open and decided to shoot the lock out with the policeman's pistol. As soon as the lock was destroyed, Mario found the keys. That started a new, violent squabble, with Mario demanding compensation for the lock and maintaining that the policeman was sabotaging his business. He threatened to bring an action for damages. Then suddenly they were friends again.

I was lying with Elisabetta under the bed. My head was splitting and I wished I was dead. Otto was on his knees beside the W.C. with the seat round his neck like a horsecollar. Carl and Rita were sitting in the wardrobe squabbling about the height of the ceiling, which Carl insisted was too low to comply with the regulations.

"Come along, you drunken swine," Mario called impatiently. "Get your trousers on. Time for mass. The others are already on their way."

The church of St. Andreas was pleasantly cool. We squeezed together into two pews and our faces assumed serious expressions.

Rita was like a Virgin Mary. At least, our idea of the Virgin Mary.

One by one we went up to the altar. Otto handed Carl his pocket flask. Going to mass was a bit of an undertaking for them and they needed mutual support.

My upper-class girl was kneeling beside me.

Otto clasped his hands in an awkward, clumsy gesture. I looked up at the figure on the cross and found myself mumbling:

174

"Thanks, Christ, for helping us last night when the blood-hounds came. Help those they caught, as well."

At that moment a shaft of sunlight struck the figure's face. How tired He looked. I felt a grip on my arm. It was Mario, still in his sweater, the sweat-rag round his neck. He stank of beer.

"Come on, Sven. Have you gone to sleep?"

"Go to hell," I snarled.

The grip became firmer, almost brutal. Otto came up. He dealt me a chop with the edge of his hand on the back of my head.

"Don't get uppish, you young bugger. No nonsense in church. Don't try to throw your weight about, as if you knew God personally."

They dragged me out. Carlo wanted to purloin a silver salver as we went, but Otto and Mario thought that would be too much.

"If we'd run into a priest outside and he had had it under his arm, that would have been different. One on the back of the head and away with the silver; but you can't pinch things inside a church. There are limits."

Carl gave in, but he was disappointed and furious, so furious that he dealt an organ-grinder a great wallop on the head, making him drop his organ, and shouted at him:

"How dare you churn out those tart's tunes beside a church, you heathen macaroni?"

A couple of hours later we said goodbye to Mario and the girls and decided we would go sightseeing. We visited a number of bars and taverns, kitbag and pack on our shoulders.

After a bit, we stopped for a beer and to visit a brothel. We also found ourselves in a picture exhibition, but that was really a mistake. Carl took a fancy to a picture of a naked girl, but when he heard the price he wanted to beat up the exhibition committee. They threatened to call the police. That kind always does. If they had offered us a glass of beer, they would not have had four big plate glass windows to replace.

We entered a smart restaurant in Via Cavour and found that a head waiter and four other waiters did not like us. It all started when a woman in the cloakroom refused to accept our kitbags and pack, became worse when Otto decided to change his socks in the foyer, but the balloon really went up when they refused to serve us. Carl got most excited and called them all sorts of names, then he stormed out to the kitchens, picked up a large dish of ravioli and stormed out, sweeping the staff aside as if he were a typhoon loose in a forest of young trees.

A couple of elderly policemen managed to entice us out and into a tavern in a side street, where we were more welcome. Carl never stopped swearing at the upper classes till we got there. He still had the dish of ravioli under his arm. A present from the smart restaurant, which no doubt thought it a cheap price to pay for getting rid of us.

When we reached the tavern, Carl held the ladle threateningly under the noses of the two policemen.

"You two lousy pavement-admirals realize that we came with you voluntarily, don't you?"

Over a beer the two assured us that they were absolutely clear about this.

Later that night we found ourselves at a fountain. Carl was swimming round in the basin demonstrating to me how to get into a lifebelt in dirty weather, while Otto and I manufactured waves. Then a window opened and a vulgar, sleepy voice spewed out threats and curses at us for our noisy life-saving demonstration.

"You bloody querulous spaghetti," Carl shouted from the water. "How dare you disturb the German Navy during life saving practice?"

Otto picked up a stone, threw it and hit the bellowing Roman full in the face. He was beside himself and tried to jump out of the window, but his wife clung on to him desperately. After all they were on the second floor. Then Otto threw another stone, but this time hit the adjacent window. Then all hell was let loose. The entire street was roused and a great fight started. It was rather like a minor revolution, from which we withdrew when it was at its height and people had forgotten what had started it.

The next morning we decided that we would all go to the hospital, but Fate willed otherwise. As bad luck would have it, we found ourselves in the company of an Italian sailor on his way to the naval base at Genoa, He had with him a bersaglieri corporal just out of hospital in Salerno, where they had given him a false leg. He did not like his new leg, which hurt him, so he carried it under his arm and hobbled along on a crutch. Originally he had had two crutches, but he had sold one to a shepherd. Not that the shepherd was in need of a crutch, but he was a man with an eye to the future.

"You never know what can happen in a war like this," he had said. "Something tells me that sooner or later there's going to be a shortage of crutches."

They had come up to us, while we were sitting on the steps in Via Torino eating grilled sardines. We offered them seats and a share, and the five of us finished the dish. Then we all wandered on through narrow alleyways, fried potato cakes in a tin over an open fire in a little square. Then we were suddenly overcome with a crazy urge for cleanliness and went to the public bath. Unfortunately there was a fuss, when we broke down the door to the women's section and we had to run for it. Stark naked, clutching our clothes and things, we made good our escape across a seemingly endless succession of fences and sheds.

We parted company on Ponte Umberto. The two Italians felt that they had better delay no longer. They had already been a month on the journey. Their papers were stamped, but the stamps weren't quite genuine. We waved as long as we could see each other, then we just shouted.

"Boys, we'll meet when the war's over. The first third of November after peace," the Italian sailor shouted from a side street.

"That won't do, sailor," Carl shouted back. "Suppose the war stops on the fourth of November, it would be a whole year till we met. What about exactly three months after the war. Meeting here?"

"Do you mean where you are or where we are?" yelled the sailor.

We were now too far apart that it was difficult to hear each other. People stopped and looked at us uncomprehendingly. Carl put his hands round his mouth like a megaphone.

"Meet in the middle of Ponte Umberto and each bring a case of beer."

"O.K. What time'll suit you best?" shouted the Italian.

"Eleven fifteen," Carl yelled.

"Will you come by train or ship?" bawled the sailor.

"Don't ask such silly questions. Do you go by train unless you have to."

"There's a bus every hour from Anzio to Rome," came the sailor's voice from the distance.

We shouted a few more times to each other at the top of our voices, but we were now so far away that our answers were only faint echoes.

We reached the hospital in Via di San Stefano early in the morning next day. We arrived in a cab, the driver of which was sitting on the passengers' seat and the three of us on the box, taking it in turns to drive. It had taken a little persuasion to get the cabby to accept the arrangement, but he had done so eventually.

"Now for the difficult bit of keeping to the channel," Carl said as we turned in through the gate.

"I'm keeping hard aport, so we should be all right," said Otto who was steering.

The orderly stared at us in bewilderment. He had never seen such an arrival before. Otto swung round smartly and drew up by the steps.

"Let go the hook," Carl ordered.

We said goodbye to the old cabby and his horse over a couple of bottles of beer.

"Where are you for?" the orderly asked peevishly.

"Have we asked you, where you're going?" Carl retorted. "What bloody business is it of yours?"

"I have to ask you," the orderly replied.

"Well you've done that; so shut up," Carl said.

The man shrugged and made his way back to the gate. An arrow indicated the way to the office.

"I promise you I'm not taking much from those iodine-heroes," Carl said. "If they're nice and polite to me, there's a slight possibility I'll be polite to them. Otherwise, they'll rue the day they had anything to do with Carl Friedrich Weber."

Paying no attention to a notice that said "Knock and wait", we burst into the office.

A medical unteroffizier in a tailored uniform was seated in a rocking chair, both feet on the desk, busily anointing his hair with brilliantine and arranging it into waves. There was a big portrait of Adolf Hitler on the wall behind him.

"Hallo, there!" Carl said, dropping his rifle and kitbag with a clatter on the floor.

The highly-scented unteroffizier did not deign to look at us.

Carl made another attempt to draw his attention to our presence.

"Hi, you boil-smith. Customers!"

The hospital-hero picked his teeth with a laryngoscope, and gazed out of the window.

"You must have come to the wrong address."

"We bloody well haven't. This set-up is a hospital isn't it?"

"Correct. You are in Ospedale Militare, speaking to the chief clerk. Here one gathers up one's weary bones into the regulation attitude and vomits a report on why one happens to be here."

"Oh, bugger off," said Otto.

"What did I tell you?" Carl snorted. "Let me get hold of his throat. Such a shitting medical squitter!"

"Come on, chum, be sensible," Otto said, doing his best. "We have to come into dock here."

"You've come to the wrong place, then. You happen to be in hospital and not a shipyard."

"Don't let's talk with him," Carl said. "Let's give him one on the muzzle and then bugger off."

Otto made another attempt.

"I don't know what you call it in your medical lingo. We are to bunk here. For repairs. Overhaul."

The medical unteroffizier was busy studying his gleaming hair in a mirror on the opposite wall. He dabbed his face with eau-de-cologne.

"In other words you mean that you are to be admitted? I presume, then, that you are in possession of papers from your MO. Are you wounded?"

179

"Yes," Carl nodded. "But that was a bloody long time ago. That's not why we've come."

"I've got a bad prick," Otto volunteered.

"Then you've come to the wrong address. This is the surgical wing." The man smiled condescendingly.

"How can you be bothered to argue with the bugger," Carl said. "Kick him in the balls, chuck him through the port-hole and let's get out of here."

The medical unteroffizier paid no attention to these well-intended warnings.

"You must report to the Department for Skin and Venereal Diseases, which is in the medical hospital. The Town Major's office will tell where that is; the movement control officer at the station will tell you where the Town Major's office is, and any policeman will direct you to the railway station."

"Don't you know where this bloody prick hospital is?" Otto asked in irritation.

"Of course. I have to."

"Then spit it out," Otto exclaimed indignantly.

"Sailor, I am head clerk of a surgical hospital, not an information bureau."

"What actually do you do, when you are not a soldier?" Otto rsked.

"Actually, I cannot see how that can concern you," the unteroffizier replied smoothly, "we two will never associate in private life; but as you are obviously interested, I shall for once break my rule and tell you. I am head clerk, 2nd class, in the municipality of Berlin."

"Now, I've had enough," Carl exclaimed, hitching up his trousers. "Head clerk municipality, pah! Clerk! Lousy pen-pusher. The lowest thing on earth." He picked up a bottle of ink and flung it at the wall behind the man. Books followed. In no time at all a large bookcase was emptied.

Carl and I jumped onto the desk and seized the man by the hair and banged his face down against the top. Otto opened a tin of strawberry jam and rubbed the contents well into the man's brilliantined hair, while Carl poured brilliantine and eau-de-cologne over his tailor-made uniform. We tore a couple of cushions to pieces and let the feathers fly.

Then we emptied a couple of jars of marmalade, smeared it on the man's face, rubbed it into the feathers until he looked like a sick hen. A nurse peered in, but disappeared in a hurry when a medical dictionary hurtled close past her head.

Before we left, Carl rammed a bundle of papers down the throat of the yelling unteroffizier. Then, well satisfied with ourselves, we left the office we had wrecked. The orderly at the gate let us pass without fuss.

"We'll be cured before we get to hospital," Otto wailed. "We've been three weeks on the way already."

We had got a good distance up Via Claudia, when a Kübel drew up beside us and two steelhelmeted bloodhounds jumped out.

"You're under arrest," one of them said.

"Don't know anything about that," grinned Carl.

His belt buckle struck the first MP a wicked blow in the face. The man dropped to the ground and crawled about, blinded and moaning. The street emptied in a matter of seconds. A cab with two women passengers disappeared at a gallop.

The second MP snatched at his holster. I leaped onto his back and sank my teeth into his ear. Carl dealt him a kick in the stomach, and smashed his fist with a resounding thud into the shouting man's face. Then we pounded both their faces on the cement.

I hopped into the Kübel, started the engine, engaged second gear and jumped out. With a crunching noise the car crashed into a building on the corner of Via Marco Aurelio.

We walked on. At the Colosseum Carl had an idea. After rummaging in his kitbag, he produced a bottle of rum and with this we walked back to the unconscious bloodhounds.

"Rinse, please," Carl said, pouring half a glass down each of their throats. We sprinkled their uniforms all over, until they stank of rum a mile away, and then we chucked the empty bottle into the front seat of the smashed car.

"The cork," Carl remarked thoughtfully.

Otto let out a great guffaw, a real belly laugh and, going back to the two policemen, he stuffed the cork into one of their trouser pockets.

"And now where's a telephone," Carl said, grinning delightedly.

We all three squeezed into a telephone box. After a lot of squabbling we managed to find the Town Major's number. Otto was to do the 'phoning, as he had the most convincing voice.

"Herr General, oh, well, then, Herr Oberleutnant, it's all the same to me what you are. Who isn't to be impertinent? What the hell's that to do with you? Do you think I haven't seen these sword-swallowers before? You want to know whom you're talking to? Do you think I'm weak in the head? Why am I ringing? What the hell's that to do with you? Hallo, hallo! The swine's rung off." Otto was openmouthed with astonishment.

"Bloody cheek they have," Carl growled. "Give me that 'phone! Have you the number? You did it all wrong. I'll show you how to do it." He asked for the number. "Give me the duty officer," he snarled. "This is Professor Brandt speaking. Until a moment ago I thought the military police were here to maintain order, but then what do I see? Your damned constables fighting with drunken civilians whom they drive round in their service vehicles. It's scandalous, Herr Hauptmann, that you allow such things. Your men are now lying dead drunk at the corner of Via Marco Aurelio and Via Claudia having smashed their car." Grinning all over his face, Carl banged the receiver down.

We resisted the temptation to stay and see what happened next.

We spent a further day and night together, then I parted company with them at the V.D. clinic of the medical hospital. As I walked away they shouted from a first floor window:

"Don't forget our meeting on Ponte Umberto, when the war's over."

"I'll never forget that," I shouted back.

I walked backwards all the way to the corner, so as not to lose sight of them. I waved and they brandished their sailors' caps.

"We'll celebrate peace at Mario's," Otto bawled.

I walked off, but I was only half way down the street, when

I had to turn and run back to the corner. It was such a pity to leave them. They were still in the window. When they caught sight of me, they swung their caps and sang the sailor's farewell. Then I ran off down the narrow street, as hard as I could go. I had to get away from them, or something would happen.

I went and sat in a park, filled with longings. The wind was in the south and you could hear the guns at Monte Cassino like an uninterrupted menacing thunder. I went to the Movement Control at the railway station to get my leave warrant changed, intending to go to the airport and see if I could find room in a transport 'plane.

An oberfeldwebel looked at me searchingly:

"Don't you know what happened yesterday?" He stood there weighing my leave papers in his hand. Then slowly he tore them across:

"Major offensive. All leave stopped throughout Army Corps South."

XI

Palid Ida's brothel was no ordinary brothel. It was not officially a brothel at all, though every soldier from Sicily to the Brenner Pass knew it.

There were several ladies in hiding from the Gestapo among Ida's staff and one or two whom the partisans were after. Ida got them all yellow passports. She divided her girls up according to their appearance and milieu. There were four departments at Ida's: privates, NCOs, officers and staff officers. Only the choicest girls who spoke two foreign languages and could quote Schiller and Shakespeare, attended to the needs of the last. Ida had a weakness for Schiller, and in her enthusiasm for him had had painted on the wall of the room in which clients were received:

> *Und setzt Ihr nicht das Leben ein*
> *nie wird   das Leben gewonnen sein!*

One night Porta and Tiny altered two words, making the quotation better suited to its surroundings.

Ida was an American. Just before the war, she had come to Paris on the classic tour of Europe. The German advance had proved too swift and she had not managed to get away. She told herself that the war was going to be a long one and decided what she was going to do. It was no surprise to her when the Americans finally came in. She used an oberleutnant as a springboard into the German commander's bed after which she had achieved all-round security.

At the beginning of 1942 she moved her residence from Paris to Rome, taking six French girls with her. It was not a bad start.

KILLER PATROL

We strewed dirty jokes around us and put on airs in front of the grenadiers and paratroopers. We were going on a special mission behind the enemy lines. They regarded us with a certain amount of awe. Everybody had heard of these special jobs.

"Are you lot volunteers?" a stabsfeldwebel with a knight's cross round his neck asked.

"When we go to the bog, yes," Porta laughed.

They helped us pull the new close-fitting battle-dresses over our black panzer uniforms. Tiny sharpened his close-combat knife on an old grindstone.

"This is so sharp I could cut the balls off a colonel without him noticing," he announced.

We moved our arms and legs about to take the stiffness out of the battle-dress. The sides of the camouflage caps could be pulled down and butttoned under the chin. The peaks could also be pulled down to cover one's face. They had slits in them for one's eyes.

We had just spent two whole days at Palid Ida's. It had been a good party. We had each had three girls, one or two of them even being officers' girls. The grand finale had been a glorious fight with some ack-ack men.

Porta and an Italian had had an eating competition. Porta had won with a score of two and a half geese, half a goose ahead of the Italian. The Italian had collapsed and they had to use a stomach pump on him. Porta's face was pale, but he managed to keep it down. If you were sick during or shortly after such a competition you either lost or were disqualified. Porta knew the trick, which was to sit absolutely still for an hour keeping your mouth firmly shut. It was a mystery to us, where he put it all. Long and thin, he would sit down at table and eat until there was not a crumb left. He would get to his feet with his stomach distended like a pregnant bedbug, yet it all disappeared, God knows where, for, a few hours later, he would be as thin as when he first started. Porta was a real champion, where eating was concerned, and his powers were famed on both sides of the front. Three times the Americans invited him to an eating race. Twice he refused, but the third time he accepted and he and a huge negro corporal met for the contest in a shell hole in No-man's land, everything being scrupulously checked by both sides.

Porta won. The negro died.

We were in Mike's dug-out lying on our bellies studying the map, which was spread on the floor. One-Eye lay between the Old Man and me.

"What about the artillery commander?" Heide asked. "He has a cool head, I hope."

"No need to worry," One-Eye said. "I know him. He was at the artillery shooting grounds at Leningrad. He knows his job. In ten minutes he'll pump 800 shells at them. The Yankees here will be lulled by that, thinking that the Indians are going to get whatever's coming."

Porta settled his yellow tophat on top of his camouflage hat. One-Eye narrowed his eye. The sight of it always made his face twitch, but he had long since given up trying to fight against it. But now, when he saw Tiny cramming his light-grey bowler on to his own head, he could scarcely contain himself; but all that came was:

"You two are crazy!"

Tiny tried to cut his nails with the wire clippers. Pieces flew all over the map.

"As you're so fond of using those," One-Eye growled, "you can crawl out first through the wire in your damned bowler. Cut the bottom two wires."

"I can't count," Tiny said beaming.

One-Eye overheard the remark.

"Porta, you follow Tiny," One-Eye went on. "Three minutes exactly between each man. It will be light shortly before five. Half an hour later the morning sun will have gone. Our artillery commander is coming here in person. We must send them the usual morning salutation, otherwise they'll smell a rat. So you must be in your places by then. The gunners have them marked on their maps. They will be firing only the 10.5s. The guns are already aimed. Your worst time will be from half past six until fourteen hours. I'll go through that again. And you listen, too, Tiny. This is the last time. Make a mistake and you'll be massacred. At 5.32 10.5 shelling as a bluff. This will stop at 5.48. At 12.45 mortar fire right in front of the Americans' noses. 12.57 automatic covering fire for 30 seconds. Then you come in: fingers out of your arses and forward. Sven, you deal with the advance machine gun nest. There's only one man there. He's relieved at 13 hours. Five metres beyond is a dug-out with six men in it. As soon as you have cut the throat of the machine gunner, you will liquidate those in the dug-out with hand grenades. Heide, you deal with the two rear machine guns. They are both on stands, but at the bottom of the communication trench with a tarpaulin over them. Their crews are in a shared dug-out three metres to the right. They have made three dummy dug-outs. They get into the proper one through a small hole in the lefthand wall, but you can't go wrong. There's a pile of empty tins outside the entrance that they've been too lazy to clear away. Two hand grenades will be enough. One far inside and one in the middle. As soon as Sven and Heide have reached their objectives, you others get moving. It's ten yards up there and you have to cover it in 2.5 seconds, no more, no less. You will rake the trench, but don't link up. Always know where each of the others is, so that you don't bump them off. Shoot at everything that isn't wearing your kind of camouflage jacket with green and black rings. In the whole world there are only 22 of you who have it. If you see a German field marshal's uniform, shoot the man down! Every single man in the Americans' position is to be killed. Not one must escape to tell the others what has happened. Your job is to shock and make them afraid. They must and will believe, it's ghosts or phantoms behind them. This sort of thing will put their coloured troops into a fine panic. Barcelona you won't move from your hole. Be a limpet. Your job is observer, while the others are clearing the trench. Green Verey light and you run as if the devil was at your heels."

"Oh, we always do that," Porta said cheekily.

"Shut up and listen," said our general. "Two seconds after that light signal, our artillery will start up and you, Barcelona, will put up a world speed record and catch the others up. The adjacent sectors won't know what to make of it all. If all goes as we plan, things will be pretty confused. You have five seconds to get off the height. Our guns will lay down a barrage right on your heels. We'll cover you to the river, where partisans will help you across. You then have 145 kilometres to your objective. How you get there is your affair. But you've got to." He pointed to a spot on the map. "At this point exactly you will have panzerfausts and demolition charges dropped to you. If anyone gets wounded, he must deal with it himself. You are most strictly forbidden to cart wounded along with you. Hide him and go and see if he is still there when you come back. Only one thing more: this task has got to be carried out, if only one of you gets through. The operations hut lies in this wood here, and the tanks stand camouflaged at the fork in the road there. There are fifteen mechanics at the most with them. They live in tents."

"Have they no security?" the Old Man asked in surprise.

"No. They feel quite safe. It doesn't enter their heads that there could be any danger. As soon as you have destroyed the tanks, two of you will attack the staff hut, while the rest of you fire on it from the south. You will seize the first staff officer you see and you will, you must, bring one back alive. The others are to be killed. No one must have any idea what has happened otherwise the whole point of the action will be lost. Then off you go back to the bridge. But, I forgot this before, you will leave two men at the bridge who will fix demolition charges, while the rest of you are dealing with the tanks and the hut. These two will blow the bridge up as soon as the last of you has got back across it. If the enemy is so close behind you that you can't get across, you must sacrifice a machine gun group to make sure that you get the staff officer across. You go on north until you come to the river. You follow that eastwards." His fat finger pointed to a place on the map. "This is an English divisional HQ. Wipe it out." He chucked down some colour photographs of Allied uniforms. "There you see the staff tabs and badges."

"Then we must hope they aren't in their nightshirts," Heide grinned, "or do they have badges on their bums?"

"That you must find out for yourself," One-Eye said curtly.

We co-ordinated our watches and checked our weapons for the last time. Everything was firmly fixed. Nothing rattled.

"Don't forget the soldier's books and identity discs of any who get killed," One-Eye reminded us. "Otherwise someone in the SD might suspect a smart bit of deserting. And one thing more. And this goes specially for Porta and Tiny. Don't plunder the dead. If they catch you with gold teeth in your pockets, they'll string you up. They have no sympathy with gold-collectors."

"But they do it themselves," Porta said defensively.

"I know, but nobody knows about it." One-Eye took hold of Porta's collar, "and nobody knows about it here either. Do I make myself clear enough, Porta?"

"Jawohl, Herr General."

"Today I'm not your General. I am One-Eye! Three days for not being able to remember it. You'll report to the hen-house to do it, when you get back."

"Right," whispered the Old Man.

A minute later Tiny disappeared over the parapet. In the north numbers of guns were rumbling away. I stared at the luminous hands of my watch. 90 seconds. My hands felt over my equipment. 60 seconds. My legs were quivering. 45 seconds. I began to tremble violently. It was impossible to keep my hands still. 30 seconds. I looked at the others. The ones I had been with so long. I wished we still had our Finnish teacher, the Lapp, with us. A sergeant who came from up by the White Sea and who taught us their methods of fighting.

As usual, the Legionnaire had his Moorish knife between his teeth. He winked at me. He knew I was afraid.

Only five seconds now. How slowly the hand moved. Three seconds. Two seconds. A hand descended on my shoulder and I leaped forward, found the wire cutters where Porta and Tiny had put them and cut away. The revolting barbs tore my skin to ribbons. I scraped on my back under the dangerous stuff. Then threw the cutters back.

I lay for a moment getting my breath after the tremendous

effort. Dear God, let me be wounded now, while those in the trench still have time to get me back. I could be in hospital in a lovely clean bed in just a few hours. The nurses would coddle me. Hospital was a thing you dreamed of, when you lay out in No-man's land. But I wasn't wounded. I had to go on. After Porta. One never is wounded, when one wants to be. In a moment or two the Legionnaire came. I looked at my watch. Two minutes had gone already. Now he was crouched there ready to spring, a panther in human guise. It was good to have him with us. It gave me a sense of security.

I rolled over and began crawling towards the American positions. Then I reached the bush where I was to hide till the afternoon. My hand slipped on something slimy, and a nauseating sickly smell filled my nostrils. I had crawled into a blown-up corpse. I vomited. I put my field glasses in front of me, camouflaged them with leaves and grass. As long as it was dark, glasses weren't dangerous, but when day came, if the sun's rays struck them for an instant, they might give me away and that would be that. Then the enemy would know that there was something brewing in No-man's land, something there that shouldn't be there.

But I had to have them. I had to study the man I was to kill. The years had changed us strangely. We no longer attached any importance to killing a fellow human. Not even in close combat. Tiny and the Legionnaire had lost count even of those they had killed with their bare hands. It had become almost a habit to thrust your knife into a man's midriff. I shall never forget the first time I saw a person die. And that was not even my doing. It was an infantry feldwebel sitting on the tailboard of a troop-transport. A stray Polish bullet hit him in the head and I only just had time to pull the tank up. It was one of those two-men tanks, a Krupp-Sport. We both jumped out to move the body out of the way and were sworn at by a leutnant for halting the column.

That was the first man we had seen killed and it suddenly brought home to us the gravity of war. It was not nearly so nice as we had had it painted to us.

Someone was crawling along close to me. I drew my knife, I pulled out my pistol.

"Boo!" I heard behind me and almost screamed with fright. Then in the moonlight I caught sight of a light grey bowler and a row of strong horsey teeth glinting in a broad grin. It was Tiny, the great idiot.

"Did you shit your pants?" he asked in a whisper. "I could see you miles away, you limp prick." Then he disappeared over a hummock and was swallowed up by the darkness.

I began digging myself in with my short-handled trenching tool. A job for a mole. I daren't make too much noise.

The guns in the north had stopped firing, and all that broke the threatening silence of the night was an occasional rifle shot or a short yap from a machine gun. Using my glasses I tried to make out my surroundings, but there was nothing but darkness. I was glad it was just ordinary infantry we had facing us. We would deal with the infantry quickly enough. They did not know all the devilish tricks the marines were expert at, and of course we almost felt that we and the marines were related because of Mike.

A star shell went hissing up into the sky and slowly sank to earth in a flare of dazzling light. A machine cannon bayed evilly. In the distance, tracer was like a string of beads against the black sky of night. It was nearly three. They would change over soon.

There they were. A clink of steel. Someone laughed. A faint glow of light. The ghastly idiots! Smoking in an advanced position! My fingers itched to get at them and I knew that all the others would be feeling the same. Death is the only punishment for that sort of madness. They couldn't be tried troops. They wouldn't do a thing like that. This must be their first time up at the front. Recruits! It would be child's play for us.

A couple of crickets were fiddling away just in front of me. Then one of them hopped up onto my back. Another couple joined in. They thought I was a corpse, as well they might, I was lying so still. That was perhaps the worst part of this sort of enterprise having to sham death. Perhaps at that moment someone was scrutinising me through glasses.

I shall never forget the first of these long distance patrols I was on. It was in Finland. The patrol was led by a Finnish ensign, a Lapp. He was called Guvi but whether that was his surname or Christian name no one knew. Every other word he said was 'Satan and hell'. It was said that he owned a large herd of reindeer with which he lived, when not in the army. Just before we set out to destroy a railway line far behind the Russian lines, Guvi came to me and brandishing his long Finnish dagger under my nose, said:

"Satan and hell, you bloody German, just you listen to me. This is the first visit you're paying to our neighbour. Satan and hell, fancy being burdened with you! You Germans ought to stay at home and leave these jobs to us Finns. You can only fight with guns and tanks. Satan and hell, that's not proper fighting. We Finns are the only ones that really fight. I know how to deal with our neighbour. I am responsible for twenty-four men. Satan and hell, I can't stand having to cart you along, you ghastly German. If anyone's nerves goes, when we get in among our neighbours, I know it won't be any of my lot. If you lose your head, we shall be compelled to kill you. If you are wounded, don't use your pistol to put an end to yourself and stop yourself falling into enemy hands. Use your knife. Drive it in a hand's breadth and a half down from your left shoulder, slanting upwards and you'll cut right through your German old woman's heart. Satan and hell, that's an order. No one is to fall alive into the neighbour's hands and talk."

But it wasn't me he had to kill on that trip, but one of his own lot, a corporal. A stupid athlete with all sorts of prizes to his credit. I saw Guvi do it. The athlete lost his head while we were lying among some trees waiting for a column we were to liquidate. Suddenly, the athlete got up on to his knees, his machine pistol at the ready. In the silent frosty polar night the noise when he undid the safety catch was like a pistol shot. Like lightning Guvi was there, and plunged his knife down by his collar bone. One of the others sat on his head, so that his rattles and gurgles were smothered in the snow.

The same thing would happen to anyone who lost control of his nerves out there in No-man's land. He would be killed instantly. We would be forced to do it. I wondered what had happened to that Finnish ensign, the Lapp Guvi? I wondered if he was lying, a frozen corpse, somewhere by the Murmansk railway? Or had he lived to become a captain as he so dearly wished? His great dream was to be able to wear silver stripes on his trousers instead of green. And his reindeer? Had he ever seen them again? How he could drink, that Lapp! And there wasn't a Lotta for miles around he had not been in bed with. When he came out of the sauna with birch twigs in his hands and rolled himself in the snow, he always said of the girl he had just had in there:

"Just reindeer cunt!"

And when we set off in an aged Ford to paint the nearest town red in one of our brief rests between patrols behind the Russian lines, Guvi always managed to start a fight with someone. I was his interpreter, where the Germans were concerned. He understood German, but talked only Swedish. Wonderful old Guvi! None of us who knew you will ever forget you! You were the typical Finnish soldier, feared like the devil and loved like God.

The eastern sky was beginning to grow red, – changing shade every minute. The world's arse-hole, that filthy mountain Cassino, looked almost lovely in the early morning. The sun hung above the monastery as a great round glowing bowl. It was God's morning.

The morning mist came off the river and hid us for a while, until the wind got up and blew it all away.

It was just before eight. Another change-over. Helmets glinted. I pressed the glasses to my eyes, got them adjusted. There they were. The one coming now was the one I would have to kill. He would be relieved at ten o'clock and come back at twelve. He had two medal ribbons on his chest, and his eyes were of a strange blue like that of a hussar's uniform. He began picking his teeth with a close-combat knife. The man he was relieving showed him something. They both laughed. It was dirty postcards they had. He was called Robert, I heard: Bob like myself. Strange coincidence, here was a Bob lying waiting to kill another Bob.

Carefree, he leaned against his machine gun. Blue tobacco smoke rose up above him. He had shoved his helmet onto the back of his head, where its chin strap bumped against his cheeks.

But what was this? My blood froze in my veins, as I saw

him take his field glasses hanging on his chest and point them at me. I did not breathe. A fly settled on my eyelid. I let it sit there. A man with a fly on his eyelid must be dead.

A bird flew down right in front of me. It had red tips to its wings. Right in the middle of No-man's land. Don't you know, little bird, that life in No-man's land means death? It hopped round me, even perched on the barrel of my machine pistol. A dangerous branch to perch on.

The sun was burning the back of my neck and the insects were almost driving me mad. Now he was being relieved again. Unless his platoon commander had something special for him to do during the next two hours, he would come back for his last watch. I wondered if he had a girl at home in the States. What his father was. What the place where he lived was like. A terrace house, where the paper boy chucked the paper over the gate every morning? Or back premises somewhere with teenagers copulating in the basement? Had he come straight from college, exchanging schoolbooks for rifle? Or was he a west-side boy, who once in a while held up a homo or knocked out a policeman?

If only they would start an attack of their own, so that our whole patrol came to nothing. Why the devil did it have to be us? Who had to get that staff officer for them? I was half out of my mind. I would soon be compelled to move. I had been lying stock still for ten hours. I bet there were fakirs who would find it quite difficult to do as much.

There I could see some helmets. The final relief. But what was this? There were many more of them. Bob was there too. I recognised him easily. What was the meaning of the great migration? Then I understood. Platoon leader's inspection. He picked the barrel from the machine gun, shouted, giving the section commander a blowing up. A parade ground lion. I knew the kind. They wouldn't let up even in the front line.

Wait, you little turd, I thought. You haven't a chance. You have exactly one hour and fifty seven minutes to live. Tiny and Heide are going to deal with your dug-out. They are personal friends of the man with the scythe. You won't escape them.

Now, God help me, he was going to put his men, who only had a few minutes to live, on charge. He did not know that of course. But even so, he was the kind whose greatest ambition was to become First Sergeant. He wanted six stripes and a star, whatever it meant in the way of death and prison for his men.

Bob stood at attention and let the filth run off him. A horse-fly was buzzing round my head. Then it settled on my hand. I wondered if I could remain still, if it stung me? I had always been afraid of horseflies and bees. It stung. I watched it as it bored its sting into my hand. A searing pain swept up into my arm.

I watched the man through my glasses, US Private First Class, he was just lighting his last Camel. Enjoy it, chum! You've only seven minutes left. I hope they'll send your mother the Congress medal. She deserves it. Send your boy to Italy to be slaughtered. At twenty. Just when life is beginning. And to end like that. Just a soldier.

Just a soldier. I had heard that often enough. Said a little disparagingly. But it's we who have to give our lives for your factories, your industry. It's over our dead bodies you get your new and better contracts. And when it's over and you're sitting in your elegant offices, exchanging contracts and giving orders to Krupp, Armstrong and Schneider; we soldiers can beg on railway platforms or rot in a POW camp. Last year's leaves are soon forgotten.

He sang softly.

Again he pointed his glasses at me.

God, don't let him discover me in the last two minutes. He put the glasses down and began to sing again.

There was a roar behind me. The heavens opened and spewed fire. The rocket-projectors. They plunged down in front of the American positions. It was an experience that could have inspired Liszt to another rhapsody. I moved the muscles of my feet in my boots. The blood began to circulate. If my leg went to sleep it would be a catastrophe. I drew my left leg under me. It had the most strength in it for the start. The rockets would stop in five seconds.

US-Bob did not know the rules of the game. He had curled up in the bottom of his trench, afraid of the whizzing shells.

I squinted to the side. There was Porta, the long idiot. His yellow hat glowing like a buttercup in a green field. I drew my knife, the knife I had taken from a Siberian guardsman long ago.

Now! I leaped forward. Bullets were whizzing past me like angry wasps, but I was not afraid of them. They were our own infantry's covering fire. US-Bob's helmet and face appeared over the parapet. The impetus of my leap knocked him over. He shouted savagely, tried to kick me in the crutch. Two pistol bullets went singing past my head. I buried my knife in his neck. He contorted himself and blood gushed foaming from his mouth. I kicked the machine gun over, cast a last look at US-Bob. He had bored his fingers into the wall of the trench.

He had flung his head back and was staring at me, eyes wide open. I felt I wanted to fling myself down beside him and comfort him, but I did not have the time or the right. I was only a soldier. I gave his helmet a kick.

Two figures appeared out of a dug-out. I put up my automatic pistol and shot from the hip. I saw Porta's arm go back and two grenades went hurtling through the air. There was a hollow bang inside the dug-out. Porta's yellow hat could be seen above the parapet, a challenge to fate. Two Americans came running. They were roused now. Things were exploding everywhere.

Heide landed beside me. A sergeant and three GIs ran straight into the bullets from our spitting machine guns. We trampled on the bodies. That was the dug-out One-Eye warned us about. Bluey-yellow flames were licking from its opening that was camouflaged with branches. Instinct made me turn to see a shadow leaping wildly at me. I bent forward and curled up like a ball. A heavy body crashed down beside me. I fired two bursts from my pistol into it. I fired without uncurling, parallel to the ground.

But he had not had enough. He leaped up like a steel spring. My kicking boots hit him twice in the face. I dropped my machine pistol, as his fingers closed on my throat. I jerked my knee into his groin. Momentarily his grip slackened, long enough for me to get my pistol from my flies and empty the whole magazine into him. I was frantic with fear. He was twice my size. Then he was over me again. I was smeared with blood. The point of a knife pierced the skin between my ribs.

I rolled over, got hold of the handle of the knife in my boot and stabbed it again and again into the quivering body. The grip on my throat relaxed. I gasped for breath, kicked him in the belly, stamped on his face.

Two of the others tore past us. Olle Karlsson's flame-thrower hissed down the length of the trench. I saw Tiny seize a man by the chest, fling him to the ground and trample him. I picked up my machine pistol, re-loaded, fired into a dug-out. Someone shouted. I tore the china ring from the handle of a grenade with my teeth, counted four and flung it hissing into the black space.

A green ball of light went soaring skywards. Barcelona's signal! Now our infantry would come, and under cover from them we would press ahead. Rocket projectors were hammering away at the positions on either side of us, smashing them. I saw some of the others leap out of a trench. There was Porta's yellow hat. Then Tiny's grey bowler appeared. I tore after them as hard as I could go. It was a race with death. Our splendid gunners were dropping their shells just behind us. I caught up the Old Man, who, panting, was breasting down the far side of the slope. It was wonderful that he could manage it at his age.

We came within sight of the river. Two Italian commandos, disguised as poor farmers, were waiting for us.

"*Avanti, avanti!*" one snarled, producing a machine pistol from the reeds.

They rushed ahead like marathon runners and it was all we could do to keep up with them. The shells came closer. Then the Italians stopped and pointed to the river.

"This is where you cross. Others are waiting for you at the broken crucifix on the far side."

The Legionnaire stared down at the muddy water. He turned to the Italians:

"Are you sure? I cannot see anything."

With an oath, one of the Italians waded out into the river. The water only came up to his waist.

"We helped build your underwater bridge. Do you think we can make a mistake?"

The shells were coming closer and closer, like a sequence of dynamite explosions. In single column we waded out and over the underwater bridge. The water was whipped up by shell splinters. We hid in some reeds on the far bank, while Heide bandaged a long gash the Old Man had in his arm.

"That was all nice and easy," Porta remarked with a laugh.

"Do you think so?" the Old Man muttered. "Killing has never become a pleasure where I am concerned."

"Cardboard soldier," Tiny jeered.

The Old Man undid the safety catch of his machine pistol.

"A word more, you psychopathic murderer, and I'll shoot you like a dog!"

"What are you getting excited about?" the Legionnaire said placatingly. "You kill the other, or he kills you. *C'est la guerre!*"

"I killed an elderly unteroffizier, a father," the Old Man said in a thick voice. "I took his pocket book," he said and produced a worn old thing, opened it and held out a well-fingered photograph of a man in sergeant's uniform. He had three stripes on his sleeve. A woman was standing beside him and in front of them sat three little girls and a happy-faced boy of ten or twelve. Across the photograph was written in English: "Good luck, daddy!"

The Old Man was beside himself. He cursed us and the world in general. We let him work it off on us. It did happen sometimes that a man you had killed became a person to you and, when that happened, your nerves could play you tricks. There was nothing anyone could do except keep an eye open and make sure the Old Man did not do anything silly, such as desert or commit suicide, both things that could have the most unpleasant consequences for one's family.

Twenty-four hours later we reached the bridge. Two infantrymen were guarding it. They were Canadians. Tiny and Barcelona killed them. It was done like lightning. We left two of our own at the bridge. The JU52 that was to make the drop was there to the second, but it had scarcely dropped the container before two Mustangs appeared out of the moonlight and the JU went hurtling down in flames. A body came tumbling from it. Its parachute did not open.

"Amen," whispered Heide.

We toiled up and across some hills and then lay up in cover, while a battalion of Scots marched past. They were training and kept practicing machine gun drill and individual forward rushes, and Tiny took a dislike to a sergeant with a large, red walrus moustache who, he said, maltreated his men, and announced that he was going to kill him. We had the greatest difficulty in pacifying him.

The next day we reached the tanks. We decided to rest before we got going and went into a thicket of pines. There we quarrelled savagely about the distribution of tinned rations. Heide was knocked unconscious with a hand grenade and Barcelona received a great gash across the whole of one side of his face. Then the Old Man discovered that Porta and Tiny had collected gold teeth despite One-Eye's prohibition. That would have meant death for the lot of us, if we were captured. The discovery led to a battle royal. The Legionnaire did one of his famous somersaults and planted his boots firmly in Tiny's face.

Then we sat down to drinking. We emptied our field bottles. Quarrelling broke out again when the Legionnaire said that we were just toy-soldiers, refuse from the Prussian midden.

"You French, syphilitic legionary snout," Porta shouted at the top of his voice, forgetting where we were. "You say they castrated you. Nobody believes it, your prickless owl. It was the Turkish music that has eaten it away."

"*Tu me fais chier,*" the Legionnaire shouted and flung his knife at Porta. It pierced the crown of Porta's top hat. Porta was furious. "May God strike all French cunts with syphilis," he yelled, seized up his machine pistol and emptied the magazine into the ground at the Legionnaire's feet. We ran for cover from the richochetting bullets, and our two guards came running up thoroughly scared. Porta shot at them and cursed them wildly. He almost killed Olle Karlsson.

Shortly afterwards peace was restored and we began playing "land" with our close-combat weapons. This was the only game in which it was impossible to cheat, so we quickly tired and took to dicing instead. A fresh fight started. Tiny tried to strangle Heide with his steel sling and it took us a quarter of an hour to get him on his feet again. Then Barcelona kicked Olle Karlsson.

After this intermezzo we began playing pontoon, but then we began to droop. We covered ourselves with branches and leaves and tried to go to sleep. We longed to sleep, but the Cola chocolate made that impossible.

A large column of trucks appeared in the distance.

"We'll deal with that lot in a jiffy," Porta said. "They're just service corps oafs. Carpet slipper soldiers with lace up their arses. Let's wipe them out, and bugger off. There's no end of powder in those carts. The bang they'll make will be heard in Rome and make the old Pope wiggle his ears."

But the Old Man would not hear of it. He was always the steady, unimaginative craftsman. He could not appreciate a stunt. He had been given an order and it had to be carried out regardless. They knew what they were doing when they made people like him feldwebels. We others did not go in so much for details. More than once we had put in a fake report involving millions, while we sat in a shell hole laughing.

Then another squabble broke out:

"You're the most chicken-hearted bugger I know," Porta shouted at the Old Man. "Not even the most avid homosexual ape would have anything to do with you. You can think yourself lucky we happen to like you, but we warn you, even our patience can come to an end. One day we'll carry you out feet first."

The transport column passed us. It would have been a good harvest. We glared at it hungrily. But, as usual, the Old Man had his way. They did well to make him feldwebel and section leader. No one else would have survived with us. The Old Man did not even realise that he went about with a lighted dynamite cartridge in his pocket.

When the sun went down, we set out again. Mosquitoes buzzed round us. We kept our lighted cigarettes hidden in our mouths. A company marched past, as we stood among trees snuffing the smell of their Camels.

"We could lay those footsloggers flat. Every one of them," Porta muttered.

"What a lot of gold teeth," Tiny said dreamily.

"Old Man," they wheedled, "let us bonk them on the head. We'll swear you've done it all on your own, when we get back.

200

They'll give you the knight's cross. I'll bet they will. Think of your wife, Old Man, she'd get a pension for life. It's worth thinking about."

But the Old Man was not to be persuaded. He would not even answer. Glumly we glowered after the disappearing column.

"There was enough gold there to start a whore-shop," Tiny said, raising his eyes to heaven.

Porta and I were in front and we almost ran into the tents. We dived into the cover of a couple of pine trees and halted the others. There were three tents. We could hear them snoring. At a signal from Barcelona we tore the tent pegs out, capturing the occupants, as in a sack. We stabbed and hit. In the course of a few minutes all was quiet. There had only been a couple of stifled cries to show there had been a fight. They had died before they were properly awake. We crept across to the tanks. We strangled the guards with our slings and threw their bodies into the bushes. We inspected the tanks with interest. They were M4's and M36's, Jacksons's with comical rollers like railway waggons. We began laying booby charges. Some were to blow the tank up when the engine started, others when the hatch was opened. The Legionnaire had the best imagination: he arranged a shell case seemingly casually on the fore hatch. If it fell off or was picked off, it set off a charge. We buried S-mines that were connected to charges under the tanks.

Tiny who was searching for bodies with gold teeth stumbled across their petrol depot. It was buried in the ground and camouflaged with branches. It was so well done that it roused Tiny's suspicions. We fixed a couple of panzerfausts in a tree with an ingenious arrangement of cords that would set them off and blow down into the petrol, if one moved one of the drums. We built three other panzerfausts into the crossroads.

Porta wailed:

"It's damned undemocratic all the gold that's going to be lying round here doing nobody any good. What do you say, Old Man, suppose Tiny and I stay behind and do a bit of collecting? You can give a true report of what happened here. We'll catch you up all right. I guarantee that."

"Shut up," snarled the Old Man.

We tossed a French helmet in among the bushes, and put a tin of spaghetti and a pocket book with an Italian soldier's letters in a reasonably visible place. That would make them rack their brains, we thought. We hoped they'd think it was Italian partisans and deserters had done it. That would make them hunt for the perpetrators in the hills to the south and leave us in peace to finish the rest of our assignment.

It was late in the afternoon, when we reached the bridge. Nothing is such fun as blowing up a bridge and we were looking forward to it. We fought for the detonator, for each of us wanted to be the one to ram the handle home. The Old Man cursed us. Barcelona made a great fuss, swearing that this was his job, he was explosives expert having been with the engineers in Spain. In the end we decided to dice for it.

A heavy truck appeared up the road leading to the bridge and behind it we saw a jeep.

"Stop that nonsense and get a move on," the Old Man scolded. He wanted to take the detonator, but Tiny hit him on the fingers with his pistol. "Keep your claws off it, you bloody carpenter. Your pissing bridge stays where it is till the dice have said who is to blow it up."

Julius Heide kept count. I was the first out with a throw of only seven. Porta was luckier with eighteen. Tiny went wild when he got 28. No one paid any attention to the Old Man, he only had 14, Rudolph Kleber had 19. Then Heide threw 28 and we thought Tony would kill him.

"You repulsive Jew-hater, you cheated. May you become valet to a Jew. Twice I've tried to inform on you, you trickster!"

"So. . . ." Heide said thoughtfully. "It was you set the Security Police on to me, was it?"

"That's right," Tiny yelled, "and I shan't give up before you're dangling from a butcher's hook in Torgau. The day they condemn you to the block, I'll apply for the job of executioner. I promise you I'll make at least three bosh shots. The first chop you'll get right up the arse."

But no one bothered to listen. We were too preoccupied throwing our dice. But no one beat 28 so Heide and Tiny had to throw again. The truck entered a steep curve and changed whining into first gear. Tiny shook the shaker high above his head. He did not care about the truck. He pranced round the detonator three times, rubbed his nose against a kilometer stone, which he thought would bring him luck; then he gave the dice a last shake like a professional barman and with an expert sweeping movement threw them onto Porta's green cloth. Six sixes. Incredible. But there they were. Tiny was beside himself with delight.

"You can't equal that, Julius Jew-hater."

"Why not?" Heide said smiling and gathered the dice.

"Stop that now," the Old Man said. "The truck's nearly at the bridge."

We didn't care. Heide spat on the dice. He shook them four times to the left, twice to the right. He raised the shaker above his head and hopped on bent knees round Porta's green cloth. Then with a fine sweep he banged the shaker face down onto the cloth, where the dice lay hidden under the shaker. Then he raised one side of the broken leather shaker, laid his head on the ground so that one eye could see inside.

"If you move the shaker as much as a millimetre it won't count," Tiny called warningly.

"I know," Heide hissed. "But I have the right to tap the top with a finger."

Tiny nodded.

The truck and jeep were now only fifty yards from the bridge which they were approaching very slowly, just entering a hairpin bend. We were beside ourselves with excitement.

"Lift it up, blast you," Porta exclaimed.

We began betting among ourselves what Heide's throw would amount to. Heide appeared to have plenty of time. He tapped the bottom of the shaker four times with his finger, then slowly lifted the shaker away. There they lay grinning; six ones. The least you could throw. He hit at the ground in fury and, if Porta had not snatched up the dice, he probably would have sent them flying.

Tiny rolled over and over in delight: "I've won, I've won," he yelled. "Heads down, boys, now you shall hear a proper bang." He fondled the detonator. The truck drove onto the bridge closely followed by the jeep. Grinning broadly, Tiny undid the catch, pulled the handle up, patted the wires:

"Little darling, now you're going to let a fart that'll echo all over Italy."

We others crawled away quickly and took cover behind rocks and boulders. Tiny began whistling as if he hadn't a care in the world:

Eine Strassenbahn ist immer da!

The truck was almost across.

"The idiot! Why doesn't the bugger blow it up?" Barcelona growled. "This isn't fireworks, but a serious military task."

"He wants to get the jeep as well," Rudolph said.

"He's crazy," growled the Old Man.

"God! Have you seen that! There's a red flag cn the truck. Stop Tiny!"

Heide called in a voice of fear.

We tried to attract Tiny's attention, but he was almost out of his mind. He just waved back to us, his face beaming. It was ghastly! A 15-ton truck laden with ammunition.

Tiny waved to the truck and jeep.

"Heh! Yankees. I'm going to show you where Moses bought the beer."

Two people in the jeep stood up and stared in our direction. A negro looked out through the window of the driver's cab.

"Greetings to the devil," Tiny shouted and rammed the handle down.

We squeezed flat. There was a bang that must have been audible for a hundred miles. The jeep flew up into the air like a ball. A pillar of flame shot up. The truck vanished, was pulverised.

The blast threw Tiny a hundred yards away. Splinters of red hot steel rained round us. A heavy wheel came racing up the slope from the bridge. It tore past Barcelona scarcely an inch away. It would have killed him. It drove into a large rock further up, bounced into the air like a ball, dropped and began rolling back downhill, heading straight for Tiny who was sitting up wiping blood off his face. When he caught sight of the wheel, instead of jumping aside, he began running down hill, with the wheel chasing him. His legs went like drum sticks, we could not believe he could run so fast. Then he stumbled, fell and went rolling on like a ball towards the blown-up bridge, still pursued by the wheel. A cloud of dust hid him from view, then there was a great splash as he and the wheel shot into the river. A short while later, he appeared on the muddy bank cursing and swearing profusely.

"You bloody murderers," he shouted. "You tried to make a fool of me. You fixed a boobytrap for me. That's why you let me win. You shitting swindlers." He worked his way up the slope at incredible speed, his long close-combat knife glinting in his hand. He made for Barcelona.

"You fake Spanish orange, you lost on purpose. This will end in court martial. Murder case, bugger and blast."

Barcelona ran for his life, calling in desperate tones:

"Let me explain! Let me explain!"

"You can explain as much as you like after I've slit up your arse, as I will when I catch you." In his fury he flung his knife at Barcelona.

The rest of us tried to stop Tiny before he could kill Barcelona, which he loudly proclaimed to be his intention. The poor Old Man let his pistol fall and clasped his head in his hands.

"I shall go mad. This isn't a military unit. It's a loony bin."

"Like master, like man!" laughed Porta.

It was the Legionnaire rescued Barcelona. He tumbled Tiny with a ju jitsu hold and got his steel-like fingers round his throat. But Tiny was not easy to hold. It was not until he had six of us sitting on him that he gave up struggling. Barcelona wanted to kick his face in, but the Old Man stopped that idea.

The Legionnaire tried to convince Tiny that he had got things all wrong.

"Do you mean to tell me that it was an ammunition truck," Tiny said in amazement. "The swine. It didn't have a flag."

"It did, but a little one, *mon ami*," the Legionnaire smiled.

Tiny was profoundly shocked, when he learned that an ammunition truck had been going along with only a pennant. "That's the most impudent thing I've come across," he exclaimed, "driving about with powder and dangerous things like that without a proper flag showing. Bugger it! I might have

205

been killed. Any decent court martial would call that attempted murder. It wasn't those idiots' fault that I wasn't bumped off by that wheel." Then he paced out the distance from the bridge that the blast had thrown him: 221 paces. "What do you say to that!" He banged an indignant fist on a mole hill. "I've a good mind to write to General Mark Clark and complain about that flag."

"One should always complain about that sort of thing," Porta said with a sly smile.

"Tiny's right," Gregor Martin agreed. "Let's write and complain. Heide knows English."

We were enchanted by the idea. Tiny wanted to do it straight away and pointed a commanding finger at Heide:

"Unteroffizier Julius Heide, you are hereby appointed Obergefreiter Wolfgang Creutzfeldt's chief pen-pusher and, note this, you write what you're told. No funny stuff with high faluting upper-class phrases. The shitting American general shall bloody well know who's writing to him." He thought for a moment while Heide spread a sheet of paper on a suitable flat stone. "Let's see. We'll start with: 'Bloody General Arse-hole! . . .'"

"You can't put that," Heide said. "They wouldn't even read a letter that began like that. That's wrong psychology. You begin: 'Dear Sir'."

"Keep your pansy phrases for your own use. In the first place this letter isn't to be written in psychology, but in English. Do you expect me to be polite after nearly getting one of their filthy trucks on my head? The man's got to have it straight from the shoulder. I would be interested to know what idiot has given him an army."

Heide shrugged.

"All right! Dictate away. But you won't get an answer."

Tiny began walking round the stone with his hands clasped behind his back. He had heard that big business men did that, when they dictated letters to their secretaries.

"Stop this fooling," the Old Man called. "We must move on."

"Go on yourself then," Tiny said. "I must get this letter off first."

"What next?" Heide said impatiently. "I've put 'General Arsehole'."

Tiny sucked a dirty finger.

"Your toy soldiers must in future see that your refuse-collectors carry the regulation red flag when they drive about with powder. I blew up a bridge today and was damned nearly killed, because one of your rubbish carts came along without a red flag showing. If this happens again, you can expect a visit from me and then things will happen to your snout. This bloody war has to be conducted in a decent fashion. Don't forget that, you ape, or you may find that your arse has been pulled up over your head. Don't think we're afraid of you, you flat-footed American. Yours sincerely, Obergefreiter Wolfgang Creutzfeldt, to his friends, Tiny, but that does not apply to you. To you I am Herr Creutzfeldt."

This letter was fixed to a balk in what remained of the bridge. Then the Old Man got angry and threatened us with his pistol.

"Pick up your things. Single column. Follow me. And put some life into it!"

We followed him cursing and swearing. We climbed up into the mountain. Every time we topped a rise, we thought it was the last, only to discover that there was another ahead of us. When finally, angry and sweating, we flung ourselves down on what may have been the tenth or twentieth rise, I no longer remember, we were oblivious to the lovely view. We squabbled over trifles, as we always seemed to, and threatened to kill each other. When a lizard ran over Gregor's boots, he became quite wild, rushed after the agile little creature, caught it, and cut it into tiny pieces and stamped furiously on the pieces.

All at once, Heide and Barcelona were rolling round together in a savage rough and tumble, all because Barcelona had insinuated that Heide had Jewish blood in him. The rest of us sided with Barcelona, finding lots of indications, if not evidence that he must be a Jew.

"By God, I believe he is," Porta exclaimed eagerly. "Nobody's more critical than a relation. That explains his hatred of Jews, the swarthy hook-nose. From now on you shan't be called Julius, but Isaac. Isaac Heide come to Daddy!"

"We'll give you the Talmud for a birthday present," Rudolph said jubilantly.

"And tattoo the Star of David on his bum," Tiny said, "and give him a fall-flap to the seat of his trousers, so that he can show his true colours, the bloody Jewish Schmaus."

Heide rushed at Tiny swinging a kriss above his head. He had found this knife when we attacked the tanks.

"Take larger strides, little Isaac," Tiny called half choking with laughter, "or you'll wear out your soles and Papa will be angry."

Heide flung a stone at Tiny, but hit Gregor who dropped to the ground, half unconscious, but savage with pain. He stumbled to his feet, seized a hand grenade, tugged the fuse-cord out and flung the hissing thing at Heide. It struck him on the chest and fell, hissing, among us. Fortunately, in his rage, Gregor had forgotten to wait before he threw it. We scattered in all directions like chaff in a storm and dived for cover. The grenade exploded with a hollow bump. Miraculously no one was hurt.

"Shoot him!" Tiny shouted.

The safety catches of twenty machine pistols were undone. Gregor seized his, loaded it and stood there, legs firmly planted, knees slightly bent, ready to shoot, cursing us. Heide came up behind him and the next instant they were rolling round, biting, scratching and snarling.

Gregor was rolling down the mountainside. Faster and faster. If he hit a stone, he would be killed.

"It's only what he deserves," Barcelona grinned maliciously. "Such a puffed-up louse."

"Do him good to lie at the bottom with some broken bones," Porta said. "He can think of all the mistakes he's made, when the sun gets up and roasts him alive."

But Gregor managed to halt his wild career. He began crawling up again, blood pouring from his face. He was filled with murderous intent, waited watching Heide's every movement. He wanted to get behind Heide, who stood there ready to kick him in the face. Twice he landed a kick, but Gregor stubbornly crawled up again. His face was a bloody pulp.

We lay on our bellies watching them with interest and giving good advice.

"Kill him, Julius," Tiny called.

Heide snorted. There was nothing he would have liked better.

Gregor was almost at the top for the fourth time.

"Give up," Heide jeered, sure of victory. "Chuck up your dog-badge and go down to the bottom and die."

"Wouldn't dream of it, you pistol-bog," Gregor shouted.

Then Gregor changed his tactics. He became wily. He chucked a knife at Heide, when he was almost up, and that did it. Heide's eyes followed the knife and as a result he started his kick too late, giving Gregor time to seize hold of his ankle. In a shower of stone and gravel the two of them rolled, closely entwined down the mountainside. Then they let go of each other and got to their feet, hit each other savagely, fell groaning to the ground. They drew their knives; then, with arms held out from their sides and bodies bent forward, almost at a right angle, they circled round each other, watching and waiting. Heide struck first. With a twist of his body, Gregor avoided the blow and tried to plant his knife in Heide's stomach. Groaning, they slashed and stabbed at each other. Heide landed a violent kick on Gregor's groin making him double up with pain, then raised his knife to finish him off, but he miscalculated. Gregor had learned the Legionnaire's trick: a back somersault and then one the opposite way and the soles of both his boots struck Heide right in the face. He screamed like a butchered pig. Gregor seized him by the ears and pounded the back of his head against a piece of rock. Heide lost consciousness. For a moment Gregor stood, swaying on his feet, then he too collapsed.

Tiny rubbed his hands in delight.

"Now I'll crawl down and finish them off. Couple of bloody proletariats!" He toyed with his dental forceps. "Heide has a whole jaw full of gold teeth and Gregor has two. They've been on my waiting list for ages!" He began clambering down, but when he was only half way, the two of them came to.

It was Gregor first saw Tiny with the forceps in his hand

and from that moment he and Heide were allies. Tiny felt cheated.

"You're written off. Give me those pegs," he shouted and went for Heide, who was nearer to him.

A fresh fight started. Although Heide and Gregor were considerably more agile than Tiny, they could not match his strength. He picked Heide up, swung him round his head and flung him against a stone. Gregor leaped onto his back and tried to bite his ear off, but Tiny just shook him off, as a cow shakes a fly from its ear. He raised him high above his head and dashed him to the ground. When he had done this four times, Gregor admitted defeat, but he was not left alone until he had handed over everything he had in his pockets.

Heide tried to escape, darting like a squirrel up the slope, but in a moment Tiny was over him, seized him and flung him several yards away, shouting:

"I'm after your pins. Haven't you tumbled to that?"

Heide capitulated. He was allowed to keep his gold teeth, but he had to hand over 275 dollars, the Pope's ring and his Russian machine pistol. That was the worst blow. We had only two of those splendid weapons. The Legionnaire had one, and now Tiny had the other. We were prepared to commit any crime to get hold of a Kalashnikov. Not a few had lost their lives trying. The owner of a Kalashnikov slept with it tied to his arm, yet even so some had been stolen. We also had four PPSH's, model 41, another Russian pistol. With one of those you could have bought a battery of heavy howitzers, but as Porta said to the gunner who had proposed the deal:

"How in heaven's name am I to cart four heavy howitzers about with me?"

The gunner had even offered Porta the battery's twenty-four horses, but as, at the time, we were stationed in a stores depot, Porta was not interested.

Five times Heide tried to steal his Kalashnikov and ring back, and the last attempt very nearly succeeded. That was the night we left Cassino, the day before we were given tanks again. Tiny all but killed him. In fact, he was only saved by the appearance of One-Eye, who came along just as Tiny was tying Heide to the muzzle of an anti-tank gun. Heide went to mass three times to try and make sure of God's support in his fight with Tiny, but obviously God did not wish to be involved.

We had some difficulty in finding the hut from which we were to get our British Staff Officer. The sentries were half asleep at their posts and had their throats cut without their making a sound. We surrounded the hut. Having eaten all our narcotic chocolate we were now chewing Indian hashish to calm our nerves. We had been out six days. A faint glow came through one of the black-out curtains.

"They've closed themselves up like a bull's arsehole in the fly season," Porta muttered. "They'll shit a fine turd when they see us."

"Do you think they'll have any gin?" Heide said dreamily. "I'm very fond of gin."

"And corned beef," Porta added. "A couple of tins of that mixed up with mashed potato can make a corpse smack its lips."

"Let's knock politely," suggested Tiny, who was lying behind a fallen tree gazing at the door of the hut. "When they open it a bit, I'll stick my good Communist Kalashnikov in their mugs. Then things will start moving. Staff buggers like that always shit their pants, when they look into the muzzle of a MP."

"We'll have a colonel this time," Porta said. "We haven't had one of those yet."

"And I want to lead him," Tiny demanded. "I'll have a rope round his neck and have him trotting behind me like a goat going home to be milked."

The Old Man asked for quiet.

"This has got to be done quickly," he whispered.

"Everything we do is," Porta said.

Tiny pointed to the hut:

"Did you see the shadows on the curtains? They had bottles in their hands."

We fell silent and gazed in amazement as a woman in uniform walked briskly across the open space.

"God, they've got cunt as well," Porta breathed ecstatically.

"It was a WAAF," Heide explained.

Tiny gazed at him uncomprehendingly.

"Do they bark?"

"Idiot!" hissed Heide.

The woman opened the door. In the light from inside we could see that she was pretty. A pretty girl in an ugly uniform.

Barcelona had found the telephone wires and reported that he had cut the 'gabble strings'. The Old Man nodded, satisfied.

"Three stay here to cover us, while the rest pay them a visit."

"They'll piss in their pants," Porta crowed.

"That tart must wash before we fuck her," Tiny said.

"*Claro,*" Barcelona bleated. "Camp followers must practise a little hygiene when visitors come."

"Don't forget their corned beef, when we've laid them cold," Porta reminded us.

A window in the hut opened and a man looked out. He had red tabs with gold embroidery on his lapels.

"That's our man," Heide whispered. "He's longing for us."

A figure appeared out of the darkness, startling us. It was coming straight towards us. The Legionnaire crouched ready to leap, put his machine pistol down and drew his knife. It was a giant Englishman.

Then we heard a familiar chuckle.

"Tiny," Barcelona exclaimed.

"That's me," grinned Tiny. He was wearing an English greatcoat and helmet. "I ran into a sentry round at the back there. Deaded him with my sling." He showed us two gold teeth.

The Old Man cursed him.

"Sooner or later you and Porta are going to dangle because of these gold teeth."

"He was black," Tiny went on by way of explanation and held up a neatly severed ear. "Here's one of his listening-flaps. He told me their password. His relief's coming in ten minutes, so I'll just breathe 'Wellington' in his ear before I throttle him and collect his ear, if he's black too."

"You're crazy," the Old Man said. "The sight of those ears makes me sick."

"Why on earth?" Porta asked, uncomprehendingly. "Those brown devils cut our ears off, so they must expect us to take theirs. Nobody can object to that."

"It's going too far," the Old Man said.

"I suppose nobody's got a camera?" Tiny asked. "I'd like a snap of myself in these Churchill rags. Strange what thoughts come to one when one wanders about alone in the dark. Back there it occurred to me that it might be a good stunt to pick you all off and shout alarm to the Tommies. When it was all over and you were dressed by the right in your common grave, no one would be able to contradict me, when I said I had been forced to join you. Who knows what they mightn't have led to? Saving a whole Churchill staff isn't a trick that's performed every day. It was my chance of having a statue."

"A strange thing to think," said Porta. "You had better give up thinking, Tiny, or you'll come to a sticky end."

"What do you think they want the staff officer for?" Heide said.

"Produce him to the propaganda boys, as if he was a randy chimp in a zoo," Porta, the omniscient, explained. "I wonder what they'd say if we came back with a corporal instead of an effing colonel?"

"They'd only send us back to get one," the Old Man said dryly.

"Well, it's time for me to totter along and get that other ear," said Tiny with a broad grin. Jauntily he sauntered across to the hut, his English helmet on the back of his head, his carbine bumping on his back. He had his Kalashnikov hidden under his greatcoat.

"*J'ai peur*," the Legionnaire muttered. "I'm going after him. He's bound to have forgotten the password."

It was a good thing the Legionnaire had such foresight, because Tiny lost his temper when the relief guard began cursing him and forgetting everything shouted at him, in German:

"Shut up, you striped pig. If you want to talk to me, speak German."

The Englishman leaped back, scared, only to die in the steel grip of the Legionnaire's fingers.

There wasn't a second to lose now. We all rushed forward, kicked the door of the hut open, knocked the window in. Our automatic pistols spat death. Porta and Heide seized a staff

213

officer, flung him through the door and knocked him unconscious with the butt of a pistol. All the others in the hut were killed.

We disappeared at a run.

Two figures appeared ahead of me. I fired from the hip. They crumpled and fell over, dead, on the path.

Tiny came racing up, still wearing his British greatcoat and helmet.

"Get rid of that British muck," the Legionnaire called.

"I got fourteen gold teeth," Tiny cried delightedly.

Automatic weapons chattered away behind us. The Legionnaire pulled me down into a hollow beside the path. Porta and Heide appeared dragging the unconscious officer. Olle Karlsson came up, called something incomprehensible and turned towards the muzzle flashes we could see in the darkness. His automatic pistol barked angrily. Then he uttered a piercing screech, doubled up and rolled round and round on the path.

"*Milles diables,*" hissed the Legionnaire.

Three of the others came running and disappeared into the darkness. Then Rudolph Kleber ran up. He kneeled down, sent short bursts into the darkness. All at once he let his automatic pistol drop, clapped his hands to his head and fell forward.

The three others came back and tried to drag him along with them. I wanted to shoot, but the Legionnaire shook his head and put a warning finger to his lips.

One of the three fell, almost cut in half by a burst of machine gun fire. The other two began to run, but one gave a sudden yell and put his hand to his eye: "I'm blind, b-l-i-n-d."

An Englishman, bareheaded and in his shirtsleeves, came into view. He had a light machine gun clamped under his arm. Seven or eight others followed him. One of them was armed with a Mark IT jungle rifle, a thing we all coveted. The Legionnaire pointed to him and nodded. The blinded man was on his knees scrabbling round in circles. The Englishman in shirtsleeves put the muzzle of his gun to the back of his head and fired a burst. Then he grinned: "Damned Kraut!" he said.

I pressed the butt of my PPSH into my shoulder. A whole flock of men appeared out of some bushes. They were panting

214

and cursing and we kept hearing the word 'Kraut'. They kicked vengefully at the dead on the path. Rudolph groaned and a corporal raised his Sten gun and emptied the magazine into his quivering body. Then I saw red. We would show them. The Legionnaire began singing: "Come now death, come only death."

The Englishmen on the path went rigid. Then deep from the Legionnaire's throat came the ringing Moroccan battlecry: "*Allah-el akbar*" and simultaneously he opened fire with his Kalashnikov. They went over like ninepins.

We stood up and fired at any who still moved. The Legionnaire laughed shrilly. He dipped a finger into a pool of blood and drew a cross on the forehead of each of the dead. He flourished the jungle rifle. He pulled the body of the corporal who had killed Rudolph out of the heap of corpses and ground his ironshod heel into the dead man's face.

We caught the others up. The officer, a lieutenant-colonel, had recovered consciousness. We placed a noose round his neck and explained that if he made any trouble, he would be instantly throttled.

"Who is in command here?" he asked arrogantly.

"What concern of yours is that?" Heide said. "Be careful we don't all get tired of you."

"Shut up," snarled the Old Man, shoving Heide angrily aside. "Herr Oberleutnant, Feldwebel Willie Beier. I am in command of this special detachment."

The officer nodded.

"Then teach your men how to address an officer."

"Oh, piss on the shit," Porta called. "Oberleutnant lousy prisoner-of-war. Bang him a couple on the knob. That's what we'll get if they catch us. What a bugger. Oberleutnant!"

The Englishman did not even bother to look at Porta.

"You must maintain discipline, feldwebel, or I'll complain when I meet your commander."

Porta gave his top hat a flourish worthy of a seventeenth century French aristocrat, put his chipped monocle in his eye with a foppish gesture, produced a snuff box and took a pinch. He blinked at the British officer.

"Sir Lieutenant-Colonel, may I introduce myself." He took

another pinch of snuff and went on speaking through his nose. "I am the famous Obergefreiter by God's grace Joseph Porta of Weding. Perhaps I may be of assistance to you, for example with a kick up the backside." Porta walked round the man, inspecting him curiously through his chipped monocle. "Feldwebel Beier, where the devil did you get this sardine? A comical figure, I must say!"

The British officer turned furiously to the Old Man:

"I will not stand for this."

"I'm afraid you will bloody well have to," grinned Barcelona.

Porta again stepped up to the British officer, who was jawing away, and began to count aloud:

"One, two, three."

The officer looked at him uncomprehendingly.

"How many gold teeth have you, Sir? I got up to three."

The lieutenant-colonel's voice rose to a high squeak of fury and he threatened the Old Man with all sorts of disasters.

"Let him alone. He'll only make things unpleasant for us, if we get him back," the Old Man said irritably.

Despite Tiny's violent protests, the noose was taken from our prisoner's neck. The Legionnaire stuck close to him.

"Mon Lieutenant-Colonel, one squeak and I'll slit your belly open" and with a smile he produced his Moorish knife.

We could hear the guns firing up at the front. Day had come and things were on the move, long transport columns and marching infantry. For a while we marched alongside a battalion of Moroccan troops, who took us in our camouflage suits for some kind of Special Unit. One leap and the British officer would have been safe, but the point of the Legionnaire's knife was pressing into his left side and in his back he could feel the muzzle of Barcelona's automatic pistol. In front of him was Tiny's huge back. It would have been certain death to have made the attempt.

We went into cover behind the American lines and waited for the night. The front was disturbed. As far as we could see were lines of tracer.

We fought our way through shortly after midnight, leaping from shell hole to shell hole. Two Indians, who were in our

216

way got mown down and we lost three men in our own infantry's fire.

Exhausted, we collapsed in the battalion commander's dug-out. One-Eye came across to us, gave each of us a hug and Mike offered us his big cigars. Padre Emanuel shook our hands. People from the other sectors came and welcomed us back. We had lost half our number, among them Rudolph and Olle Karlsson.

We were given five days leave. As we walked along towards the rear, a big field-grey Mercedes swept past us. In the back seat sat our British prisoner beside a German general. We were spattered with mud.

We spat at the great luxurious car. Then we began envisaging what we should do when we got to Palid Ida's whore-house, and at the thought of her girls all else was forgotten.

XII

The mountain was trembling like a dying animal. A thick yellow cloud of fumes and dust hung above the monastery, which was slowly being coloured red by the licking tongues of flame. We knew that there were still some monks up there; but we did not know that at that moment they were celebrating mass below the basilica.

"They must have been pulverised," Barcelona muttered as he looked, appalled, at the smoking ruins.

Major Mike emerged from a great pool of mud. The padre was with him.

"Volunteers to go to the monastery."

We stacked our rifles. The mortars stood silent. We ran up the slope, and the Americans, English and French watched us intently. We ran across the remains of the walls. Padre Emanuel was in front and just behind him the MO. We put on gas masks as we entered the monastery and gathered those we could find in what until recently had been the central courtyard.

In silence they filed out of the monastery, carrying a large wooden crucifix at the head of the long line of them. We went with them as far as the bend. There they began chanting a psalm. The sun came out. It was as though God for a moment had looked down from his heaven.

The Americans were standing on the parapets of their positions staring at the strange procession. On our side, paratroopers and tank gunners rose out of their positions. Someone ordered: "Remove helmets!" Was the voice English or German? We all removed our helmets and stood with heads reverently bowed.

The last we saw was the crucifix, seemingly gliding through the air.

Then we ran back to our positions and the muzzles of our machine guns again pointed forward.

Gefreiter Schenck suddenly collapsed at my side. Two hundred yards in front of us an American flame-thrower team died. A French lieutenant went charging down the serpentine road. He had gone off his head.

For a few brief minutes we had been human. Now that was forgotten.

DEATH OF THE MONASTERY

The monastery was a heap of ruins. It was being shelled without intermission. There were fires everywhere.

One at a time we ran across the open space in front of the gate and slithered head over heels down into a cellar. Some paratroopers, who were digging themselves in, made fun of us.

"Have you sold your tanks?" they jeered.

The flames lit up the word PAX carved over the gateway. The central courtyard, the one with the statues of St. Benedict and St. Scholastica, was piled with broken masonry. We dug ourselves in.

That night 200 heavy bombers attacked the monastery. In the course of a couple of hours they unloaded 2500 tons of bombs on top of us. Our fox-holes were levelled with the ground.

Porta and I were lying side by side. We saw an enormous piece of masonry being sent soaring into the air. We watched it.

"Run," shouted Porta.

We scrambled to our feet and bolted. With a thunderous crash the masonry struck the exact place where we had all been lying. One third of the company was buried under it. It was hopeless to think of digging them out.

When day broke, we hauled our machine guns out of the earth and slime, arranged their tripods, loaded up, checked the belts. All was in order.

"They'll be coming soon," Porta predicted.

Mike crawled across to us. He had lost his helmet. One eye was covered by a loose flap of skin.

"How're things?" he asked, puffing at his fat cigar.

"Hellish."

"And there's worse to come."

Mike was right. Things got much worse. The holy mountain quivered like a dying bull in the ring. Colossal lumps of stone flew in all directions. Tiles that were hundreds of years old were ground to powder. Fierce fires broke out.

We abandoned our position and withdrew to the crypt. Nobody could have remained out there and lived. We found room behind the altar and stretched out there. The yard-thick ceiling was beginning to give. It was going up and down like a stormy sea. Some of the paratroopers tried to shore it up. It was no good. With a crash the ceiling collapsed, burying the paratroopers.

Our new minstrel, Gefreiter Brans, got shell-shock. He seized his trumpet and began playing jazz. Then he got it into his head that he ought to blow us all up. Tiny managed to wrest the T-mine from him and flung it out into the yard, where the roar of its explosion was drowned in the thunder of bursting shells.

A paratrooper who had had both legs crushed by falling masonry lay in a pool of blood in the middle of the floor.

"Shoot me, shoot me! Oh God, let me die!"

The ever-ready Heide raised his P.38, but the Old Man knocked it out of his hand. Medical Orderly Gläser bent over the shrieking man, jabbed his morphine syringe through his uniform and emptied it into the pain-racked body.

"That's all I can do for you, chum. If you'd been a horse, we'd have shot you. God is merciful." Gläser spat viciously at a crucifix.

Padre Emanuel laboriously made his way through the piles of masonry, white with dust. He bent over the wounded paratrooper, held the crucifix to his lips, clasped his hands and prayed. His face was gashed by a shell splinter. Gläser wanted to bandage him, but the padre thrust him angrily aside and went across to a SS-Hauptsturmführer, who was in a bad way, having had his belly torn by an incendiary.

"Bugger off, padre," the dying officer hissed. "And take your God with you." He poured oaths and curses over all and sundry.

Padre Emanuel was deaf to it all. There was no putting him off. He held the holy cross over the cursing Hauptsturmführer.

The man's guts welled up out of his ripped-up belly.

Gläser rushed across and tried to restore the bloody mass to its place. The wounded man bellowed. Porta toyed thoughtfully with his pistol. Tiny picked up a club. If the man did not die soon, we'd kill him. His screams chilled even us to the marrow.

Gläser had no more morphine.

"Gag that bugger," Porta called, desperately.

Padre Emanuel moved on to the others who were dying. There were many. As soon as they were dead, we chucked them outside. It wasn't a pretty sight, when the rats started on them.

A ten-ton bomb hit the crypt, and there was a hail of beams and masonry. We were imprisoned behind the altar, which was built in a cloister

Fresh bombs kept exploding. We were almost suffocated with the dust. Hour after hour it went on. We lost our sense of time, had no idea whether it was day or night.

Padre Emanuel was sitting in the middle of the floor, his uniform in tatters, his face bloody and begrimed. He looked round, searching for a place to try and laid hold of a great balk. He was as strong as an ox.

We watched mockingly while he struggled with the balk. It would have taken a tractor to shift it.

"God's servant is very keen to get out of the Master's house," said Heide, grinning. "Take a seat, Padre, and peg out with the rest of us. It's lovely in God's heaven. Or don't you believe your own bunkum?" This was Heide's favourite topic. He hated God, the same way as he hated the Jews.

Padre Emanuel turned towards him. On his mouth a broad grin, but his eyes flashed dangerously. Slowly he walked towards Heide, who scurried nervously back against the altar and drew his knife.

Emanuel landed a kick on his hand that sent the knife flying in a wide arc. He seized Heide by his tunic, pulled him from the altar and banged him against the wall by the side of the great crucifix.

"Julius, mock God once again and I'll smear your brains over the wall. You won't be the first whose head I've bashed in. Don't get me wrong, even if I am a priest. If there's anyone here afraid to meet his God, it's you, Julius."

The blast from a huge bomb flung us in a heap together. Padre Emanuel gave his head a shake, spat out some blood. The Old Man handed him his water bottle. The Padre smiled gratefully.

A big stone whizzed past his head. Heide was standing with another stone ready in his hand.

The Padre drew himself erect. He stuffed his crucifix into a breast pocket, tore off his stiff dog-collar and went towards Heide with the alert watchful movements of the practised wrestler.

Heide hit at him with his stone, made a lightning dart to one side and landed a dirty kick. But the Padre was made of tough stuff. He seized Julius by the throat and flung him to the floor. The whole thing took only a few minutes. Then Heide had had enough.

The Padre returned to his balk as if nothing had happened. Tiny spat on his hands and went to his help. They set their feet against it, the two of them, the priest and the killer, each as strong as a horse, and the incredible happened: The balk gave. They grinned at each other proudly. No one else could have done it. We managed to dig a little tunnel and got out into the front chamber.

The basilica had fallen in and there lay a colonel with arms stretched out, eyes wide open.

"What the hell are you gaping at, Colonel?" Porta exclaimed. "If you're dead, chum, shut your peepers!"

A flock of rats scurried across the floor. Furiously I flung my steel helmet at them. One of them dropped something it had been carrying off. It was half a hand. On one finger was a swastika ring. Gefreiter Brans, our minstrel, gave the hand a kick.

Padre Emanuel bent over the wildly staring colonel. He had been killed by blast. His face was like a soft-shelled egg. Everything beneath the skin had been crushed. It was a thing we had often seen, when the big mines did their weeding out.

"Put him over by the wall," ordered the Old Man.

Tiny took the corpse by an arm and began pulling it along.

All at once he found himself holding just the arm. For a moment he was at a loss. Then he gave the hand a shake: "Good luck, old fellow. Never meant to pull your paw off!" Then he flung the arm at a flock of squealing rats that were trying to clamber up the wall.

Porta was gazing avidly at the corpse's long black officer's boots.

"I rather think I'll acquire those two foot-warmers."

A paratroop lieutenant looked the other way and mumbled something about plundering bodies. Porta pulled the boots off the colonel. They fitted as if they had been made for him. He caught sight of Eagle sitting in a corner and insisted that he salute the boots. As a stabsfeldwebel reduced to the ranks it was his simple duty to salute a colonel's boots, said Porta.

Eagle refused as always, but after being beaten about the head he gave in and saluted the boots.

"You are and always will be a half-wit, Stahlschmidt! The next time you get up on your hind legs, you'll have your bum kicked by a pair of colonel's boots."

The bombardment continued without pause. The monastery was swaying. We sat scattered about the place, hands clasped round our weapons. Time no longer existed. Porta tried telling a story, but no one could be bothered to listen. It was about a man in Bremen who traded in dogs. A certain Herr Schultze.

Oberfeldwebel Lutz went mad and ran head first, like a goat, at the wall.

A swarm of rats came pouring through the basilica. There were hundreds of them. All crazed with fear. They climbed squealing up our legs. They had only one thought in their heads: away from that hell of flames. We went at them with our infantry spades. The moment they smelled fresh blood, they went for each other: an inferno of snarling, bleeding scratching shapes.

Padre Emanuel stood with his back to the wall hitting out savagely with an infantry spade. On his one shoulder sat a rat, half its hair singed off it, hissing at the others attacking it. The Padre dropped his crucifix and a rat bit at it furiously. Tiny crushed its head with his heel. We ought to have been grateful to the rats. They saved us from madness.

There was a momentary pause in the bombardment, but shortly afterwards it resumed with renewed fury. Later we learned that two thousand flying fortresses were used to bomb us. In that one day and night more bombs were dropped over our little area than were ever emptied over Berlin.

At that moment Padre Emanuel was holding his crucifix out towards us and blessing us. We had made another altar out of boxes and broken beams. It had cost him a few cuffs and blows to get us to do it; but if the Padre intended to say mass there was nothing we could do.

We gathered round him. He glared down at us.

"Remove helmets!" he commanded. "Kneel for prayer!" Tiny was a bit slow in getting to his knees and received a swinging box on the ear to encourage him.

Then the Padre prayed. It wasn't a prayer he could have learned at the college, but it was a prayer that gave us courage. And then he began to preach. His booming voice drowned even the roar of the exploding shells.

"Don't you imagine that God is afraid of you," he said pointing an admonishing finger at Tiny. "That box on the ear came to you at God's command. You snivel with fear at the thought of dying, but have no scruples about killing others. This Company has lost 86 killed in three days. That's a lot. There will be more yet. You had better seek God through me, while there's still time."

He went on for a quarter of an hour, storming at us from his make-shift pulpit.

"He ought to have been a general," Porta whispered. "Some commander he would have made."

A rain of shells struck the monastery.

The Padre was flung out of his pulpit. With blood running over his face from a deep gash, he climbed back into it. Raising a machine-pistol above his head, he held it out towards us threateningly.

"Don't kid yourselves that this is the only power in the world. Don't shut the door in God's face. Life is only on loan. Machine-pistols have nothing to say where God is concerned. I know you. I know what you're thinking there. Don't you grin, Porta. Not even your dirty Berlin wit will get you out of it with God. Don't believe what's on the buckles of your belts. God is not with you. Any more than he is with the others. A war is the height of human stupidity. The Devil's work. Some have called this war a crusade. That is blasphemy. It is a war for plunder. The world's greatest act of manslaughter."

A colossal crash put a full stop to his sermon. The basilica collapsed. The flaring Hindenburg-candles were extinguished. We worked furiously to get out of the smoke-filled room, crawling on our bellies through piles of stone. There was a different sound to the bombardment now. It was no longer the nerve-destroying scream of the bombs that predominated, but the whine of shells. Artillery. More concentrated. Quite different. Regular. More congenial.

We dug ourselves in. The monastery disappeared. We could not understand how God could let it happen. We pledged ourselves to the devil and at the same time prayed to God. The sun went down. The sun rose. Time after time the ruins of the monastery were tossed into the air.

We lay each in his hole gazing out fearfully at the flame-covered, shell-devastated ground. How long yet?

A figure came tearing down the path towards us. A long leap and he landed in our hole.

It was Eagle. He was the battalion runner. He was breathing heavily. Mike gave him a thump.

"What's up?"

"The Battalion's wiped out, Herr Major," he gasped out between breaths. "No. 3 Company's been buried alive."

"Nonsense," snapped Mike. He beckoned to Porta. "You and Sven find out what's happened."

We picked up our machine-pistols, stuck a few hand grenades into the tops of our boots, clapped Eagle on the shoulder.

"Lead on, old jail-fart."

"I can't," he groaned and cowered in terror on the floor of our hole.

Porta dealt him a kick.

"Up with you, you fat swine. Perhaps you can't, but you will."

Eagle was almost beside himself with fear. We belaboured him with our butts. It was no good. We rubbed his face in the dirt, gripped him by the tenderest parts of his body, did everything we could, nothing worked. Yet what our brutality had failed to accomplish, Mike's voice of command achieved.

"Stahlschmidt," he roared. "Pick up your rifle and get going! That's an order."

Eagle shot to his feet, stood at attention in that rain of shells and barked:

"Jawohl, Herr Major!" And off he dashed, so fast that Porta and I had the greatest difficulty in keeping up with him. "Follow me," he yelled. Then he thought he saw an American, emptied his magazine into him, but it was only a corpse.

We ran across the contorted ruins, seeking funky cover in deep shell craters. We edged our way past pieces of red hot metal. A six inch shell tossed a corpse into the air: the remains of an Englishman. One foot dropped off and struck me on the back of the neck.

A warning whine automatically made us run. We became coated in slush. Only our eyes moved in the thick mud masks that now covered our faces. What had once been No. 3 Company's position was now a lunar landscape, out of which a single arm in a sleeve of camouflage cloth protruded like some lonely flower.

"A direct hit," Eagle explained. "I had just left the Company HQ, when it landed. It must have been a 12 inch."

"One can see it wasn't a rifle-grenade," Porta growled. Then his eye fell on an enormous dud lying in a shell-hole. "Have you seen that copper snozzle? Fine lot of dough there! Will you give me a hand if I gently remove it? There's at least three nights at 'Palid Ida's' there."

I gulped. The thought gave me a sinking feeling in my midriff. There wouldn't be as much as a button of us left, if that dud went off. But I didn't dare refuse. With our united strength we pulled the copper snozzle upright. Porta spat on it, made the sign of the cross over it, knelt three times. Eagle was deathly pale and I, no doubt, the same.

"Hold on to her now, or you'll have shat your last turd," commanded Porta, producing some tools from his haversack, which he laid out neatly beside the great shell.

We got 3d. a lb for copper and there must have been at least 2 cwt of it on that monster. Porta and Tiny were avid collectors. They had had a whole lorryfull some time before. More than once they had crawled out into No Man's land and pinched the rings off the shells right in front of the American positions. But the other side had its collectors too, and it had happened more than once that rival groups had come to bitter blows over a couple of duds.

Thoughtfully Porta weighed a pair of parrot-beaked pincers in his hand. Just as he was about to take a grip of the point of the shell with them, there was a wail overhead that sent us diving for cover on the bottom of the shell-hole. Earth, stones, steel rained down over us. Cautiously we peered over the rim to see if that was all.

Porta spat and ordered Eagle to sit astride the shell. Eagle blubbed and begged for his life.

"This is murder," he squeaked desperately.

"Will be, if you don't do as you're told," said Porta dryly and began pulling on the pincers.

I got a grip with another pair and pulled in the opposite direction. Porta exerted all his strength, while Eagle tried desperately to keep the shell from shifting.

Porta groaned and sweat poured from his face, not the sweat of fear, but of exertion.

"If it begins to fizz, run like bloody hell: Or we'll be enjoying the view from the top of the moon!" He let go of the pincers, spat on his hands and took another grip. "I'd like to meet the chap who screwed this on. I'd tell him something." He shoved his yellow tophat onto the back of his head, squinted across at Eagle who was as white as a sheet. "Are you comfortable, Stahlschmidt?"

Eagle gave a sob. "Blast the day I landed in this shitting company."

"Now she's coming," exclaimed Porta jubilantly and turned his pincers round. Having removed the cap, he knelt down and peered inside. Then he thrust his hand in.

I expected the thing to go off any moment. Nobody normal would dismantle a shell in that way, unless he was tired of life.

Eagle bit his lips till they bled. His eyes were popping out of his head. He looked like a sick hen.

"Where the hell is the fuse?" swore Porta, his whole arm inside the shell. "I don't understand a fart of this. There's a mass of wheels and cogs in here. Now she's beginning to tick. Listen!"

"It's a time one," Eagle yelled desperately.

Porta lit his lighter to get a better look.

I came out in gooseflesh all over.

"Oh, shut up," he exclaimed, surprised. "Queer lot of shit inside here, and the whole lot's moving. It's like the guts of an alarm clock."

Eagle gave vent to a hoarse screech, leaped off the shell and took to his heels. Porta was too preoccupied with his interesting shell to notice. He hauled out a strip of asbestos, a tube that looked like glass followed, whereupon the shell began to whistle like a kettle.

I was seized with panic, flung down my pincers and ran, landing in a shell-hole twenty yards away. I peered back towards the great shell. I could see Porta's top hat going up and down like a pump-handle.

Five minutes passed. Then he beckoned to me.

"Come over and help, you funk-bag. I've got the clockwork out of her."

Somewhat faintheartedly I crawled back. Eagle had vanished. A pile of screws and wheels lay in front of Porta.

With a deal of baroque gaiety we went on dismantling the shell.

"Peculiar type," Porta said, wondering, "I can't find a fuse. There must be one in there somewhere."

"Do you think it can still explode," I asked, apprehensively.

"Must be able to," Porta said. "Let's hope she won't till we've got all the copper."

There was an impressive pile of it heaped between us, by the time Porta announced himself satisfied. His final act was to lie flat beside the shell and put his ear to it. "Now she's ticking again." He said, "Shouldn't we try to dismantle her altogether, so that we have some idea how these work? Be a bit dangerous in future, if we don't."

"Come along, for Christ's sake," I yelled, thoroughly frightened, and ran as hard as I could.

Shortly afterwards Porta came trotting along after me, weighed down by copper. Scarcely had he caught up with me, before the ground seemed to rise up to heaven and a wall of air knocked me flat. Our friend had gone off.

Porta crawled round searching for his top hat. He found it behind some scorched bushes. A splinter had gone right through it, tearing off the oak leaf band and cockade.

Eagle was lying at the bottom of a deep crater weeping. He was badly shocked. He became quite savage when he saw us. We had to hit him across the head with a spade.

Only forty men were left of No. 2 Company, which was commanded by the one surviving NCO. No. 3 Company had been wiped out altogether. No. 4 Company now consisted of seven men, of whom four were badly wounded. The Company Commander, a lieutenant aged eighteen, sat in a corner of the trench, an enormous bloody bandage round his belly.

"How's things, lieutenant?" Porta asked in his free and easy way.

The lieutenant made an attempt at a smile. He gave a machine gun beside him a pat and said:

"We're ready to receive them, when they come, the shits. They'll know we're here."

In the place that should have been No. 1 Company's position, we found a dozen machine-gun barrels sticking up from the ground and a heap of bloody lumps. That was all that remained of the Company.

Out of the 700-strong battalion only 117 were left. Then the reserves arrived, running the gauntlet of that gully of death. Shells kept ploughing into the monastery. An ammunition column on the serpentine approach road received a direct hit and bits of human body and truck, earth, stone and iron came raining down on all sides. Battalions and regiments vanished. New ones appeared. There was not one of us, who had not some wound. But only the dying were carted off. Gefreiter Knuth went to the Field Dressing Station with three fingers shot off one hand, but the doctor kicked him out. He had no time for "minor" injuries, nothing less than an arm.

Shortly after sunrise the shelling stopped. The holy mountain lay enveloped in yellow, poisonous fumes. We listened. A flute-like note we had not heard before: a new kind of shell?

A paratroop major swung his gas mask over his head.

"G-a-s, g-a-s!" The warning cry went up from man to man. The shells exploded with a strange sort of pop and out welled a greeny-yellow vapour.

We began to cough. It stung our lungs. Our throats were sore. We felt we were choking. Our eyes smarted. One or two went off their heads and leaped out into space.

"G-a-s, g-a-s," the alarm was passed from shell-hole to shell-hole.

We tore off our helmets and dragged our masks over our faces. The glass steamed up, blinding us. We sweated, felt the iron fist of fear gripping our throats. Now bayonets glinted at the end of our rifles. We were ready for a desperate fight.

Day was turned into night. We looked ghastly with our black masks over our faces.

It was not gas, but smoke shells. That was bad enough. Several men were suffocated by this "harmless" smoke screen.

Then they came. Sure of victory. The first thing we heard was the death-promising clank of tank-tracks. Dense shoals of them emerged waddling out of the smoke. Their great snouts dived into shell craters to struggle out again up the almost vertical sides. The clattering steel tracks crushed dead and wounded alike. They had their hatches open, commanders standing erect in the turrets, looking round for victims in the greeny-yellow venomous smoke, grinning, sure of victory.

"Go to hell, kraut, here we are with the Shermans!"

They fired off a broadside, a hurricane of fire, and showered the ground with their machine guns. Their flame-throwers spat out at a company of grenadiers that were squeezing petrified against the wall of rock.

But they had reckoned without us tank men in our new role of infantry. They could not rattle us with their clattering tracks. We knew how to deal with such vermin. Heide knocked his LMG's legs into position with his underarm, adjusted the visor. We screwed the caps off our hand grenades, stuffed

231

them into our belts, sticks up. The rings we pulled out with our teeth.

The roaring steel monsters were quite close now. A crazy hatred took possession of us. Now we were going to exact vengeance for the thousands of shells they had been flinging at our heads.

Tiny came running up with a bunch of hand grenades under each arm. In his right hand he had a T-mine. He stopped a few yards in front of a Sherman, flexed his knees and threw the mine. It brushed the face of the young commander in the turret. A tremendous explosion. The commander was flung out and up into the air. The great tank turned a somersault and lay, – its tracks working wildly in the air.

Tiny was already at work on the next. Porta was hanging over the cannon of another. He dropped two grenades with the pins out into the barrel, then rolled off. The tank passed over him, but he knew the trick of squeezing flat to the ground and he was not even touched. The next moment he was up on the rear platform of another.

Heide took up position between the rollers of a burned-out tank, covering us with his machine gun.

The Americans stopped. They did not understand what was happening, as one after another of their tanks was transformed into a funeral pyre.

"*Allah-el-akbar!*" The Legionnaire's battle-cry rang out again. "*Vive la Legion!*" He dragged a tank-commander from the hatch of his turret and tossed his hand grenades in instead.

I took hold of a T-mine and heaved it at the nearest Sherman. It caught on the track and hung there. The blast flung me back under a burning tank, where two charred bodies lay. Up! On again! Another mine.

The next moment we were fighting hand to hand. Wild, implacable murder.

A torn-off tank turret landed with a crash among us. Half the tank commander was still in the hatch. The gun was spinning round like a top. Bloody sheafs of flesh.

Mike came storming up, a pistol in one hand, a samurai sword in the other.

"To me and follow me," he roared.

Paratroopers, infantrymen, grenadiers, gunners, stretcher-bearers, anti-tank gunners and a padre followed the bawling major with the samurai sword.

The Legionnaire, Porta and Tiny caught him up. Between them they had Eagle. He was bare-headed, having lost his helmet, his legs were going like drum sticks. He must have been right off his head, but he fought like a lion. He had one of the new English automatic rifles with a bayonet at the end, which he stuck into everything that came his way.

Some Indians stuck their hands in the air. They had turbans. The next moment they were spinning round like live torches.

Heide was yelling savagely. He had picked up a dead storm-trooper's flame-thrower.

Wild confusion reigned at Divisional HQ. An orderly officer, spattered with blood, was standing in front of One-eye and his chief-of-staff, reporting the position.

"Most companies have been wiped out, Herr General-major. All our positions razed to the ground. All batteries silenced. All contact lost, but we're fighting everywhere."

"Everything destroyed and yet fighting. Who the hell is doing the fighting?" One-eye shouted hysterically. "How the hell am I to lead a division that doesn't exist?"

The telephone rang. It was the forward artillery observer from the monastery.

"Herr General, large tank units attacking from the north-east and south. We have no anti-tank guns available. For God's sake send reinforcements!" A hysterical sob ended the conversation, as the wretched gunner's nerve went.

One-Eye darted across to the big map on the wall. He spat on it. It was no help. Everything was in confusion. He yelled at the adjutant, who was standing holding a telephone in either hand:

"What the hell are you gaping at, Müller? Take your fingers out of your arse and get those shits in the rear stirred up! Up with the reserves. I demand reinforcements! Every cook, every hospital orderly. Empty the dressing stations. Take their crutches and give them rifles instead. This isn't the time to lie farting in hospital."

The situation maps were swept from the table and trampled

under dirty boots. Maps were no use any more. This was the overture to Death's *danse macabre*.

The orderly officers were sent off. One-Eye threatened to court-martial them if they did not get there.

"I forbid you to get killed," he shouted.

A badly wounded lieutenant staggered in and collapsed on the floor. Just before he died, he managed to stammer out: "Herr General, No. 4 Company wiped out. Fighting continues. Sherman's fought to a standstill in front of our positions!"

One-Eye banged his stout walking stick on the table and seized the dead lieutenant by the collar.

"Answer me, man, before you die! What positions? Who's fighting?"

But the lieutenant's head fell back lifeless and blood ran from it across One-Eye's hands. He flung the dead eighteen-year old aside.

"There should be a punishment for dying like that," he swore. He flung a pistol at a Hauptman, yelling: "Don't stand there gaping! Get me situation reports from the Companies. I want to know who are these ruddy spectres who're still fighting."

The same crazy confusion prevailed in the HQ of the other side. The Americans and New Zealanders were attacking them under command of that headstrong general, Freyberg. On his orders the monastery was razed to the ground. He wanted his own Verdun, and he got it. When he heard of the resistance his tanks and troops were encountering, he flung his helmet tn the floor.

"Impossible!" he roared. "There can't be anyone alive up there. You must be seeing things. It must be ghosts!"

If so, they were ghosts armed with machine guns and flame-throwers. Fresh units were thrown in and bled mercilessly in front of the remains of that formerly lovely monastery.

British tanks came roaring up the serpentine road. Scots infantrymen clung like bunches of grapes to their turrets. A furious blast of machine gun fire shaved them away. Soldiers in blood-soiled rags chucked mines under the tanks vulnerable bellies.

General Freyberg took his Bible oath that he would take the monastery, whatever the cost.

Fresh units were sent in: Scots, Welshmen, lads from Texas, cotton-pickers from Alabama, Australians, New Zealanders, warriors from the mountains of Morocco, Indians in turbans, melancholy blacks from the banks of the Congo, battle-happy Japanese. And heading them all a Polish division thirsting for vengeance.

They wept. They roared. They cursed. They fell and toppled in that hellish machine gun fire. They were beating the air. There were no positions, and yet they were being fought.

The tanks got stuck. Their aerial-photograph maps were of no use. Their own artillery had transformed everything. Where, three days previously, had been a road or a path, was now an impassable area of rock. We were lying in a dug-out, Porta, Tiny, the Legionnaire and I. Two GI's put up their hands. Porta chucked a hand grenade at them.

"The red light's out, chums. All seats sold."

The GI's collapsed in a rain of steel. I planted the legs of my MG42 firmly in the churned up mud. The next moment it jammed. I opened the breech. Heide prised the treacherous cartridge out with a bayonet. I got ready to load. New cartridge belt.

Snarling, the quick-firing MG spat steel from its muzzle. When the barrels got too hot, we pissed on them to cool them. Gregor Martin came with three new ones.

Eagle landed beside us, laden with ammunition. God knows where he had got it. He had been pretty well scalped by a shell splinter and half of one ear was missing. He relieved Heide as my helper.

I pressed the butt to my shoulder, jammed the feet against a stone. The MG spat death and destruction. Khaki-clad infantrymen crumpled and dropped a few yards from us. Another stoppage.

Eagle handed me a bayonet: up with the cap and out with the jammed cartridge. The cap shut tight with a click. Loading action again. The 42 had been on strike only a few seconds, but they were closer because of it.

Heide had also got hold of an MG. He was on his knees, the great gun pressed to his side, shooting. His kidneys and

235

bones must have been shaken loose, but we knew what was at stake. The moment they reached us, we should be killed. Neither side was taking prisoners.

The bodies piled up. Porta and Tiny were throwing hand grenades. Gregor Martin pulled the cords, handed the grenades to them and counted. It would have turned any hand grenade instructor's hair grey; but every grenade exploded exactly at waist level in front of the enemy soldiers.

Then a mortar began punping its shells out. That was Mike and the Old Man. Mike handed the shells to the Old Man.

A Sherman stuck its great snout over the ruined monastery wall. We stared at its belly that towered there in front of us; in a matter of seconds it would tilt down and crush us.

Porta leaped to his feet and flung a T-mine at it. A column of fire. The tank became a raging hell. A human voice shrieked in panic. It was the tank commander, stuck in the turret. His torso twisted convulsively. His arms flailed like windmill sails. His lower half was burning.

An American infantryman gave him the *coup de grace*. We changed position. A couple of paratroopers with a great bundle of panzerfausts joined us.

The Legionnaire was kneeling. Holding a flamethrower that spurted fire in all directions.

Allah-el-Akbar! Viva la France!" he shouted idiotically, as if we didn't know we were fighting a French general.

They were beginning to waver, the Americans and the death-defying New Zealanders.

Then all at once One-Eye was there among us, in one hand a Nagan, in the other his gnarled stick.

"To me!" he ordered. "Follow me!" He had lost his black eye-patch and the empty socket glowed redly. His general's badge on his shoulder-straps glinted in the light of the flame-thrower's darting tongues. Stout and broad, he trundled like a steam roller down the slope, closely followed by men from every conceivable arm.

On his right stormed Mike, an enormous cigar nicely centred in his mouth. On his left ran Porta, his yellow top hat on the back of his head. A bloated general with his body-guard.

With savage fanaticism we rolled and fell down the steep side of the sacred mountain. Crazy hand-to-hand fights were fought on piles of shattered masonry. We bit, snarled, kicked and thrust.

An American captain, armed only with a bayonet, rushed at a Panzer lieutenant. His uniform was in tatters. He was bathed in blood. I turned my machine-pistol on him. He was invulnerable. He killed the lieutenant. His bayonet snapped. Foaming with fury, he flung the handle at me. He picked up a stone and went for a paratrooper who had taken up position with an LMG behind a rock. The raging captain smashed his head with the stone, seized the LMG and swung it in a semi-circle with tracer bullets fanning out from him.

A panzerfaust blew him to bits.

An American corporal of marines and a German para-trooper lay entangled in death. The American's teeth were buried in the German's throat.

A French major sat on a stone trying to stuff his guts back into his ripped-up belly. An American negro sergeant was lying with both legs caught and crushed beneath the track of a burned-out tank, firing hurricanes of bullets from a red hot machine gun. Beside him was a great pile of empty cartridge cases. A hatchet split his skull for him.

When we ran out of grenades, we flung duds at them. The air was full of whining and whistling. Clouds split. Flames shot down from the heavens. The ground splintered. Barrage. The shells, American and German, killed friend and foe in-discriminately. The staff in the rear had panicked and set in motion a giant mill that ground down everything.

We leaped for cover and flung ourselves down together with our opponents of a moment before and shook furious fists at the gunners we could not see.

I found myself lying beside a GI at the bottom of a shell-hole. Too frightened to speak, we watched each other. Who would shoot first? Then with an oath he flung his machine-pistol aside and held out a packet of Camels. I laughed with relief and offered him a Grifa. He smiled. We both roared with

237

laughter, and fell on each other's neck. We began jabbering away, great laughing explanations of which neither understood a word the other said. We exchanged water bottles. He had gin in his. I Schinkenhagër in mine.

Two figures came tumbling headfirst into our hole. It was Porta and Tiny. They started back when they caught sight of the GI. Tiny undid the safety catch of his Kalashnikov. I kicked it out of his hand. I gestured reassuringly to the GI. We crawled deeper into our hole. Our water bottles went the round. We swopped buttons, ribbons. The GI. became quite crazy, when he saw the red Commissar's star on my purse.

We diced, smoked Grifas and Camels, and emptied our water bottles. The GI. showed us a tattooing of Donald Duck on his chest. When he moved certain muscles the beak opened. We laughed so much, we almost died.

Then the shelling stopped. Cautiously we peered over the rim of the shell hole: three Germans and one American.

"Now I am going home," said the GI.

We slithered back to the bottom of the hole and took a fond farewell of each other. We exchanged home addresses and field post numbers, promising to write, as soon as we had time. We covered him with our automatics against possible murderous devils as he ran bent double across the shell-ravaged ground.

"I in person will strangle anyone who picks him off," said Tiny.

We saw him jump down into a dug-out, then wave his machine-pistol.

A machine gun began to bark beside us. Figures in field grey leaped across our hole. The attack rolled on.

Figures in khaki emerged. A brief salvo from Gregor Martin's machine-pistol. They folded up. A group of them was lurking behind a great block of stone. A hand grenade went whistling through the air. The lurking group was transformed into a bloody heap of flesh. On! On! An Englishman crouched to jump. The next instant a knife sat quivering in his back.

More shells. Masses of infantry shot up from the ground. We withdrew. Groaning, sweating, gasping for breath we flung ourselves into what had once been a trench, set up our automatic weapons in position. We tore our shirts into strips and used them to clean the earth and filth off our weapons. What made us fight on so obstinately? Was it the monastery, the holy mountain, our country? No. We were fighting for our bloody lives. All that we still possessed. We were as poor as church mice. Did not own as much as a clean shirt or a pair of boots that did not leak. We had forgotten what soap looked like. We were no longer human, but machines that had run amok and were killing everything living.

One-Eye landed in the hole beside us. His empty eye-socket was full of earth. He lit a cigar at the red-hot barrel of a flame-thrower. His one savagely flashing eye stared at Porta.

"I shall put you in for a decoration. If anyone deserves one, it is you!"

Porta grinned impudently.

"I'd rather have a case of beer and a nice little cunt to my-self."

A wave of gunfire, the like of which we had not yet seen, made further conversation impossible. The holy mountain shook. An earthquake of giant proportions. We pressed our-selves to the ground, dug our fingers into the mire, made our-selves small, became insects that sought shelter in cracks in the rock and under protuberances. The valley and the mountain were on fire. Every millimetre was plastered with shells of the largest calibre. The village of Cassino vanished.

A paratrooper went off his head and began climbing. He swarmed up the rock faces like a monkey, a feat that under normal conditions would have been front-page news. As it was scarcely anyone noticed. Our nerves could take no more. We lay with our faces in the mire. Smoke shells. Gas masks on. Barrage. Then they came. First the Poles, the Carpathian Brigade.

"For Warszaw!" they shouted.

We withdrew to the monastery. We dug ourselves in. The first khaki-clad figures appeared and were mown down. Bodies, bodies, piles of bodies. Men were burned. Men were crushed. Men were pulverised.

Some thousands of Moroccans, led by fanatical French

officers, came storming up, hard on the heels of the Polish Division, which broke in the concentration of machine gun fire.

A Polish lieutenant-colonel, bleeding from countless wounds, rose from a hole and shouted to the twenty men who were all that remained of his regiment.

"Forward, men, and long live Poland!" He had knotted a Polish flag round his neck.

"You're a man after my own heart," said the Legionnaire as he knelt and took careful aim. "You shall be seated at the right hand of Allah, my brave Pole." Then he emptied a magazine into the Polish officer's belly. "God is wise," he whispered. "It is not for us human vermin to ask why." He seized a number of hand grenades and flung them into a nest of American machine guns.

Then the Ghurkas came, wearing their broad-brimmed hats turned up on one side.

They died in our machine gun fire.

We were fighting in the ruins of the monastery. The Moroccans cut the ears off those they killed, so as to be able to show how many they had accounted for, when they returned home. They wore brown hats pulled down over their heads.

The Legionnaire exulted in murderous joy, when he saw them. He vented his savage Moroccan war-cry.

"The brown boys are here," he yelled, flinging his head back in crazy laughter. "Kill them! *Avant Avant, vive la Legion.*"

We followed him as so often before. One-Eye tried to halt us. A crazy thing to do. He flung his stick after us in a fury. We were firing from the hip, changing magazines as we ran.

The Moroccans halted in amazement. A paratrooper leaped down from a rock right in among them and spun round like a wheel, his LMG spilling out bullets.

We hit out with spades and rifle butts, we throttled them with our bare hands. Tiny flung a good dozen out over the edge of the cliff.

Porta and I were lying with a 42 in position behind a heap of corpses spewing death around us.

The Moroccans and Ghurkas had now dug themselves in. When darkness fell, we sneaked out under command of the

Legionnaire and without so much as a sound crept up on them and cut their throats.

Heide had gone back to his favourite pastime of sniping. He had a couple of the new rifles with night telescopic sights. He chortled aloud every time he hit.

Leutnant Frick became more and more indignant.

"I hit him right in the ear," Heide called delightedly. "A poor tame bugger with two bars on his helmet." Heide was using explosive bullets.

"Damned idiot," Leutnant Frick shouted, hitting at Heide's rifle.

Heide gave him a scornful look, threw his rifle to his shoulder and another shot rang out.

Away over there a shape leaped into the air. We thought the leutnant was going to spring at Heide.

"Shoot once more and I'll report you for insubordination," he shouted furiously.

"Yes, Herr Leutnant," mocked Heide. "May I ask, am I to pass on the order to the other side and then perhaps you could arrange a football match in the market place in Cassino? Are we to unload our weapons and throw our hand grenades away, Herr Leutnant?"

Leutnant Frick narrowed his eyes.

"Unteroffizier Heide, I know that you are the complete regulation soldier, the best in the German army. I know, too, that you have certain connections in the Party. But you are also the filthiest murderer I have yet encountered. You and that filthy uniform you wear are admirably suited. You are an adornment to your Führer's guards'"

"Cold feet?" laughed Heide.

Swiftly Leutnant Frick bent down, seized up a mess-tin full of spaghetti that Porta was cooking over a spirit burner, and flung the contents right into Heide's face, sending him staggering back with a bellow of surprise. Without any alteration in expression, Leutnant Frick put the empty can down beside Porta. Then he caught hold of Heide by his tunic.

"Look, Unteroffizier Heide, now you can send in a report that your superior officer laid hands on you, uttered treacherous statements, mocked the German uniform and insulted the

241

Führer. I should think that would be enough to be hanged five or six times over." The leutnant then turned on his heel and ran across to Major Mike, who was sitting in an adjacent hole popping lice.

"You are my witnesses," Heide shouted hysterically, wiping spaghetti from his face.

"What are we witnesses to?" Porta asked, challengingly.

"Don't pretend to be dumb," howled Heide. "You heard him say we've lost the war and I'll make you sign my report, you'll see. I am going to see that lousy beast dangle."

"What actually are you talking about?" Barcelona asked. "I haven't seen a sign of the leutnant and *I've* been here all the time. Have you seen a leutnant, Tiny?"

Tiny removed a piece of sausage from his mouth.

"Leutnant? Yes, but a long time ago."

"Tell me," said Porta getting to his feet, "what the hell do you mean by this impertinence: taking my spaghetti and pouring it over your head? This'll cost you something. It had bits of pork and tomato ketchup in it. Which you are going to pay for! Hand over your Grifas and opium-sticks."

"I'll shit on your spaghetti," Heide promised, furious. "I'll personally break the neck of that officer's prick." He looked round in search of more willing witnesses. He pointed at Padre Emanuel, who was sitting in a corner with Eagle. "Padre, dare you swear by Jesus Christ's holy cross that you did not hear him insult the Führer? I warn you that this matter will go before a courtmartial. Don't lie, Padre. You are in holy orders."

The Padre grinned broadly, cocked his head on one side, making himself look a complete idiot.

"Do I understand, Heide, that you stole Porta's spaghetti and poured it over your own head?"

Heide loaded his machine-pistol.

"Padre, you saw that ersatz-leutnant chuck it at my head!"

"Are you crazy, Unteroffizier Heide?" Padre Emanuel asked with well-feigned horror in his voice. "No leutnant would throw spaghetti at a subordinate's head."

Heide turned swiftly to Eagle.

"Panzerschütze Stahlschmidt, on your feet. Pull your bones

together when an Unteroffizier addresses you and don't lie
to me, your superior and Group-leader. There's a court
martial with a rope on the table awaiting you, if you do. You
heard what the Leutnant said?"

Eagle was shaking all over. His water bottle was full of
schnaps – fell from his hands.

"Well, you down-at-heel jail-bird, did you hear what I
asked?" Heide roared, excitedly.

Eagle was about to reply, when Porta banged the back of
his head with the empty mess-tin.

"You heard what Heide said about the Führer, didn't you,
Stahlschmidt? This is the moment when you decide whose
side you're on, Panzerschütze Stahlschmidt."

Eagle was deathly pale. He gulped, moistened his cracked
lips with the tip of his tongue.

Heide cleared his throat impatiently, flexed his knees.
Eagle had almost taken his decision, when his eyes fell on
Porta, who was nursing a flame-thrower in a most significant
way.

"I heard Unteroffizier Heide say that the Führer was a
great arse-hole."

Heide was beside himself.

"You great, fat, lousy traitor! I'll settle with you one day.
Meanwhile, dream of prison, because, believe me, that's
where you're going." He pointed his bayonet at him. "Stahlschmidt, I shall personally take you in chains to Torgau."

"Don't preach so much, Julius Jew-hater," Porta interrupted, prodding Heide in the stomach with the flame-
thrower. "Out with those opium-sticks of yours. That perhaps will teach you not to steal peaceable people's spaghetti.
In this country that's a sacred dish, that even the Pope eats."

"You're not getting a thing," Heide announced, self-
assuredly and kicked at the flame-thrower.

"Aren't I?" laughed Porta and sent a jet of flame spurting
over Heide's head. It was so close, we could smell singed hair.

"Stop that tomfoolery," Major Mike called, looking up for a
moment from his louse-hunt.

Heide leaped behind a rock for cover.

Another jet of flame.

Heide emerged from behind the rock, blackened and with fear in his eyes.

"Stop that. Or you'll burn me!"

"Only just realised that?" said Porta with a devilish smile and got ready to give him another burst of flame. "Hand over or I'll turn you into a handful of ashes."

A roll of narcotic cigarettes came flying through the air. Porta picked them up, smelled them and gave a nod of satisfaction.

"And now you'll get me a mess-tin of spaghetti with diced pork and tomato ketchup. And I wouldn't say no to a little browned onion."

Heide capitulated, but at the same time swore by Padre Emanuel's prayer book that he would be avenged on all leutnants in the great German army. Then Mike summoned him and sent him to Divisional HQ as orderly. Objective: obtaining cigars for Major Mike.

Heide asked for more detailed instructions.

"It's not my farting business, where you get them," roared Mike. "You can pull them out of Kesselring's arse, as far as I'm concerned, but don't you dare come back without a box of cigars. And if you aren't back within six hours, I'll post you as a deserter and put the Military Police on to you."

Swearing and fulminating, Heide set off on his quest, Porta calling advice to him, as he went.

"Holy Mother of God, look at that!" Padre Emanuel was pointing up at the sky.

We looked up and refused to believe our eyes. Innumerable vapour trails were shining in the cloudless sky. An enormous swarm of bees. Only the bees were colossal bombers.

We fought for the field glasses.

"Jesus," murmured Barcelona, "there are at least a thousand! And they're American Flying Fortresses. I wouldn't like to be where they unload."

"They're B 17s," whispered Leutnant Frick fearfully and instinctively crept further into the dug-out.

Mike let a louse go, as he stared up at the sky.

"Where the hell have they come from? They're coming from the bloody North!"

We didn't realise then that that great shoal had taken off from aerodromes in England that same morning. Swarms of fighters had escorted them across France. They had ruthlessly violated the neutrality of Switzerland, where gunners in near-mediaeval helmets had shot at them without so much as scratching their paint. Our Focke-Wulffs had gone for them, but they had kept on their course. It was not for nothing we called them the Pig-headed. Their navigators were given a course at the start, and that is what they flew, even if the devil in person appeared in front of them. The twenty-four year old pilots sat in their cockpits chewing gum. Their faces were covered with oxygen masks. A couple of bomb aimers new to the game, went off their heads. One leaped out through the bomb-hatch, followed by an oath.

Hour after hour the great engines roared. They went bald-headed through a thunder storm and on into a barrage of ack-ack. They tore off their oxygen masks. The second pilot handed a thermos flask to the pilot. The navigator put five Camels in his mouth, lit them together and handed them round. They smoked as they gazed at the red notice saying "Smoking prohibited." They looked at the muzzle flashes of the 8-8's. A Focke-Wulff, its nose painted like an attacking shark, came for twenty-two year old Captain Boye-Smith's B.17.

"Get that filthy kraut," he called to his tail-gunner.

Whether it was that that tail gunner was a magnificent shot or just wonderfully lucky, at all events his first burst hit the screaming Focke-Wulff, which shot past beneath the bomber with a plume of thick smoke streaming out behind it, then reared up like a horse before an exploding shell and described a figure of eight in the air, before hurtling down to earth. It fell in the village of Pantoni, west of Firenze, killing two children and a young wife, who was washing clothes. The pilot, Barn von Nierndorf, was killed by the first spurt of flame high up in the air.

The leading arrow-head of fifty B.17's was exactly over Monte Cassino. The air roared, as a hurricane of steel was born.

"What the hell," exclaimed Mike in the act of holding

a louse up for inspection.

We rolled over onto our bellies, crawled in under an over-hang of rock and waited for death.

The Americans in their positions were just as surprised. GI's everywhere were diving for shelter. "Damn it, they're bombing us!"

The first rain of bombs shaved the mountain. A line of houses in the valley was blown right away. A heavy ack-ack battery, lurking behind the locomotive-sheds in Cassino, was wiped out in a second.

Then the next wave came. More bombs plumetted on to the monastery. Everything was enveloped in a venomously yellow mist. The holy mountain was enveloped in a flame-spluttering hurricane. After the B.17's came British Mitchells, so-called precision bombers that went straighter for their objective.

Wave after wave came. That night One-Eye appeared with his adjutant, Oberleutnant Hartwig, who had lost his right arm at Charkov a year before. That time, when we were fight-ing in the dentist's apartment.

One-Eye summoned the company commanders.

"We're disengaging tonight," he said. "But they must not notice a thing on the other side. The paratroopers are to pull our first. Then No. 1 Battalion. No. 5 Company will be the last to go. But, no matter who is here or is not here, you leave this shit here at 2.05 precisely. One group will remain. Two batteries will lay down harassing fire higher up."

"And that last group," Porta called from the background, "is of course No. 2 Group. Haven't you nearly had enough, my heroes? Rejoice, children will read of us in school. My top hat and my dentist's forceps will end in a museum."

One-Eye looked at him thoughtfully.

"As you've suggested it, Porta, so let it be. No. 2 Group."

"Will you never learn to hold your bloody tongue," said Barcelona.

Porta lobbed a hand grenade at Eagle, who sat cowering in a corner.

"Don't look so unappreciative, you halting hero!"

The Companies peeled off at the times ordered, floating away from the positions without a sound.

"Good luck," whispered Leutnant Frick, just before he disappeared.

Major Mike patted the Old Man's shoulder.

"Be seeing you, Beier." Then the darkness swallowed him up.

Feeling somewhat nervous, we huddled behind our machine guns.

"If they get the least suspicion that our chaps have pulled out," Porta whispered, "they'll be over us in a trice."

"I'm shitting my pants with fright," Barcelona muttered.

"If they come, I'll give them one belt, but don't count on me after that," Porta said in a subdued tone of voice. "I shall run for it, and run as I've never run before. I'm not going to Texas to break stones as a defeated kraut."

The Old Man was studying his watch.

"In five minutes the artillery starts up," he whispered. "Dismantle your MG and keep yourselves in readiness. Tiny, you take the mortar."

"Wouldn't dream of it," Tiny protested. "If you want that old stove-pipe along, you can bloody well tote it yourself. The Legionnaire has given me my job. I'm taking care of the jar with the booze."

"I'm in command here, and you're taking the mortar," the Old Man said furiously. "Your brew is no concern of mine. Understand?"

"I'm not deaf," growled Tiny.

"Then repeat the order."

"What order?" Tiny was pretending to be dumb, a usual trick of his, when there was something he wanted to get out of.

The Old Man swore savagely.

"Don't play the idiot, you great bog, and listen to me. If you haven't got the mortar with you, when we get to Via Appia, I'll put you on charge."

"Come on, Old Man, show a little humanity and under-standing," Tiny pleaded. "I can't lug both the mortar and the booze."

"You take the mortar," the Old Man cut him off.

The guns began thundering. Porta took hold of the machine gun and swung it onto his shoulder. I clapped the tripod together. Barcelona helped me heave it onto my back. We divided the long cartridge belts between us. Porta blew a kiss towards the Americans.

"Good-bye, Sammy, see you later! Don't cry, when you find our dug-outs empty."

"How we love each other," grinned Barcelona genially. "Know anyone else who knocks so energetically on the door."

"That love will be the death of us," Heide said.

Noiselessly we began the climb down. A series of clattering bangs frightened us out of our wits and made us freeze to the mountain side.

"What the hell was that?" the Old Man asked in a scared voice. "Are they after us already?"

Out of the darkness came Tiny's self-satisfied voice:

"Mightily beg your pardon, Old Man. That bloody mortar leaped from my hands and slipped off down the slope. It was all because you insisted I should lug it along as well as the booze."

"You didn't spill any of that?" Porta asked apprehensively.

"By the patron saint of cannon, the holy Barbara, I swear that not a drop has been lost. I'm very conscientious where valuables are concerned."

"You super-idiot!" the Old Man growled. "You're to get hold of another mortar, and it's no concern of mine where you get it from."

"I'll borrow one from Sam," Tiny answered happily. "He's lots of that shit."

Sweating, we laboured on, clinging to every jutting bit of rock. Our hands were bleeding.

"I can't do any more," I groaned. "I'm chucking the tripod."

"No need for that," Barcelona said consolingly. "Give it me."

Where a piece of rock looking like a horse's head jutted out, I eased the tripod off my back and gave it to Barcelona, getting the flame-thrower instead. It was just as heavy, but easier to deal with.

We balanced our way along a narrow ledge. There was a ridge we had to get over. Tiny was lying on his face a bit further up. He had tied his feet to a tree. He reached down a hand: with a quick jerk he heaved me up. Barcelona came after me. Then Porta. One after the other.

"Strong aren't I," Tiny boasted. "You'd have gone on your arses without me." He threw a stone into the chasm. We heard it rolling and bouncing down through the dark. "Hell of a long way to the bottom," Porta muttered.

A star shell soared up. We flung ourselves behind cover, tried to merge with the ground. The slightest movement meant death.

Slowly the glaring light died away. Guns were rumbling in the east. That was Castellona, height 771. We did not know it, but it was the beginning of the American's break through. The 168th US infantry regiment overran our 139th. At the same time the US 142nd settled the hash of our 200 Panzergrenadiers.

There was roaring and flashing all round the horizon. Hundreds of guns were spitting fire. Blood flowed in torrents.

"Take up your arms," the Old Man ordered. "Single file – follow me!"

The Company had dug itself in between some houses. Tiny set the great jar of booze carefully on the ground.

"Shall I open the bar?" he asked the Legionnaire.

The Legionnaire nodded. A door was torn from its hinges and placed across two drums. Mugs were arranged neatly. Porta seated himself on a shell, produced a medium sized cash-box and an altar bell. Tiny took up position behind him, a flame-thrower in his hands. Our new minstrel put his trumpet to his lips and blew the Assembly.

Inquisitive heads popped up from the various shell-holes.

Mike came striding up, a large cigar in his mouth, for Heide had returned with what he had been ordered to get.

"What the hell are you up to? Stop that trumpeting. The Americans know an assembly call when they hear one, too. You might bring them over here."

"Haven't anything against American customers," Porta said. "Dollars are hard currency."

"Don't put on airs," said Mike. "You've never even seen a greenback."

Without saying a word, Porta thrust his hand into the top of his boot and pulled out two fat bundles of dollar notes.

Mike's jaw fell. For a moment he was dumb with amazement. "Where the hell did you get those freckles from?" he exclaimed.

"From General Ryder's and General Walker's boys. We happened to meet behind the monastery and I convinced them that they had no further use for this dough."

"You know perfectly well that foreign currency has to be handed in to your Company Commander or the NSFO,* don't you?"

Porta put the money back in his boot, smiling craftily.

"Yes, Herr Major, I know that. I and our NSFO are good friends." He gave a little cough and held a miniature spy's camera up for us to see. "And this little box is the reason why. I am quite crazy about photography, only I can never remember where I put the films. A couple of days ago I happened to snap our NSFO while he was busy seducing a very young Italian boy. We had a bit of a chat about the film afterwards, and we agreed that it would not be an awfully good thing, if it got to Prinz Albrecht Strasse."

Mike whistled and gazed intently at Porta's boots.

"Suppose I put in a report about the boy and the film?" he said in honeyed tones.

Porta grinned unconcernedly.

"As would only be your duty, Herr Major. But remember that every report must go through the Divisional Commander, General-Major Mercedes, and I wouldn't like to be there, when a report for the RSHA lands on One-Eye's desk. If it got through successfully, it would go on to a chap I've never met, but I've heard a lot about him. He can't stand the black boys of Prinz Albrecht Strasse either, but perhaps you know him personally? I mean Herr Generalfeldmarschall Kesselring. Who knows if he's not another who's changed his name, like the famous Herr von Manstei, who, so I've heard, used to be called Lichtenstein."

Heide spat.

"Was his first name by any chance Nathan?"

* Nationalsozialistischer Fursorgeoffizier (political).

250

Porta shrugged.

"If it was, that'll explain why he changed it. It's not a name that is exactly popular these days."

Mike leaped forward. He would gladly have gone for Porta's throat. His cigar jerked from one corner of his mouth to the other.

"One day you'll dangle, Porta," he prophesied kindly, and in his mind's eye saw Porta's body swaying from a cork-oak beside the Via Appia.

Major Mike looked tired. He sat down heavily on the bottom of the trench, using Eagle's helmet for a chair, which the latter politely pushed under his broad backside.

"A drink, Herr Major?" Porta enquired with a neutral smile.

The major emptied the mug at one draught. It was 88 per cent rice spirit. He got to his feet, broad and tall, and slowly put a fresh cigar between his teeth. Eagle lit it obsequiously.

The major did not even look at him. He fingered the machine pistol that hung on his chest, and smiled a rather forced smile.

"Porta, you should have been chief of staff. You'd give even marshals stripes on their bottoms."

"Oh, hell, Herr Major. I'm the same as that marine from Texas, a simple soldier who has learned to safeguard himself in all directions. My motto is: regard everyone as a limb of satan till the opposite is proved, and it very seldom is."

Major Mike drew a deep breath, almost swallowing his cigar.

"Once more, Porta, you would look well at the end of a rope."

Porta shrugged.

"You know yourself, Herr Major, one piece of decoration does not make a Christmas tree."

The major disappeared muttering something incomprehensible. We only caught the word "bugger".

Porta began ringing his altar bell wildly and bellowing:

"Bar's open. Bar's open."

They came in clusters and formed a queue.

"Mug in the right hand, money in the left! Payment to be made just before pouring!"

The price differed though the measure was always the same.

An SS-Oberscharführer had to fork out more than a Panzer-oberfeldwebel. On the other hand, a battalion clerk had to pay twice what had been exacted from the Oberscharführer.

Twice Tiny had to come into action and prevent a fight. One blow on the back of the head with his flame-thrower restored peace. Then in the middle of it all they were over us. Without our noticing a thing, the brown-burnoused Moroccans had cut the throats of our pickets. They came leaping down the cliff, firing at us from three sides.

The next instant we were engaged in murderous hand-to-hand fighting. Tiny whipped up the jar of booze and took it to a place of safety inside one of the houses. Then he stormed out, his flame-thrower spitting fire. The Legionnaire was standing with his back to a wall plying an axe.

Then the Jabos arrived and swept the scene with their machine cannon. The brown men had got too far in front, and the devilish fire of the American fighters sent them spinning.

The houses went up in flames. One old peasant made desperate attempts to put his out with a saucepan. Then the saucepan flew from his hand, water splashing in all directions, earth spurted up and the shadow of a fighter-bomber brushed him.

Artillery fire. Swarms of infantry. We withdrew. The few of us, that is, who survived and could drag ourselves along. We fell in by the side of the road. The ambulances were parked under cover of the trees. We placed the Old Man in one of them, though it took all our Grifas and all Porta's dollars to get him a place. One lung appeared every time he drew a breath. We squeezed his hand; then the ambulance drove off towards Rome at breakneck speed.

Mike was put in an army truck with four other seriously wounded. His right arm was smashed. We placed his box of cigars beside him, and he nodded gratefully.

We buried Eagle by the roadside. A hand grenade had taken off both his feet. We did not dig deep and he got no cross or helmet over him. We just trampled the earth down a bit.

"Burn slowly in hell, you dirty prison fart," said Barcelona.

Leutnant Frick came across to us. He had a bandage round his head that only left one eye and his mouth visible.

"Pick up your arms. We're going forward again. The

grenadiers have withdrawn, and the position has to be held at all costs. I am responsible with my life."

We swung the machine guns up onto our shoulders. Whining shells landed among us.

Barcelona collapsed. Two paratroopers carried him back. He had shell splinters in his abdomen. Heide went spinning and the machine gun fell from his hands. The back of his neck and shoulders were one gaping, bleeding wound. We sent him back with some grenadiers.

Leutnant Frick had his head severed. A fountain of blood rose from his gaping neck.

We took up position in a shell-hole full of mud, Porta, Tiny, Gregor Martin and I. The last of No. 5 Company. All the others were in hospital or buried. I suddenly found myself elevated to company commander, commanding a company of four. Other little groups, joined us, the remains of companies and battalions. We held out for another five days and nights. Then the trucks fetched us. Paratroopers covered us.

The last battle of Monte Cassino was over.

Dear Reader, if your holiday should take you through the village of Cassino, stop for a moment, when you get to the road leading up to the monastery. Get out of your car and bow your head in reverence for those who died on the holy mountain. If you listen, perhaps you will still be able to hear the roar of the shells and the screams of the wounded.

THE END

REIGN OF HELL by SVEN HASSEL

Burning, looting, raping, murdering, Hitler's Penal Regiments advanced on the centre of Warsaw leaving in their wake a bloody trail of death and destruction. They killed indiscriminately. Pole or German; young or old; man, woman, child – anyone who crossed their path was eliminated. For Himmler had sworn that Warsaw would be razed to the ground – if it took every member of the German army to do it! And against the Führer's expendable battalions, for whom life had no meaning, the battle for Warsaw became an inferno – an endless reign of hell . . .

0 552 09178 2   35p

T114

SS GENERAL by SVEN HASSEL

The 27th Panzers in Hitler's Penal Regiment had fought through the winter in the hell-hole that was Stalingrad. Now there were few survivors from the last massive Russian attack. Weary and nauseated by the horrors they'd seen on the Russian front, they crawled into a bunker near the banks of the Volga. Hunger, they had discovered, was more demoralising than fear or defeat. Then the brutal SS general arrived . . .

0 552 08874 9   35p

T115

FLAME THROWER   by ANDREW WILSON

This is the first book to describe the activities of a Crocodile –
one of the venomous flame-throwing Churchills – of which
there were only fifty in the entire Allied Armies.

Towing armoured trailers full of liquid fire which would be
pumped out of the tank's turret, a Crocodile could reduce a
fortified house to a raging inferno in a matter of seconds, or
the enemy trenches to a charred rubble . . .

FLAME THROWER is a fascinating account of the ordeals
and triumphs of a man wielding one of these formidable, even
horrifying weapons of war as they blazed their way across
France to the Rhine.

0 552 09382 3   35p   T50

THE LONG DAY'S DYING   by ALAN WHITE

Somewhere in Europe, in the middle of the second world war,
three men from a commando unit have been detailed to watch
a hill. They are fighting their own war, not only against a
professional enemy, but against fatigue, physical pain, and a
sense of having been abandoned. They are all specialists:
trained to jump by parachute, to handle a knife or a piano
wire – trained to kill.

To each of them the war is something different; their reasons
for volunteering for this dangerous work highly individual.
What those reasons are becomes apparent after the arrival
of Helmut starts the long day on its inexorable path of dying.

0 552 09307 6   30p   T51

A SELECTED LIST OF WAR BOOKS THAT APPEAR IN CORGI

All these books are available at your bookshop or newsagent : or can be ordered direct from the publisher. Just tick the titles you want and fill in the form below.

CORGI BOOKS, Cash Sales Department, P.O. Box 11, Falmouth, Cornwall.
Please send cheque or postal order. No currency, and allow 10p per book to cover the cost of postage and packing (plus 5p each for additional copies).

NAME...

ADDRESS...

(FEB. 74)...